E.T. GUNNARSSON

The Salt March

Empire Fallen Book One

Bragi Press
www.bragipress.com

First published by Bragi Press 2024

This novel is entirely a work of fiction. The names, characters and incidents portrayed in it are the work of the author's imagination. Any resemblance to actual persons, living or dead, events or localities is entirely coincidental.

E.T. Gunnarsson asserts the moral right to be identified as the author of this work.

E.T. Gunnarsson has no responsibility for the persistence or accuracy of URLs for external or third-party Internet Websites referred to in this publication and does not guarantee that any content on such Websites is, or will remain, accurate or appropriate.

First edition

ISBN: 978-1-960301-04-8

Editing by Neil Broadfoot
Cover art by E.T. Gunnarsson

This book was professionally typeset on Reedsy.
Find out more at reedsy.com

For my mother, father, and all those who get me here.

Acknowledgement

First, I'd like to thank my family. Through my first series, and now this one, they have been there helping me and pushing me through the entire journey. I love you guys, and this new series is for you.

Second, thank you to my editor, Neil Broadfoot, for helping polish this book from meh to nice.

Third, a big thanks to my beta readers, Scott Holland and Craig Bowles. Your support for the last series and this one has been tremendous.

Fourth, I must show my gratitude to my friend Jonah, who spent countless hours and nights listening to me read and edit this book. Your advice and thoughts are interwoven with the pages beyond. I hope America is treating you well.

Finally, all my readers, especially those who were there for the last series, this new one is for you as well.

Map

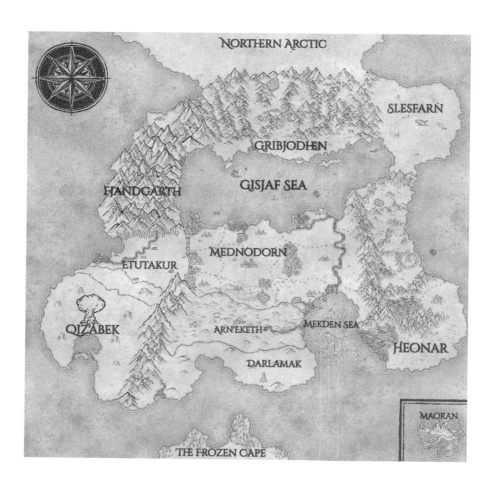

Calendar and Seasons

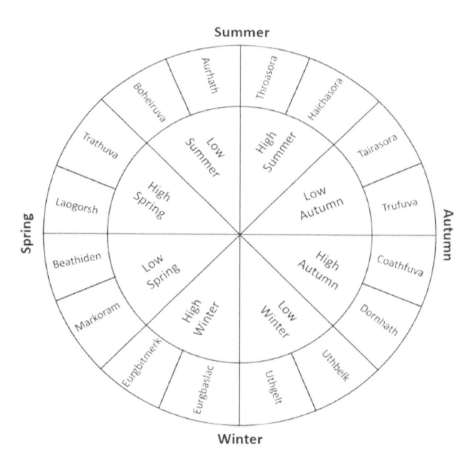

Day = 26 hours | Week = 6 days | Month = 30 days | Year = 480 days
Age = Aothill = 150 years

Basic Name Guide

The full name guide is available at the end of this book.

- **Brónmal** - "BR-OOn-mawl" - Supreme General. Son of Remtaich, General
- **Daonrex** - "DOWN-rex" - Supreme god in Tharifen, creator of man and patron of the nobility
- **Hacarad** - "HACK-ah-rod" - Brónmal's Squire and friend
- **Heokolon** - "Hee-oh-k-OH-LIN" - A person from Heonar, a person from the Heokolon Empire
- **Heonar** - "Hee-oh-NAR" - The Heokolon Empire, home of the Heokolons, East of Mednodorn
- **Mednodorn** - "MEHD-no-dorn" - Mednohail Empire, home of the Mednohail, Scourge of the Fourth Aothill, center of the known world
- **Mednohail** - "M-EH-D-no-hail" - A person from Mednodorn, a person from the Mednohail Empire
- **Remtaich** - "REM-tech" - Veteran of the First Heokolon War, Brónmal's father
- **Throfi** - "THR-AW-fee" - People of the north, a person from Gribjodhen, Fjandgarth, or Slesfarn

Prologue

A tyrant will always have the throne.

This age has ended, an era of gods and unjust rulers. Few remember a time like this one, when pagan men and warring tribes laid waste to civilization. In our time came the Uniter, the one who broke the first men and tamed their tribes.

But the first men, ungrateful, overthrew the Uniter and again plunged into their savage ways. Six hundred years I have waited. The Stygian Men stir in the West, the throne of Ardmunhaich trembles, and chaos has been born again. The Uniter has been absent for six hundred years, yet the whispers in the dark speak of his return.

Namen kube dari'ra – we will rule forever.
Astrophel, the First Accursed

1

Massacre at Hafornstalt

Brónmal hated the Northlands.

Even as High Summer approached, it still snowed. The light sprinkle came from sparse clouds and layered the ground. Despite the snow, the valleys and fjords were rife with green.

Standing on the dock, he watched the ships arrive from Mednodorn across the Gisjaf Sea. The sea calmly ebbed and flowed. Beyond the bitter waters to the Western horizon rose the Fjandgarth mountains. Great storm clouds enveloped their peaks. From the distant mountains, salty, icy winds swept over the sea and lapped against Brónmal. He shivered.

"How do they tolerate this weather?" Brónmal thought.

Throfi and Mednohail workers unloaded warships full of food, weapons, and armor onto the docks. Shouts and laughter echoed around the docks. Every dialect from the North and across the Empire could be heard while they worked. The Mednohail, Brónmal's people, were short, stocky men with dark tan skin and brown hair. While the Mednohail were often five feet tall, the Throfi were taller, usually a foot or more than the average Mednohail. They were large men whose heavy footsteps shook the wooden docks.

From afar, Brónmal watched the Throfi. He found their gray skin and silver hair strange, lacking a sense of normality. Their pink, shallow eyes made him recoil in disgust. While Mednohail wore refined clothes of linen and fibers from plants, the Throfi wore animal skins. Hide and fur from northern

1

beasts covered them from head to toe and kept them warm. Flakes of snow rested on the fur clothes and white beards of Throfi men.

"*Primitive,*" Brónmal thought. The giants lacked sophistication. They had no factories or great fields to produce clothing, just small tribes and families. Worse still, they had magic, a wretched offense to the Three. Brónmal's jaw clenched. He wished that they would simply release their devilish traditions.

Dockworkers greeted ships as they arrived. Brónmal scanned the horizon. The Godspeaker's galley, the *Apfaircada*, was still nowhere to be seen. As General of Beinthal, the third of the Nine Provinces of Mednodorn, it was Brónmal's job to prepare for the Godspeaker's arrival.

Brónmal turned to his friend and squire. "Hacarad, is the city secured? The guard must be ready for the Godspeaker's arrival."

Hacarad nodded. "Of course, Lord. I also made sure that supplies were stocked and accounted for."

"Good. Go, talk to one of the warship captains and see where the *Apfaircada* is."

Hacarad bowed. "Yes, Lord."

Brónmal adjusted his robes and watched Hacarad go down to the docks. He wanted his armor. The Throfi were friendly, but how could he trust a pagan people?

It had been an Aothill, 150 years, and the Conversion was far from completed. Brónmal hated how long it took. It was the Mednohail's *Daodamath*, or divine purpose, to lead the world into the one true faith, *Tharifen*. The Godspeaker often spoke about how men like Brónmal were shepherds of the ignorant. Here, among the ignorant, he hated them. He looked forward to the Godspeaker's arrival.

"*It is time for these pagans to learn,*" he thought.

Hacarad returned from the docks a few minutes later. "Lord, the captain says the Godspeaker's ship will be here soon. It is in the middle of the fleet. The last of the fleet will dock by nightfall."

"Wonderful. That lays my worries to rest. What do you think of these pagans? This is my third time in the North, and they never seem to change."

"These Grayskins? Strange people. They are giants compared to us."

2

"I think they are savages."

"They are. How could anyone worship the sun, moon, or death over the Three? If only they knew of their *Eirsa*."

Brónmal shook his head. "They do not know of the *Cug Baolar*. The Godspeaker explained that *Eirsa*, even the word heresy, does not exist in their language."

"Primitive language. At least they are not like the Heokolons."

"True. I pity these ignorant Grayskins. At least they are learning and converting. Are they not worth mercy because of that, Hacarad?"

"I believe we can save them. For some, it takes time to see the light of the Three and to bathe in the bliss of the Godspeaker's words."

Brónmal smiled. "Eager to see our glorious Godspeaker again?"

"It is always a blessing. May Daonrex smile upon his journey here."

"Are all the housings ready for the Godspeaker and the White Hands?"

Hacarad nodded. "Yes, Lord."

"Good. These pagans can at least prepare for the arrival of true grace."

"What does the Godspeaker intend to do when he lands, Lord?"

"Many are as ignorant as I. I believe the Godspeaker will give a speech to those here in Hafornstalt after his arrival. There will be a feast, and work will begin converting the Grayskins."

"What do you mean, Lord?"

"I heard the Godspeaker will travel for a week from farmstead to farmstead and to a few villages to help convert people."

"And we must escort him?"

Brónmal shook his head. "No, the White Hands will protect the Godspeaker. We will only accompany him, not deal with his protection. I am to speak to the village leaders on the way."

Hacarad shrugged. "Simple work then."

"Boring work. But it is far better than warring with these giants."

Brónmal looked across the small city of Hafornstalt. It was insignificant compared to any city back in the Empire. The houses, made from wood, were small and dome-shaped. Treated hides covered the roofs and kept the heat in to endure the never-ending snow. Smoke came from chimneys protruding from the center of each home. They always required firewood here. In the distance, Brónmal could hear the city stirring. As High Summer approached, the sun no longer set. The Throfi scurried to use the enduring sunlight before the long dark of High Winter took hold again.

Hacarad pointed at a group of Throfi on a dock. "I would not like to fight such giants."

Brónmal glanced at him before bowing his head. "Saying that is a mistake. I would gladly give my life for the Highlord, the Godspeaker, and the Three. If it takes one of these beasts to send me to Daonrex, so be it. Whatever sacrifice it takes to lead the world into righteousness is worth it."

Hacarad's gaze fell. "My apologies, Lord. Cowardice took me."

"There is no room for cowardice. We are servants of the Three and have nothing to fear."

"Yes, Lord."

Brónmal groaned. "Come fetch me if you see the *Apfaircada*, and make sure the Grayskins do what they are told."

"Where will you go, Lord?"

"I am going to the temple to pray."

Hacarad nodded and bowed. "As you say, Lord."

"Three bless you, Hacarad."

"And you as well, Lord."

Brónmal walked toward the city's temple. His steps carried his father's lessons about nobility. Walk upright, plant each step as if one owned the earth, and hold the chin high with dignity and virtue. On Hafornstalt, no one dared to meet his gaze. The Throfi, much larger than him, crouched and lowered their heads, fearing him. They knew him as ruthless, a righteous judicator for the Highlord, the Godspeaker, and the Three.

It took cruelty and unyielding honor to work one's way up from a knight to a General underneath the Highlord himself. Brónmal held his position with stern pride, far from the humility of a peasant.

Each street bustled with trade. There were vendors everywhere selling items from food to weapons. Many sold fish, meat, and other animal goods since crops were hard to grow in the North. The air was heavy with the reek of animals in cages, barrels full of fish, and racks of salted game everywhere. Throfi hunters and Mednohail immigrants packed the streets. Yet, unlike the streets of a Mednohail city, Hafornstalt did not stink of feces and unwashed peasants.

As if witnessing a murder, the streets became deathly silent while Brónmal marched past. Even the animals grew quiet. The crowd parted to let him through, some kneeling and bowing in respect and fear. Brónmal's gaze was like a spear, penetrating the mind and spirit of anyone he looked at. The courage of hunters and peasants faltered beneath it.

On the way to the temple, Brónmal thought of his faith. Did these Grayskins have what he had? Could they, or their children, faithfully follow the holy words of the Godspeaker, the one true prophet of Mednodorn? Could they submit as deeply as he did to the will of the Three? He pitied them. They were ignorant, closer to savage cannibals than blessed folk under the Three.

The Throfi were lucky the Mednohail held any form of mercy toward them. Brónmal knew that if any of the Nine Armies of Mednodorn sailed North, cities would burn, and they would erase the name "Throfi."

A Throfi child ran out of an alley and crossed before Brónmal. As she did, she saw him and fell to her hands and knees, head down. She begged in the Southern dialect of Throfi, words that made no sense to Brónmal. He looked down at her.

"*Monster*," he thought. She was a feral beast of the North with gray skin, silver hair, and pink eyes. Dressed in fur, she wore a necklace of bones. Primitive. He raised his chin and continued.

A smack sounded, followed by a cry from the little girl. Brónmal did not glance back. He kept walking while a Throfi woman yelled at the child.

"*Imbecile language*," he thought. His nose wrinkled. He did not understand them, and he never wished to.

The crowded, domed houses opened into a large square dominated by a cube-formed stone temple. Its roof had a bulbous, dome-like garlic shape. The dome had five spires, each adorned with smaller bulbs that made the roof crown-like. Towering over the city, the temple stood as an idol of power over the North. Brónmal looked up. He thought of it as a seed of domination,

5

soon to sprout over the entire world.

Enslaved heretics had built the temple. Its body of stone was immortal compared to the wooden homes of the Throfi. Brónmal believed stone showed superiority. While the Throfi's primitive houses would rot and collapse, the temple would stand timeless through the ages.

A pair of Mednohail soldiers guarded the grand entrance to the temple and bowed before Brónmal. "Three bless you, General Brónmal!"

Brónmal walked past them and entered the temple. The ceiling, supported by grand stone arches, rose high above a salt pool along with three statues that stood opposed to the entrance. Corpses lay in the pool, time and salt mummifying them. Brónmal went around it to the statues.

A Mednohail man dressed in black robes approached Brónmal and bowed. "Three bless you, Lord."

Brónmal bowed in return. "Three bless, Nehadrir."

"Any news about the Godspeaker?"

Brónmal gazed at the salt pool. "He is soon to arrive. I have simply come to pray to pass the time."

Nehadrir gestured to the pool of salt. "There is no nobler way to wait. I hope the dead do not bother you?"

Brónmal shook his head. "I have slain far too many heretics to be bothered by death. No, I am curious about what the Grayskins think. Do they think like us?"

Nehadrir tilted his head. "Of salting the dead?"

"Yes. It must be different to keep the dead like we do so that families may grieve and remember their mortality and sins?"

Nehadrir shrugged. "It is far better than sending the sick, dying, and dead into the frozen north. I have heard little objection. I have helped build a few ancestral altars to lay the dead here in Hafornstalt. The Throfi seem grateful that those that pass may stay for a short while longer before burial."

"I remember when we replaced my great-grandfather's body with my grandfather's. It was sad to bury him finally. It is good to see the heathens learn."

"Three bless them. We will shepherd them all to the light, eventually."

"Hopefully. I will pray now. Three bless you, Nehadrir."

"And you as well, General."

Brónmal walked around the salt pool and knelt before the three statues. The central statue depicted a muscular man. He was dressed in traditional noble clothing, large robes that reached just below his hips, and a belt around his waist. The belt shaped the robes into an hourglass and brought out the fine details of flowers and twisted designs placed along seams and folds. The statue's pants were tight, bulging with great leg muscles. A gold crown sat on his head, which was unlike the rest of the stone body. A mask covered his face, and he held a sword in his right hand. This was Daonrex. He was the divine progenitor of humanity and ruler of all things.

"*Praise to you, I am not worthy*," Brónmal thought.

The second statue depicted an old, bearded man dressed in priestly robes holding a pen. Filahaich, the patron of the common folk. His robes were long and flowing, a common priest's attire that removed individuality. Instead, with simple clothing, he was one with the church and the universe. A figure of humility and honesty, he was the role model of the peasant. He ruled outside of humanity and made plants grow. Without his hand, the world would starve.

The last statue, worn and unkempt, depicted a hooded man dressed like a peasant. Dubilfen, the patron of darkness. Clothes torn and patchy, he looked like a vile man. Sneering with a mouth of broken, rotted teeth, he was depicted with boils and rashes upon his skin. He brought plagues, disasters, and chaos. The Mednohail did not worship Dubilfen in reverence. Instead, they hoped to appease him and keep him away. He was the First Sinner and patron of heretics and criminals. It was *Eirsa* to worship Dubilfen, heresy of the worst degree.

Brónmal spread his arms upward and bowed his head, opening himself to Daonrex. He felt divine light enter him. A sensation of glowing and pulsing came from his bones. He felt love and passion.

* * *

The temple doors burst open, shocking everyone inside. Hacarad stormed in and shouted. "The *Apfaircada* is here! Prepare for the Godspeaker!"

7

Brónmal came out of his meditation. "Tell the city! I want the guard prepared for the Godspeaker! Go! GO!"

Hacarad and Brónmal left the temple. The city bells rang, drawing a crowd toward the docks while Brónmal darted to the ships. He sprinted through the streets, pushing past people and accidentally knocking over a barrel. At the docks, dozens of armed Mednohail soldiers formed a wall between the piers and the growing crowd.

The *Apfaircada* docked alongside a few other vessels. A white titan, it was an incredible wooden mass dwarfing not only the other ships but also a quarter of the city. The oldest Mednohail ship, it had been around since King Peregrine IV in the first Aothill. Nine soaring sails cast the docks in shadow, even as crewmen hurried to lower them. Its white body was adorned with gold-painted designs of flowers. Upon its bow was a wooden, shirtless man, spear in hand as if he led a charge. Along the ship's sides were three layers of trapdoors that ran from stern to bow. Within each were dozens of great ballistae of ancient design. Though the *Apfaircada* had never seen battle, it would undoubtedly tear apart any ship. Crewmen ran like ants and gathered to lower a large ramp.

Brónmal ran along the docks. "Line up!" he barked.

An army poured from the ship. The White Hands. Each man stood taller and broader than the average Mednohail. Dressed in all-white plate armor, their figures shone in the summer snow. Each had a spear and a large rectangular shield. There were a hundred White Hands, all surrounding a man dressed in bulbous white robes.

The Godspeaker, Bruidharir, stood out among any man. His brown hair had streaks of silver, with the pale fur of an albino animal decorating his shoulders and gold adorning his entire figure. Age had bent his posture, yet he walked with pride. His brown eyes had bags under them and looked as if they had seen centuries pass by. In his hand, he held a staff of silver and gold twisted together. A book with a jeweled cover and golden pages hung from his left hip, a holy scripture permitted for the Godspeaker only.

Brónmal knelt and bowed his head as the White Hands surrounded him. The Godspeaker approached. "Brónmal, Three bless you. It is good to see

8

one of the most faithful men I know here in this chilly place."

"It is an honor to see you again, Holy Godspeaker."

The Godspeaker's words gave Brónmal a taste of euphoria. "Come, Brónmal, we must speak."

"As you wish, Holy One."

The White Hands surrounded them, forming a wall between them and the soldiers lining the dock. The Throfi, new converts, cheered for what they believed to be a divine figure. They threw orange flower petals in the air and cried out in broken Mednohail. Brónmal gazed down at the petals. They were Yow flowers, the most common and hardiest flower of the North that grew all year around. He recalled the taste of Yow tea, bitter and sour, unlike the sweetness of any Mednohail tea.

The Godspeaker tilted his head. "How have the Throfi treated you?"

"As well as a pagan people can. They are strange people, though slowly turning to the light."

The Godspeaker rested a hand on Brónmal's shoulder. "I sense impatience in your voice, Brónmal. They will learn. I will be sure of it. Even animals can see the light. Not too long ago, the Throfi here were sacrificing to heathen demons. The rest of the tribes will learn what the Southern cities have learned."

Brónmal bowed his head. "Forgive me, Holy One. It is hard to watch such misguided people."

"Do not worry. You hold yourself responsible for people who can only be responsible for themselves. They will learn."

Brónmal glanced at him. "Do you intend to give a sermon today?"

The Godspeaker nodded. "At the temple. I intend to bless these people and help them see the Three. We have a few that we will usher into the light, reborn."

Brónmal smiled. "I am glad that I can be here. The priests have made all the preparations for your arrival. Do you need me to provide anything?"

"No, you have done your work. You may join me if you would like."

Brónmal's heart fluttered. "Absolutely, Holy One."

"Come then. We have no time to waste."

The army of white-armored bodyguards escorted the pair to the temple. They kept the people back, shouting and plowing through the crowd. At the temple, priests greeted the Godspeaker, exchanging pleasantries and kissing his hand. The White Hands, followed by the roaring crowd, gathered outside the temple.

Brónmal stood, hand resting on his scabbard. He watched the Godspeaker whisper to a priest, who nodded and disappeared. A moment later, he approached Brónmal. "An exciting day, is it not?"

"Yes, Holy One."

"We must speak later of the Heokolons. Mednodorn calls for its Generals."

Brónmal recoiled. "The Heokolons? What of the Easterlings? Have those wretched heathens attacked us?"

"No, but this is a conversation for another time. The Throfi await."

Brónmal lowered his gaze. Like all Mednohail, Brónmal hated the Heokolons. *"Will I avenge your failure, father?"* he thought. Only time would tell, though he itched to spill Heokolon blood.

The Godspeaker's booming voice interrupted his thoughts, repeated by a Throfi translator. "Good people of Hafornstalt! With the grace of the Three, I am blessed to be here amongst the humble Throfi once more!"

The crowd roared.

"It is my pleasure to see this temple finished in all its glory! A stone immortal, may it stand here for all eternity as a symbol of our faith in the Three! It fills me with joy to see so many of you basking in the light of Daonrex!"

Again, the crowd roared and jumped. The line of Mednohail soldiers in front of the White Hands stumbled back, eyes wide as they raised their shields. The Godspeaker raised his hand to calm the crowd. "I have served you, Mednodorn, and the Three for twenty years! But never in my life have I felt the love of Daonrex himself shine so bright here in these cold lands!"

He paused and glanced as a line of twenty-seven Throfi men in chains approached, escorted by twenty-seven Mednohail soldiers. "Yet, even in the brightest times, some still wish to cling to the darkness. Some have not seen the light, refusing to let go of ignorant and savage ways!"

Brónmal squinted while the line of men approached. The soldiers kicked out the knees of the prisoners and hit them with the hilts of their swords, forcing them to kneel and bow their heads. A priest came to them. He held a bowl in his left hand and a twig in his right. The bowl had a reddish-purple liquid called the Blood of Daonrex, which was water mixed with sap from sacred Morohm trees. While he chanted, the priest dipped the twig in the bowl and flicked drops of the liquid onto the heads of the Throfi prisoners. The crowd grew silent.

"Good people, the men before you have refused to see the light! They continue to do Dubilfen's work and conspire to bring down the holy knowledge we have brought to these cold lands."

One man jerked against his chains and shouted in Throfi. The crowd murmured, some screaming in anger. The few that could speak Mednohail cried out. "He said he's converted!"

"Silence! Many of the men before you are wretched heathens, though few have falsely converted. Let them not fool you! They are disguised demons, workers for Dubilfen who lied about their purity! They are sinners, guilty of four of the Cug Baolar! The first is *Aolfrao*, deceit! The second is *Esadif*, disobedience! The third, to the disgust of the Three, is *Aogadraod*, witchcraft! And fourth, most heinous of all, is *Eirsa*, heresy!"

The crowd jeered and shouted when the translator delivered the Godspeaker's words, but the line of guards held them back.

Hacarad walked up to Brónmal. "My Lord, what is going on?"

"I am not sure. The soldiers brought out these heathens, but I think some have converted. Where have you been?"

"Dealing with the guard. Everything is a mess. Something is going on. What have we not been told?"

Brónmal grimaced and looked around to see if anyone was watching them. All control seemed to have been taken from them, but by who? The Godspeaker?

The Godspeaker raised his hands in the air. "Good people, we cannot have traitors in our midst, heretics corrupting us! Wretched magic users, all of them in defiance of the love and grace the Three give us! We must be pure, we must be faithful, and we must fulfill our duty to the Three to lead the people into the light! If it is done through the sword, so be it."

The soldiers readied their swords. The Godspeaker continued. "May heretics and our enemies, from outside or within, know we will not be misled. By man's blood and steel's will, all will see the light! Send them to Dubilfen."

The soldiers cut into the line of prisoners, felling them with brutal, zealous stabs. The prisoners convulsed and screamed; their cries turned to gargle as they choked on blood. The crowd gasped. Men shouted as brothers and kinsmen were put to the sword, wives and daughters screaming as loved ones perished.

Hacarad shouted. "What are they doing?"

Chaos erupted. Brónmal heard women and children scream and watched them run. Throfi men tackled soldiers or kept them at bay while their families escaped.

Mednohail soldiers attacked the enraged Throfi. Brónmal snapped out of his shock and barked commands. "Wall formation! Surround the temple! Protect the Godspeaker at all costs!

The Mednohail soldiers gathered in an immense wall of shields and weapons, pushing against the attacking Throfi. Throfi men clawed at the shields. Some soldiers were ripped from their feet and hurled to the ground. Others screamed as Throfi men tore shields from their hands and broke their bones with crude bronze weapons. Brónmal clenched his hands in anger. Such primitive monsters were nothing to him, nothing without Mednohail discipline.

Brónmal shouted. "Move forward! Slaughter them!"

A unified cry came from the soldiers. "For the Three! The shield wall slammed forward. The Throfi fell back, swords and spears cutting them down. The formation inched forward. They crushed dead men under their feet, stomping and stabbing until the crowd broke. The intimidated Throfi grabbed their children and wives and ran off, leaving only a few who clung to the bodies of their fathers, brothers, and husbands. Wailing filled the air. Blood tainted the sacred grounds of the temple.

"*What happened?*" Brónmal thought. Did the Godspeaker execute heathens or massacre innocents? He walked among the dead, blood squelching beneath his boots.

Hacarad came up to him. "Why this? We were meant to convert peacefully here, so why this now?"

Brónmal hissed. "Shush! Do not question so loudly. We will speak later. I must see to the Godspeaker."

"As you say, Lord. I will help keep order and deal with the dead."

Hacarad bowed and walked toward the small army of soldiers. "To me, men! Gather the dead! Secure the streets around the square!"

Brónmal looked up. The snow continued to come down, melting in the heat of fresh blood.

Had they sinned here or served faithfully?

2

The Gisjaf Sea

T he sea rocked the tremendous body of the *Apfaircada*. Brónmal could barely see the rest of the fleet in the darkness of the moonless night. For once, the northern skies were clear. The constellations shone brightly, the jewels of the universe crafted and placed by Filahaich himself. Brónmal adored them, though he could never remember the names of them all. He was no navigator, only a soldier.

"*Finally,*" he thought, glad to be far enough south to have nights again. Though the nights in this part of the world during High Summer were only a few hours long, Brónmal took the time to see the stars. Incredibly restless from the swaying boat, he had nothing else to do.

Around the *Apfaircada*, the fleet stirred. Mednohail sailors crawled every-where on every ship, ensuring everything stayed together as they sailed home. Brónmal did not trust sailors. Men who did not fear the deep waters and life at sea seemed insane, yet he respected their discipline and hard work.

Mednodorn awaited. Brónmal looked forward to returning home. It was the month of *Aurhath*, the last month before High Summer. Soon, the green hills and forests would wither. The opposite of High Winter, High Summer meant death. *Aurhath* brought the first harvest. Brónmal looked forward to the first harvest. People would soon celebrate for the last week of the month, gather at temples, praise the Three, and feast. Better yet, the warmth of Low Summer in Mednodorn meant no wretched snow to bother him.

Brónmal leaned over the ship's side. He could taste the salt swept up from the ocean spray by the breeze. Unlike other bodies of water, the Gisjaf Sea stank. It smelled of rotten eggs, the scent of decay reeking from dead algae, seaweed, and plankton carried by the waves. Brónmal's mind darkened while his gaze fell to the dark depths of the sea below. The massacre, fresh in his mind, replayed itself in his memories: blood, the spasms of the newly dead, the cries of the newly widowed.

He did not care for the Throfi, but something was wrong. Were those converted men? Even if they were not, the murders had soured Mednohail relations with the Northlands. He had no qualms about executing heretics. The Throfi were different, more like disciplining dogs than punishing evil dissenters.

The sound of a whip crossed his memories. Discipline. He shook the thoughts out of his head and stared out at the other ships.

A voice cut through the night. "My Lord?"

Brónmal jumped. "Gah! By the Three! Hacarad, is that you?"

Hacarad emerged from the dark and bowed. "My apologies, Lord. I did not mean to startle."

"You are forgiven. I was just drawn into my thoughts."

"Thank you, Lord. May I join you? The swaying of the ship has me restless."

Brónmal gestured to his side. "Of course, friend. I am not doing anything but thinking."

Hacarad joined him and looked out into the dark waters. "You cannot sleep, Lord?"

Brónmal shook his head. "Ships swaying make me restless as well. I was just thinking of what happened at Hafornstalt."

Hacarad frowned. "A tragedy. I understand they are pagans, but they are not like heretics. Heretics know what they have done wrong."

"No need to twist your words with me. We are alone. Yes, they may not have deserved mercy, but how do we know? We do not know what those men did. I was told some had converted, not all."

Hacarad shrugged. "I am not sure either. The Grayskins accepted us and the righteous light, and this is how we treat them?"

Brónmal lowered his gaze. "It has set back relations for decades. By now, I am sure all of Gribjodhen—if not all the North—knows of the massacre."

Hacarad sighed. "Why do we worry so about the heathens? You and I have slaughtered countless heretics in the name of the Three."

"Perhaps we feel pity for them, like helpless dogs. We cut the hands off a thief because a thief knows better, but we beat a dog with a stick because it needs discipline and respect for its master."

"You may be right, Lord. But, in truth, we should trust the Godspeaker and the Highlord. If the Godspeaker wishes it, we obey."

Brónmal chuckled. "Are we then the dogs?"

Hacarad smiled. "I know no better master to serve than the Three, and for that, I am willing to be a dog."

"Well said. I am glad we have left the Northlands. Snow in Low Summer? How could they endure in such a place?"

Hacarad shrugged. "I know not. I know that High Summer awaits us when we arrive at Ardmunhaich."

Brónmal grimaced. "The drought will be fun. And marching in the heat."

"Better than snow, Lord?"

"Maybe we should turn around?"

The pair laughed. Hacarad shrugged. "Would you like to head to the red sands of Arn'eketh instead, Lord?"

"Absolutely not! Those damned Ahamari and their desert. I am glad our forefathers broke them and their worship of the ground itself."

"I have heard strange things from those lands."

Brónmal tilted his head. "Like what?"

"Despite two *Aothills* of rule, over three hundred years of our control, there is talk of revolution."

"Revolution? Their empire has been broken for over four *Aothills*. How could they ever hope to rebuild it?"

"They could never, even if they tried. Our temples dominate their lands, and their children and forefathers have worshiped the Three long enough to forget about the old ways. Despite that, I have heard from Gaothal's General, Domganmir, that some Ahamari can manipulate the surrounding sands."

"Witchcraft? Surely, they know the punishment for committing *Aogadraod*? Magic belongs to the Three."

Hacarad nodded. "Even children know full well not to mimic the Three. There have been many executed magic users in Arn'eketh, and the General says they continue to pop up like an infestation."

"Domganmir has always been useless. Fat and lazy with his easy rule over the Southern lands. Send me down there, and I will have the Ahamari begging for mercy."

"Well said, Lord."

Brónmal turned and leaned against the deck siding. "There is another thing that bothers me."

Hacarad tilted his head. "What would that be, Lord?"

"The Godspeaker wanted to talk to me about the Heokolons."

"The Easterners? We have not interacted with them in at least three decades."

"I know. That is why I worry. Why else would the Godspeaker want to speak to me about the Heokolons? War must be coming."

Hacarad gasped and walked around Brónmal. "Are we going to war against the East, Lord?"

"I do not know. He only mentioned that Mednodorn calls for its Generals. The other eight must be going to Ardmunhaich as well."

"The Godspeaker can be mysterious, Lord. We must trust him. Surely, there will be answers at Ardmunhaich. Do you think it will happen? Thirty years since our forefathers failed in the East, we might have the opportunity to avenge them."

"Perhaps so. I worry about the Throne. What of the Highlord, what of the Godspeaker? Why was our duty taken away from us at Hafornstalt?"

Hacarad waved his hand dismissively. "I would not worry or think of those things. It is *Esadif*, and such a sin is beyond you, Lord."

"You are right. We must obey." Brónmal stood silent for a moment. "I think I am going to retire to bed. The breeze is cold."

Hacarad bowed. "As you wish, Lord. If you need me, just call. Good night."

"Good night, Hacarad."

Brónmal sighed once out of earshot of Hacarad.

"Could I trust you, brother?" he thought. Perhaps Hacarad could not be trusted with his inner thoughts about the Godspeaker. Perhaps his thoughts had led him to the sin of Esadif, disobedience. Was he wrong to value serving the Three over the Godspeaker and the Highlord? Surely, he was. Yet, something had snapped. He was not sure, but he felt deceived.

He shook his head. He was above such thoughts. Ideas of unyielding, zealous loyalty filled his mind again as he descended into the ship's bowels. Sailors and soldiers filled every cabin and passageway. Between those who played games, talked, drank, and slept were the seasick. The wretched stink of vomit and unwashed bodies filled the ship's interior. Above the sound of people talking and gagging, Brónmal could hear the ship creak and rock.

Brónmal stumbled and leaned on the walls of each passageway. Like most soldiers, he felt dizzy. He hated boats. Nothing was good about the musk, the cramped spaces, the old food. The horrific idea of them sinking haunted him. Drowning terrified all Mednohail. Only a brave handful who grew up by the Mekden and Gisjaf seas dared to sail over the abyssal darkness of the depths below.

Hesitantly shuffling along, he arrived at his cabin. Like the other Generals of each province, Brónmal had an escort. They alternated shifts on the boat, two at a time guarding his room. They bowed as he approached. "Three bless, General Brónmal!"

Brónmal waved his hand. "Three bless."

They opened the door for him. He wobbled in and fell on his knees by his chamber pot. The nausea was too much. Dry heaving a few times, Brónmal panted, gave up, and crawled to his bed.

He muttered. "Curse this boat!"

Wrapping himself in his blankets, he felt some relief. The spinning in his head slowed as his mind fell to dark thoughts. The Throfi needed discipline. They needed to obey. Discipline. The sound of a whip echoed in his head. Memories of his father appeared and tormented him, imaginary pains searing his back. He tossed and turned, falling into a restless slumber.

3

The Hunt

Brónmal shivered. Aged eleven, his small body could barely keep warm. Low Winter had arrived, and the North wind from Gribjodhen blew down into the hills and forest of Mednodorn. Snow blanketed the land. The estate grounds, usually green and filled with slaves, were vacant and dead.

Only the imposing stone walls of the estate gave any color to the dormant land. The estate stood as a testament to his family's wealth. It had multiple sections, including a temple dedicated to the Three. The structure was unyielding and had stood since the First Aothill after the Reign.

Brónmal bounced up and down, waiting for his father to leave the house. His ears were cold, and he could see his breath. Just as he was about to swear about the snow, a shout came from the home. "Boy! Get in here!"

His heart sank as he ran into the house. Brónmal went into an extensive room with a staircase and three people. Two of the people wore rags. Born from executed heretics, they were slaves condemned to servitude for the sins of their parents.

The third person was his father, Remtaich. Unlike the slaves, who grew up stunted because of little food and medicine, Brónmal's father stood tall. He was the ideal Mednohail man: sun-kissed skin, brown hair, and eyes so piercing that they could burn someone from a look alone. Scars covered his skin, marks from his service in the first Heokolon War. He was merciless, decisive, and brimming with faith. Brónmal, only eleven, could only hope to be somewhat like his veteran father.

Remtaich pointed at Brónmal. "Boy! Have you prepared the arrows?"

Brónmal shook his head. Remtaich's brow wrinkled, eyes darkening. He snapped to one slave. "You! Go grab the arrows."

The slave bowed and disappeared as the other one lowered his head and helped Remtaich into his hunting clothes. Remtaich looked at Brónmal. "I should beat you for your disobedience. I will not tolerate *Esadif* from my own son. Is that what you want?"

Brónmal jumped and bowed his head.

"Then act better! I will whip you again if you disobey me! Would you treat me so if I was the Highlord or the Godspeaker?

Brónmal shook his head again. "No, Lord!"

"Good! At least you have some manners and discipline in the face of holiness. Grab your bow and meet me outside. NOW!"

Brónmal ran to the manor's armory. He entered and found the slave gathering arrows. The slave only glanced at him, not allowed to speak unless given permission.

The armory was full of various armor and weapons. Among them were trophies, like Brónmal's favorite, a suit of Heokolon armor. It was the finest craftsmanship he had ever seen, with perfectly molded plate armor lacking any crack or weakness. Next to it was a spear with a tip more like a wing than any point seen in Mednodorn. Made from special Heokolon glass, the blade was sharper than any metal yet strong enough not to shatter against plate armor.

Brónmal had heard stories of the Heokolons. They were savage pagans with cruel weapons, only matched by the zealous and righteous hordes of Mednodorn. The first war ended disastrously. His father told stories of being pushed over the Kabhain River, which separated the two empires. Out of anything in the world, Remtaich hated the Easterlings the most. Brónmal wanted to fight the Heokolons to make his father proud. Maybe one day.

He grabbed a small bow before returning to his father. The slave followed, giving Remtaich his arrows and bow. Once Remtaich was ready, he led

Brónmal out to the forest.

Brónmal followed. "What are we looking for, Lord?"

"Anything today. There's not much out with the coming of High Winter. We will see."

They strode into the snow between the skeletal figures of looming trees. Everything was still. Not even the wind stirred as frost coated the land and rendered life immobile. Brónmal shook. He hated going out in the cold, but his father made him bear it. He told Brónmal that a true soldier of Mednodorn did not fear heat or cold, only weakness. Remtaich said that only the strongest were blessed by the Three.

"*The cold is nothing; the love of the Three keeps me warm,*" Brónmal thought.

The estate disappeared behind the hills. They marched into the cold dark of the woods. Somehow, his father did not seem bothered. He did not even shiver. Brónmal, on the other hand, felt his hands going numb in his gloves.

A few birds flew between the leafless branches above. Most had two sets of wings, and only a few had a single set of wings. By this time of the year, many of the birds were white. They looked down at the pair, singing and filling the forest with sound. Brónmal glanced up at them. They were beautiful. Their pure white feathers and gentle songs contrasted against the lifeless, dormant trees. Unlike Brónmal, they were free.

"Come on, boy. You are lagging."

Brónmal hurried forward. His father paused occasionally, looking around the woods and listening for calls or sounds. "This way."

They marched between endless hills. Remtaich easily climbed the steep hills while Brónmal slipped and crawled. He stuck to the trail left by Remtaich. Uncovered by Remtaich's boots, Brónmal hooked onto tree roots and dug his hands into rocks. They continued for another hour before Brónmal spoke. "Father, what was it like to serve the Highlord?"

"An honor, boy. I would gladly lay down my life for him and the Godspeaker, the righteous Godspeaker."

"Why did they make us go to war against the Heokolons?"

Remtaich glanced back. "Have we spoken about Daodamath?"

"No, Lord."

"Well, a long time ago, when the supreme god Daonrex created us Mednohail, he created us to serve the Three unquestioningly. As loyal servants, we have. But we were not just made to serve. Mednodorn, the shining beacon of the Three, exists not only as an example of how the world should be but also as a shepherd. Many pagan people are outside the light. The Throfi, the Ahamari, the Heokolons. It is our duty to be an example to them and help them see and accept the Three."

Brónmal frowned. "Why do they believe any different from us?"

Remtaich shrugged. "I do not know. The work of Dubilfen posing as pagan gods, no doubt. They are lost, like children such as you. Like children, they will learn."

"Why do we think they are not right, Lord?"

Remtaich stopped. "Watch your tongue, boy. I will not have such *Eirsa* come from my own son. I did not raise a heretic who does not know better. They are not right because they are outside the light of the Three, outside the love of Daonrex."

Brónmal bowed his head. "Apologies, Lord. I did not mean that."

"You had best not."

Brónmal asked. "Have you ever met the Godspeaker, Lord?"

"I have. I have attended many of his sermons and speeches in Ard-munhaich." "What was it like?"

"His words fill you with ecstatic joy. It's as if you are being cradled in love. I could not fully describe it, but I would suffer just to hear his words again."

Brónmal looked down. His mind wandered into dangerous depths before he spoke softly. "Why do we listen to a man when seeking the words of the Three?"

Remtaich struck Brónmal across the face. Brónmal cried out and crashed into the snow. His face burned, the iron taste of blood filling his mouth. His father shouted, distant birds taking flight out of fear. "How *dare* you? Such heresy! You will be silent for the rest of this hunt before I cut your tongue out!"

Brónmal curled up and hid his burning cheek. He let out pained gasps, unable to speak.

"Get up! Do not utter another one of your heinous words and questions!"

Brónmal got to his feet. His head bowed while his father stormed off. He meekly followed, tears rolling down his eyes.

The woods were quiet, all life hiding in fear from Remtaich's booming voice. They went on for hours, silent. Brónmal's face tingled as it became red, sure to bruise. Angry thoughts swirled in his mind. *"Why can I not ask questions? I want to know what the Three would think, not what a man knows. What does Godspeaker know that I do not?"* He drowned his thoughts, hiding them from even the gods.

Eventually, his father slowed. Tracks. They were in sets of six, dozens seen in the snow. Remtaich pointed at the tracks. "These are from large beasts, creatures with six legs. Pay attention to each print. They are far apart and deep, yet they are consistent. They must be grazing somewhere."

The pair crouched low and followed the tracks. Brónmal examined each print. Like a dinner plate, each hoofprint was two times larger than his foot. The beasts must have been heavy, each print uncovering soil beneath the packed snow. They followed the trail for two hours before a warbling call echoed through the woods.

"They are near. Quiet down, boy."

They crept toward the source of the call, hiding among the bushes while they got up to the crest of the hill. Below was an open field. Massive six-legged beasts grazed in the area, each crowned with four huge antlers. Crobestir. They were ordinary cloven beasts in Mednodorn, yet only nobles could hunt them. Despite being great beasts with immense shoulder and hip muscles, they were skittish. Any slight disturbance put the herd on edge, a stampede just a branch snap away. Occasionally, they let out warbling calls.

Remtaich pointed at one near the base of the hill. "That one boy. Nock your arrow and aim."

Brónmal quivered. He did not want to kill, but he did not want to disappoint his father. He drew an arrow and snuck down the hill. His heart beat faster, hands squeezing the bow, feet hesitantly finding their way. A group of bushes provided the cover he needed. He crept up to them and peeked through a small gap, bow drawn. The bowstring was heavy, taking all his might to pull back. As he aimed, his hands shook, aim quivering.

Could he really do it? Why would he hurt this innocent thing? The great stag lifted its vast head, its sheer mass terrifying. It looked over the hill and released a warbling cry. Brónmal gasped and stumbled back, letting loose the arrow. Whizzing through the air, the arrow cut clean over the beast and flew over the field into a tree. A high-pitched warbling call echoed from the beasts as the herd scattered in terror.

"You fool!" Remtaich shouted.

Brónmal's father's booming shout thundered over the field, sending the stampede in the opposite direction of the pair. The beasts charged across the area. They disappeared into the woods beyond the field when Remtaich ran down to grab Brónmal.

Brónmal tried to run. "Father, no!"

Remtaich grabbed him and dragged him across the field. "You damnable child! How dare you miss?"

"It was an accident, Lord!"

"It must be Esadif! You disobey me, boy! I will teach you a lesson to disobey me!"

Remtaich grabbed Brónmal and threw him on the ground, removing his belt. Brónmal tried to crawl, only to be struck with the belt. It made a cracking whip-like sound, each lash burning. Remtaich screamed with each strike, swearing to the Three and spitting raging incoherent words at Brónmal.

"Lord! No! Stop!"

* * *

Brónmal lurched up, shaking his head. He was on the ship, far from the field and his wretched father. His heart pounded, his hands shook, and goosebumps covered his skin. The nightmare was not just a twisted vision from his brain but a memory.

He still hated his father. Remtaich could never beat the questions out of Brónmal's head, yet he could scar his body and mind. By now, he was a decrepit, wrathful old man rotting away in his estate. Brónmal was unsure what to do when he died, though he had contemplated burning the estate down. After his service as General, Brónmal could get enough slaves to build another one. It would be better than facing the nightmarish memories imprisoned in every hall and room of the accursed place. Despite his father's brutality, his noble origins and status as a veteran got Brónmal far into the Mednodorn military. Without his father, he would not be the General of the Beinthal army.

Brónmal put on his robes and walked onto the ship's main deck. He went to the bow to see if he could spot Mednodorn. The fleet still sailed, hundreds of crewmen swarming the vessels while the early morning sun rose over the freezing sea – no land on any horizon. Brónmal frowned. They were still far from Mednodorn. He could not wait to get home.

4

The Throne of Ardmunhaich

T he grand capital of Ardmunhaich. The city stood as an immortal monument to the power of Mednodorn and the Mednohail people. Three walls, each colossal, surrounded the city. Outside of them were immeasurable fields of farmland. The poor lived within the outermost ring of walls, the middle class in the middle, and the nobility in the innermost ring. Standing in the center of the city was a ziggurat. Pyramid-like, it was built in plateau-like layers that made it a tower.

Within the ziggurat was a tomb hosting the bodies of all previous Highlords, Godspeakers, kings, and prominent church members. Outside, each level had immense green gardens leading up to two massive structures. One was a castle, the impenetrable home of the Highlord. The second was a temple, the holy residence of the Godspeaker and the ruling members of the Church. No structure in the entire Empire came close to these two. The ziggurat rose above the massive walls, the castle and the church stood high above anything in the Empire.

The army marched into the farmlands outside Ardmunhaich. Peasants lined the road leading to Mednodorn, cheering as soldiers marched past. In the middle of the army was the Godspeaker. He rode in a carriage pulled by beasts called Auhmogs. Like Brónmal, the army of White Hands rode Auhmogs, surrounding the carriage like an impenetrable wall. Nervous creatures, Auhmogs were reserved for nobility as a form of transportation.

Many had tried, but few had ever ridden the beasts into war.

The peasants shouted.

"The Godspeaker has returned!"

"The Three have blessed us!"

"Three praise!"

Brónmal glanced at them. Unlike those in villages and hamlets, these were not freemen. They were bound to noble lords in Ardmunhaich, serving faithfully and providing food in return for land. At least they were not slaves or heretics.

It took an hour of marching before they drew near the gates. The mighty walls loomed over the city, standing 115 feet over the land, the height of twenty-three men. At the base of the walls were great foundations. The foundations, made from soil, were steep hills that added 25 feet to the walls. Difficult to climb, the tremendous foundations stabilized the walls. Built without magic by freemen, serfs, and enslaved soldiers, the walls of Ardmunhaich were one of King Peregrine's most outstanding achievements. Archers patrolled them. Shouts came from above, the walls rumbling as the gates moved.

The cheering outside became muffled as the gates opened, revealing a crowd of thousands. Two lines of soldiers flanked the path from the outer to the inner city. A horde of people pushed against them. Temple bells rang, flower petals rained down, and hundreds wept joyfully.

Brónmal waved. Zealous singing and cheering filled the air as people celebrated the arrival of their Godspeaker and great men like Brónmal. He was not the only General called to the great city. The other seven Generals followed behind him, the eighth awaiting them at the center of Ardmunhaich. Brónmal had only met the other Generals a few times and respected only two. The first was Baufrius of the Northern province of Eidthal. A Northerner like Brónmal, they thought highly of each other. They shared the same customs and communicated with the same dialect, naturally putting them on good terms. The second was Trudumal, the Ardmunhaich General and the Empire's Supreme General. He was old, wise, and a role model for all Generals. Out of all great men, Brónmal respected Trudumal almost as much as the Highlord and Godspeaker.

Cages hung from the dense buildings above the road, heretics trapped within them. Condemned to death, they were starving and nude. The sun blistered their bony bodies, birds pecked at them, and scum covered them. Some were dead. Those alive sat, a few reaching out to plead. Brónmal looked up. These were the warnings to the sinners in Mednodorn, each trapped heretic acting as a display of the Church's power.

A mile separated the outermost wall from the middle, yet the whole area was packed. There were no spaces between buildings, mud and feces covered the roads, and the people were dirty. Brónmal could smell them—the poor stank, filthy, and unwashed. Most were serfs, though among them were slaves and indebted peasants. They dressed in rags and worn clothing, their skin dark from years of labor beneath the sun. Children among them did not have shoes, running barefoot in the city's filth.

"*Wretched peasants,*" Brónmal thought. Though they loved him, he kept his head high. He was, indeed, better than them, more loyal to the Three than they ever could be. They were insignificant. Like most of Mednodorn, they were bodies with which to build monuments. To him, they were nameless and faceless, mere tools for the nobility and divine rulers.

The second gate opened, and another wave of cheers erupted. The inner city had wealthier people, freemen, and women. Most were traders, artisans, craftsmen, and skilled folk. They had finer clothes and wore jewelry. Women had braided and combed hair, men were shaven, and the air did not reek like refuse and rot. The buildings here had some space between them. Their structures were made from stone and brick, more robust than the outer ring's wooden houses. Vibrant ribbons wrapped around poles flapped in the wind, white flowers rained from the crowd, and the people sang and wept.

Hacarad urged his Auhmog up beside Brónmal's and spoke over the crowd. "What a welcome, is it not, Lord?"

"Quite the welcome! Praise the Three! It is a good day to come to the throne of the Empire!"

"Escorting the Godspeaker himself, no less!"

"Indeed."

"Lord, do you know why the other seven Generals are here?"

Brónmal shook his head. "Not a clue, Hacarad. We have all been called here; that's all I know."

"Perhaps something is going to happen?"

"May it be good."

"I pray for us it is, Lord."

The center of the capital was only three-quarters of a mile across. They met the innermost wall. It stood fifteen feet higher than the other two walls and was thicker. Men in finer armor guarded these walls. They stood watch faithfully. The inner gates opened, revealing the inner city. The nobility greeted them just as joyously. Dressed in fine clothes and glamorous jewels, their perfume filled the air. They showered the men with petals from exotic flowers, delicate pieces of cloth, and other luxurious jewelry.

Brónmal, like many of the Generals, had visited Ardmunhaich often. His name meant something to the nobility; he even knew some of the young noblewomen. They cried out for him. He waved back, making them blush or throw red love ribbons at him. He caught a few, chuckling with Hacarad as they approached the steps.

The ziggurat awaited. A small wall separated it from the rest of the inner city, standing only twenty-five feet high. Divided into nine layers, the ziggurat had four grand staircases leading up to the top, where the castle and temple were. Each layer had gardens. Slaves took care of the gardens while White Hands patrolled everywhere.

Priests rushed to greet the Godspeaker as he left his carriage. The soldiers on beasts dismounted, surrounding the Godspeaker in formation and marching up the steps. Hacarad followed Brónmal. The army fell into a rectangular formation at the top of the stairs, standing in front of a massive Morohm tree separating the castle and church.

Awaiting them was the Highlord, Dachfranir, together with a small escort. Dachfranir was a burly Mednohail man with white hair and a beard like a lion's mane. His eyes were green, a rare color most now associated with royalty. His kingly robes were large and fur-adorned, and he wore a golden crown. The crown was ancient, belonging to every Highlord before him, going back six hundred years, all the way to King Peregrine IV. Among the escort was the ninth General, the Supreme General of Ardmunhaich, Trudumal.

The Godspeaker approached. The Highlord bowed, kissing the Godspeaker's hand. "It is an honor to welcome you back, Godspeaker."

The Godspeaker smiled. "It is an honor to see you again, Dachfranir. Three bless you, my friend."

The Highlord gazed over the White Hands, the eight other Generals of Mednodorn, and the servants of each. He raised his hands and spoke in the voice only an emperor could conjure. "Good men of Mednodorn, it is with great praise I welcome you back to the throne of the Empire! It has been long since I have seen some of you, though I welcome you all back as friends and loyal servants of the Three!"

The men cheered. "Praise the Highlord! Praise the Three!'

The Highlord smiled and continued. "Though I cherish this unity and meeting of brothers, I do not bring you home for no reason, good men! I bring you home for a change, to prepare for the coming Aothill. A new age is coming. Soon, the comet Serkur will burn the sky and usher us into a glorious new era. The Godspeaker himself has envisioned this, and you men will be at the helm of our great Empire!"

Again, the men cheered. The Highlord continued. "In this new age, you men will help guide the world into the light of the Three. We have already begun this guidance in the North, yet the entire world must see! It is our Daodamath, our glorious destiny, to see this fulfilled!"

The men erupted. "Praise the Empire!"

"Good men, I recognize this is with little time and little ceremony, but great things do not need to be complex. I have brought my good friend, advisor, and leader of the swords of Ardmunhaich here. Trudumal, step forth!"

Trudumal, the Supreme General of Ardmunhaich, stepped forward. He was an older man, just like the Highlord. He had seen decades of battle and served in the first Heokolon War. His face was scarred. With a frail body, the once-great warrior was thin and aged. He was bald with a white, wispy beard. He stood unsteadily, posture slightly bent and hands shaking. Despite his broken body, his spirit was unwavering. His gaze frightened all soldiers, his voice raspy and commanding. He bowed. "Praise the Highlord, praise the Three."

Brónmal stared at Trudumal. This was his role model, the example to emulate and impress, the reason to overachieve. There were hushed rumors he was more loyal to the Highlord than the Godspeaker. His fanaticism appeared through the sword and the spear rather than prayer and submission. He was a man of action and did not listen to anyone but Dachfranir.

The Highlord continued his speech. "Trudumal has served me for decades. He has led every battle, and despite what his advisors think, he has always led at the front of war as the tip of the spear! He was the first to go into every battle and the last to leave. Surely, the Three have blessed him. Despite that, old men like us break, and with a new age, the young men will lead."

"*What is going on?*" Brónmal thought as he looked around. All the men stirred.

"After decades, Trudumal has chosen to step down as General of Ardmunhaich to allow the new to take his place! Trudumal, my brother and friend, if you wish to ease their minds, do so."

Trudumal bowed to the Highlord and stepped forward. He spoke as if he had eaten only gravel his whole life, a voice as scarred as his body. "I see before me, worried men. I had believed you all had more faith in the Three and the Highlord. Do not worry. It is shameful."

"*Three bless you, Trudumal. I bestow my trust in you as my father did,*" Brónmal thought, head bowed in reverence. The men grew still and silent.

"Though I wish I could have died in war, the Three seem to have other things in mind for me. I will continue to serve but as an advisor rather than a warrior. It is wise to let younger men pave the way when getting out of bed on your lonesome grows hard. I feel confident. I feel blessed by the Three knowing that the future is in hands like yours, the most faithful of all Mednohail."

He turned. "May I, Highlord?"

Dachfranir nodded. Trudumal turned to the men again. "It is with pleasure that I may announce my successor. This man has served faithfully all his life, from his youth as a commander to a General. It is no simple task; earning what he has takes great fortitude. Brónmal! Step forward!"

Hacarad let out a gasp while the army burst into roaring cheers. Brónmal's heart sank. His hands quivered while he tried to contain himself. He nervously stepped forward out of the ranks.

Trudumal approached. Brónmal knelt, almost falling as he bowed his head deeply. He whispered. "Praise the Three. I am not worthy."

Trudumal rested a hand on his shoulder. "You are worthy. Stand like an honored man."

"*I am not worthy, I am not worthy,*" Brónmal thought while he stood. Trudumal drew his sword. It was a sacred sword carried with him as a sign of nobility. It was sharp, its blade covered in swirling marks and its hilt golden with jewels. He touched the blade to each of Brónmal's shoulders. "Raise your hands."

Brónmal's eyes flickered. His heart fluttered as he raised his hands, the sword placed horizontally across them. Trudumal stepped back. "This, and the armies of Mednodorn, now belong to you. Serve with honor, serve with loyalty, serve with faith. Three bless you, Supreme General."

The army behind him shouted. "Praise Brónmal!"

Trudumal stepped back as the Godspeaker approached and sprinkled the Blood of Daonrex upon him, staining his clothes with reddish-purple dots. The Highlord approached and shook Brónmal's hand firmly. "It is an honor to welcome a new General for a new coming age."

The Highlord looked over the rest of the army. "Praise Brónmal, may the Three bless him!"

The army chanted. "Praise Brónmal! Praise Brónmal!"

After a few chants, the Highlord waved them into silence. "Good men! The priests of the temple are going to have mass to welcome you back. Go now in peace to the temple!"

The army marched to the temple, leaving only a few White Hands behind with the Godspeaker and the Highlord. The Highlord gestured to Brónmal, "This way."

"*How could I deserve this?*" Brónmal thought. He felt weak and dizzy as if he would pass out on his feet.

The three men, escorted by nine White Hands, marched into the grand castle of Ardmunhaich. Inside the great doors was a throne room. It was long and tall. The ceiling extended higher than most churches and had floors above it. On either side were balconies that overlooked benches that led up to a massive platform. At the top of the platform was a throne. Carved out of the base of a statue, it towered over the throne room. The sculpture depicted King Peregrine IV, the first Highlord and the uniter of the Empire four Aothills ago. Above it, windows let light flood the throne room.

"*Glory to the Three, I am not worthy; find me in solemn humility and grace,*" Brónmal thought, mind swirling with prayers and doubts.

Dachfranir marched up the steps and sat on his throne. The Godspeaker stood beside him. The nine White Hands stood along the steps in a cone, and Brónmal stood in the middle at the very base of the steps.

The Highlord made himself comfortable and leaned forward. "I am sure you have many questions, Brónmal."

"No, Highlord. I am loyal to you, the Godspeaker, and the Three. Whatever you wish of me, I will provide and serve faithfully in this new position."

The Highlord chuckled. "That is good to know, but even the most loyal are curious. You must be wondering why there was so little ceremony, unlike the Generals of the past. Times are changing, and we must look beyond our lands. There will be time to celebrate once you come back."

"*Look beyond our lands?*" Brónmal thought, brow furrowed.

The Highlord gestured to the Godspeaker. "Bruidharir here has seen a glorious vision of the future. The Mednohail will rule and shepherd the world into the light in the next age. The new age begins with the East. The Heokolons have gone unpunished for too long."

Brónmal's eyes widened. It was time to avenge his father's legacy. Dachfranir nodded. "Indeed. It has been far too long since we failed in the East, yet the people hunger. Veterans seek revenge, the youth seek glory, and we seek the good and just salvation of all."

"Highlord, are we going to war?"

"Indeed, and you will lead the army of Ardmunhaich and the army of Beinthal to the East. You will cut off the head of their emperor, burn their lands, and bend them to your will."

Brónmal fell to his knees and bowed. "It is an honor, Highlord! Why me?"

"You are the most faithful and unquestioning of men. I knew your father, and Trudumal served alongside him. We both knew he raised a fine, vigorous young man who prizes the Three above all else. We examined the other Generals, yet your deeds, mind, and spirit are above all others."

"Thank you, Highlord. Three bless you."

"Do not worry, Brónmal. There will be time to meet the men of Ard-munhaich and plan for the invasion of Heonar. We will talk often about this. There are many things to consider, reasons beyond our Daodamath."

"What do you mean, Highlord?"

Dachfranir pointed out of the castle doors, "Out there are millions, the faithful of Mednodorn. They will come to die, and in their lives and deaths, we need salt—salt for food, salt for the dead. Our mines are overburdened, our stores empty."

"*We march beyond the demands of faith?*" Brónmal thought. He tilted his head and spoke. "What will you have me do?"

"Above all else, secure the lands of Western Heonar before the mountains of the East," the Godspeaker said. "There, in the plains, is salt in the very ground. You will find plenty to enslave for salt mines there."

The Highlord nodded. "If you secure the land beyond the Kabhain River, the Empire will have enough salt to last for Aothills. You secure the fate of millions if you succeed."

Brónmal bowed his head. "I will do this for you, for the Three, and for Mednodorn."

The Godspeaker raised a finger. "Do not fail. We must assert our power over the world. We must dominate the wealth and riches of the unworthy. My word must reach all; I demand it. We are done here; you may go join your men. Celebrate now, for the future holds much work."

"Am I dismissed then, Holy One?"

"You are."

"Thank you, Three bless."

Lightheaded, Brónmal stood and walked out of the castle. He glanced back, his jaw clenched in thought. Did he hear the Godspeaker speak words of greed?

5

The Army of Ardmunhaich

Echoes of metal boots filled the air as the White Hands escorted Brónmal and the Highlord from the city. The White Hands and their snow-colored armor shone in the light of High Summer. Like a white spear, they parted the terrified and awe-filled crowds. To the people, they were power incarnate.

The news spread fast. People cried out in praise at the presence of the new Supreme General. People waved, shouted for Brónmal, and tried to shower them in flower petals as they did when the Godspeaker arrived.

While the White Hands marched, Brónmal and the Highlord rode upon Auhmogs. They proceeded out of the inner city. Gate after gate opened, the crowds in the streets parting for the escort and cheering at the sight of the pair. Brónmal rode with a high chin. He was the third most powerful man in all Mednodorn; his voice and would now be able to command legions of faithful. He rode straight, face stern, staring ahead like a noble. Within, he felt powerful as the people reached out to him.

"Love me, for I am your shield. May I earn my place, Three willing," he thought as people cheered.

Dachfranir looked over at Brónmal. "How does it feel?"

Brónmal raised an eyebrow. "Pardon, Highlord?"

"How does it feel to be the Supreme General?"

"I feel blessed, Highlord."

Dachfranir chuckled. "You do not need to be polite. I know you have deeper feelings than that."

"May I speak openly then, Highlord?"

"You may."

Brónmal looked up at the high walls of Ardmunhaich, taking them in while he formulated his thoughts. "I would never have expected to receive such an honor. Not in this life."

"Why not?"

"I was born from a failure father, a man who stumbled in the face of glory. I come from the end of the Empire, and I was like any noble child. I expected to be a regional commander, maybe for a village or perhaps a minor city. But then I became General of Beinthal, and now this. It is truly an honor."

"You know, as well as I, the only way to ascend is through service. That is how mere peasants become nobles. It is not our origin or the promise of one's merit. It is faith, loyalty, and action. I did not select you over the other eight Generals or any other candidates merely for your ability. Men like your father did great things during the first Heokolon War, but this war is not theirs. We need men we can trust, men like you. Men that soldiers look up to."

"What do you mean, Highlord?"

"You are the most faithful, and you are of the people. Do not think that you can get away with your own thoughts. Even I know you prize the Three above both the Godspeaker and myself. I see it in you. Most men do not have that quality. They believe I can save them, that the Godspeaker can save them, but we are mere men."

Brónmal recoiled, unsure of what to say. "Highlord, I do not..."

"Silence. Be glad that I am not like the Godspeaker, who would force you to prostrate yourself before the Empire and undo your guts for the masses. This is between us. The Godspeaker is the true ruler of Mednodorn. I harbor no troubles with this. I can lead the military and manage the Empire for him, but I am far from an icon. As long as he captures the hearts and spirits of the people, then why should I rule? But, in the masses, there are men like you who prize the Three, their faith, above all else. It is a lost perspective, buried in the sin of *Esadif* – a necessary loss. Even with faith, you cannot drive thousands of men into their doom. They need an icon, something material to protect and adore. Only with a great prophet, a figure of faith and good, will they lay down their lives in treacherous lands like the East. To serve something greater, they must see it, they must hear it."

"*I am no great zealot or a great leader; even Father knew that,*" Brónmal thought. He frowned, his eyes locking on the horizon beyond the fields surrounding Ardmunhaich. "Will the men respect me as they did Trudumal?"

"That is up to you. You must command the soldiers' hearts and invigorate their spirits. I know you are capable of this."

Brónmal nodded. "Y-Yes, Highlord."

"Trudumal was just like you when he first came to Baradun. Nervous, unsure how to succeed the last Supreme General. The men could feel his lack of spirit. But, in his first battle, when he chose to lead the charge, to be the tip of the spear, the legions knew they had a worthy successor."

"If I must be the first into battle, then I will be."

"It is a tradition at this point. May the Three guard you."

Brónmal squinted ahead and asked. "How far is Baradun? It's been years."

"Not far. We are nearing it."

The escort departed from Ardmunhaich's borders, leaving behind immeasurable fields of farmland. After an hour, they arrived at a great plain. In the center stood a massive stone fortress: Baradun, the ancient war citadel. This was where the Mednohail had trained every soldier since the start of the Empire six hundred years ago. Its walls were thought to be immortal. The citadel sat on a leviathan stone hill, each side of the stone steep and impossible to climb. The fortress itself was hulking, its walls thick and reinforced with metal. Each wall was lined with slits and holes to shoot from and pour oil out of, while the top of each wall was covered with metal panels. The entrance held five gates. Made from iron, they weighed thousands of pounds. Each gate had grand mechanisms to open it, requiring hundreds of men to budge. This was where the Highlord and Godspeaker would take refuge if Ardmunhaich ever fell. No one thought that would ever happen. None had ever besieged the edge of the Empire, not even during the first

Heokolon War.

Brónmal looked at the war citadel with awe. Outside, thousands of men lived in tents. Here, they trained, enduring a whole year through High Summer and High Winter before they were ready. With little protection, they were hardened against the elements, against pain, against weakness. Baradun turned farm boys into soldiers. Many, like Brónmal, arrived at the fortress at the beginning of Low Summer. Brónmal remembered that training was harsh, and living outside through all eight seasons was harsher.

Outside the tents, hundreds of battalions trained, running and sparring all day. They trained while the scorching heat of High Summer approached. Brónmal was glad those days were over. He had passed out many times during High Summer and nearly lost his fingers during High Winter.

"*Cursed fields. At least Father prepared me for this place,*" he thought.

The very sight of the White Hands sent commanders running. They gathered the entire army of Ardmunhaich and the future soldiers of every single province. Thousands of men formed into square formations outside their tents, silently standing as the escort passed.

Brónmal straightened up, riding tall and proud. The Highlord looked over the sea of peasants-turned-warriors. "Are they not something to behold?"

Brónmal responded. "They are, Highlord."

"Must have been quite something to be here. Do you remember your days here fondly, Brónmal?"

Brónmal chuckled. "Absolutely not. I only got to spend a week in the fortress. Most of my time here was in the tents."

Dachfranir laughed. "That is how you make men of steel with unyielding will and unquestioning loyalty. Much has changed since your training here."

"What do you mean, Highlord?"

"We have new ways, new weapons to break the Heokolons. Nothing this world has ever seen, not since the Reign."

Brónmal recoiled. "The Reign?"

Though Brónmal knew little of the dark time, the mention of it made his skin crawl. A broken age, it was the time of the immortal Arathmalok, who ruled the world with an iron fist. He ruled for six Aothills before being overthrown, leading to the First Aothill. The scars of the Reign still existed. In the West, beyond Peregrine's Wall, was Etutakur. It was a cursed land. Magic polluted the very soil, creating strange and corrupted things like sideways rain, floating islands, and monsters. The men in the West were once Mednohail. Now they were the Stygian Men, the forsaken apostates. They served Arathmalok during the Reign and now lived as magical aberrations, scarred forever for their treachery.

Dachfranir looked Brónmal over. "Do not fret, Brónmal. You will see."

They marched past the endless formations. The escort went around Baradun, arriving at a small field opposite the training grounds. Brónmal looked it over. Men in robes wandered the area, working on strange machines and objects Brónmal had never seen. They had papers with glyphs and unknown symbols in hand. Mysterious circles dotted the area, surrounded by candles with objects in the middle. The men chanted around these circles, channeling strange, orange energy from the air.

"*Magic in this sacrosanct place! A sin!*" Brónmal thought. He drew his sword and pointed. "Aogadraod! How could witchcraft be in such a holy place? This abomination must be purged!"

The Highlord held out his hand. "Hold your weapon! Calm yourself, Brónmal!"

Brónmal stared at him. "What is this?"

The Highlord gestured at a wooden structure. It was round, similar to a house's roof, with multiple trapdoors and holes, each reinforced with metal. "Behold the secret weapons of Ardmunhaich."

"Secret weapon?"

"It is called a War Carriage. It is animated, like us, and moves on its own. It was built to house many men with crossbows who could shoot out of it. This weapon is what we will use against the Heokolons. It will protect from arrows and swords."

Brónmal shook his head. "This is Aogadraod! Sin!"

The Highlord raised a finger and shook it. "This is not some lowly craft like that of Bogarthdraod. These men are not witches manipulating the power of the divine. They are blessed by the Godspeaker himself, who oversees their study. Think of them as seekers of the deeper answers and the universe's inner workings. They act with grace and humility, obeying the Three."

Brónmal panted, so offended and shocked that he could barely muster words. "Am I to be taken for a fool?"

"Watch your words! If you are to speak of sin, I expect not a shred of it from you. I will not tolerate disobedience, especially in the face of just acts. This is not witchcraft, taking advantage of the peasantry and working with Dubilfen. This is Gluvadraod."

"Gluvadraod?"

"Indeed. It is animation magic, magic that gives life to objects. It is a gift from Filahaich, bestowed to the Godspeaker through visions. This War Carriage is alive and is not the only thing we have developed."

"*How could magic be gifted to the Godspeaker? Why would any of the gods but Dubilfen bestow us with such heresy, such a transgression against them?*" Brónmal thought.

Dachfranir whistled. "Bring a Snakebow and a Flamebow!"

The robed men nodded and ran around the field, coming over with three objects. The Highlord gestured to the first weapon. "This is a Snakebow. It is like a crossbow, but instead of a string, it uses animated wheels to shoot bolts. We have tested it on Heokolon armor from the first war. It will kill any Heokolon."

Brónmal examined the Snakebow. It looked like a wooden pipe attached to a crossbow butt and trigger. How could it fire with just wheels? Without string, it seemed useless.

"*How can a pipe be of any danger to anyone?*" Brónmal thought and frowned.

Dachfranir gestured to the next weapon. "This is a Flamebow. Like the Snakebow, it attaches to this oil barrel and spits fire. It goes quite far. It's stunning to see."

The Flamebow was like the Snakebow but made of metal. A hose attached it to a barrel that stank with strange fumes.

"*Do you plan to simply pour liquid on the enemy and light them on fire? Ridiculous,*" Brónmal thought, his brow furrowed, jaw clenched. "What are these unholy contraptions?"

"They are not unholy. They are divine gifts, weapons of war to crush the Heokolons. Demonstrate the Flamebow!"

A pair of robed men grabbed the weapon. One held the rifle end while the other carried the tank. They moved to a range of dummies covered in scrap armor. The man with the rifle pointed his weapon, pulling the trigger and causing a sloshing sound to echo from the tank. A cascade of molten, tar-like flames spewed from the gun, coating the dummy in sticky, flaming goo.

"*What atrocity is this?*" Brónmal thought, recoiling. What a horrendous weapon. Was this what the Highlord planned to bring down on the Heokolons for the second invasion?

The Highlord chuckled. "Is it not monstrous? Divine flame to bathe and cleanse the sin of those pagan Easterlings."

"It is, Highlord. But how could such a wicked thing not be the product of Dubilfen? Men with swords have honor, but this? How is this honorable?"

"There is no honor in war, especially in the lands of the East. Your father must have taught you this."

"He did, Highlord."

"We plan to win this war at any cost. Be it through flame, machine, steel, or blood. We will have victory."

"As you command, Highlord. Three bless us."

The Highlord gestured. "Come. Do you want to greet your commanders?"

Brónmal nodded. "Gladly, Highlord."

The pair left the field. They rode toward the great fortress gates, leaving behind the dreadful creations. Brónmal looked up.

"*Three bless us. Have we stumbled from the light, out of the embrace of salvation?*" he thought.

Lowering his head, he prayed for his soul.

6

The Church

Brónmal rode behind his father. The forest around them seemed painted, comprised of rich red, purple, and orange colors. High Autumn was coming to an end. Among the leaves were the skeletal figures of naked trees, dormant for the coming winter. In the absence of green, dull grays and whites awaited the forest.

The pair came to the city of Beinthal. Surrounded by two ring walls, it was the smallest province capital in Mednodorn. As High Autumn came to its end, the city began to stir. People gathered from all over the province to celebrate the second yearly harvest.

The guards saluted Remtaich as he rode through the gate. "Three bless, Lord!"

Remtaich nodded. "Happy harvest, Three bless!"

The second harvest happened in the third week of Dornhath, the last month of High Autumn. It was the end of the week. The peasants celebrated, free after a full six days of harvest and labor. They drank in honor of Filahaich. People sang and stumbled in the streets; many danced, and a few praised Brónmal and his father.

"Praise Remtaich! Praise Brónmal!"

Remtaich waved. The people loved him. Though he was not a village lord or the king of Beinthal, they praised him for his nobility and honor as a veteran. No one blamed the old veterans for their loss against Heonar. Only the veterans carried their shame, their hearts wrapped in guilt. Instead, people sang songs of revenge, waiting for the day of another invasion into the East.

Brónmal winced. Would they love Remtaich so much if they knew of his bruises? His chest ached, his back seared from lashes, and his hands were covered in blistering sores. To raise a warrior, Remtaich made Brónmal train with weapons until his skin tore. When he failed, he was beaten. Out of many lessons, Brónmal was taught to fear weakness and to loathe laziness.

Remtaich responded to the people. "A good harvest to you! Good harvest, Filahaich bless you!"

A woman cried. "Three bless you, Lord!"

The outer ring of the city burst with festivities. Peasant children ran in the streets and played games. Men and women stumbled to the city's square to participate in the festival's main event. Even though drunk, they bowed and made way for Remtaich and Brónmal. Remtaich glanced back. "Chin high, boy. Ride with the nobility you were born with. Do not meet the gaze of the commoner; look above them. You will be their shield and sword but never their equal."

Brónmal raised his chin. "Yes, Lord."

The pair rode into the city's central square within the inner wall. A massive stone church loomed over the square. Like all Mednohail churches, it was cube-shaped, with a tremendous bulbous roof crowning it and casting its shadow over the people. Growing from the church was a grand staircase. In the center of it protruded a stone stage shaped like a spear.

A crowd separated by classes gathered in the square. One section had farmers and serfs who had traveled to the city for the celebration. Another had craftsmen and free people. The last had the nobility, the lords, and ladies of Benthal's realm. There were no slaves in sight. As they rode past, Brónmal recoiled from the stench of the lower classes. They were unwashed and dirty from a week of harvesting.

The pair joined the nobility. Clean and washed, they did not offend Brónmal's nose like the peasants did. Some people greeted Remtaich, though everyone else watched the center of the square.

A massive mound of rubbish sat in the center of the square. People went up to it, tossing branches, weeds, poor parts of the harvest, and unwanted belongings onto the pile. Priests walked around it. They dumped barrels of tree oils onto the heap and blessed it with chants.

"*The pile is huge this year,*" Brónmal thought. A mass of waste, it was the first great offering to Dubilfen, a great gift to plead for his mercy through his absence.

Remtaich smacked Brónmal's head. "Sit straight, boy. Only the lower-class slouch, straighten up like a lord."

Brónmal inhaled and straightened up. "Sorry, Lord."

"Do not apologize to me. Be better."

The crowd rose into a thunderous cheer. The Archbishop of Beinthal walked out from the church, accompanied by guards and priests. Ancient by Mednohail standard, the sixty-year-old man was frail. Stuffed into yellow-white robes, he seemed like a ripened fruit. Bulbous like a frog, his neck puffed over the robe's collar. One of his eyes was discolored, its edge red, and the pupil slightly slanted to the left. His right eye was a hazy green, staring the crowd down. He waved, soon lowering his hands to silence the crowd.

"Good people! For thirty years, I have served this humble city and the Three! It is with joy that I announce that I feel the love of the Three more than ever on this day! Filahaich has blessed us! I know many of you are joyous of the recent fortune of a good harvest and that you are glad that the harvest week is over!"

He inhaled, the pause making people lean forward in anticipation.

"Behold before you the pyre of Dornhath! Into it, we throw our sin, the unwanted grain, the wretched rubbish so that we may be clean! We gift the unwanted to Dubilfen! May he be appeased, and may our crops, animals, and lives be untouched. If any of you have more to rid yourselves of, do so now."

Only a few of the crowd had anything left to throw. While they rid themselves of their garbage, priests came out of the church with torches. Once everything had been thrown on, the Archbishop continued. "Good people! The pyre is complete! Priests, good servants, burn the sin away!"

The priests stuck their torches in the pile. The mound, soaked with tree oil, burst into flame. Within seconds, the whole pile burned. Pops and snaps echoed while the fire consumed the garbage. The peasants and free folk went wild, screaming out their love of the Three.

Brónmal raised his voice. "Praise the Three!"

Remtaich grabbed him. "Silence, boy! You do not shout like a peasant. You are solemn, humble, and quiet with your contentedness for the Three."

Brónmal whimpered. "Y-Yes, Lord!"

The Archbishop spoke again. "Good people! We have one last gift for Filahaich and Dubilfen! Priests, bring out the beast!"

The crowd fell silent as the priests brought out an animal. It was an Axin. Not much taller than the average man, its hill-like shoulders peaked at five-and-a-half feet. Its neck and head were heavy and square. Rolling from its head were two horns that curved forward and back toward the beast's chest. Its tail curled, flicking now and then. The livelihood of the peasant, many families had one or two Axin that helped with labor. At the end of their lives, they were typically eaten by the local village in a feast.

This one was huge. It was a great bull, its muscles broad and its horn vast. Out of all Axin, this was the largest in Beinthal, measured and brought by the city's priests. It had been pampered and fed honey, milk, and oats for the last month.

The priests brought it to the base of the stone podium. The creature wobbled drunkenly, its glazed eyes lifting lazily. Its mouth foamed; the intoxicated creature could not keep its jaw closed. Unaware, it cooperated as the priests laid it on a stone table.

The Archbishop looked down at the beast. "Good people! Gaze upon the bull of the second harvest! This year, we have found a giant, a beast worthy of pride. We give its life and its flesh to Filahaich and Dubilfen. We offer it to Filahaich to show our gratefulness. We offer to Dubilfen, so that he may be absent and that High Winter may be free of struggle and death!"

The crowd cheered.

"What cruelty. Poor thing is not even aware of all this," Brónmal thought. It was evil to him. This poor creature left a green pasture and a herd to live in the city. Gorged with milk and honey, how could it envision such an end?

46

Hazy-minded, it could not even fear the crowd around it.

The Archbishop shouted. "Priests! Draw the blade!"

A priest approached another by the head of the great bull. He gave the other priest a scythe, sharp and glistening in the High Autumn sun. The man who took the blade bowed to the Archbishop. The Archbishop nodded. "You have my blessing to deliver the sacrifice unto the Three!"

The crowd fell silent in anticipation. The priest walked around to the neck of the beast, raising the scythe in the air.

Brónmal looked away and held his breath. Remtaich grabbed him, pushing his head up and pinching his chin. "Look, boy, do not fear death or blood. You must witness its passing, for it is an honor for this lowly beast."

Brónmal reluctantly blinked and stared. The priest looked at the crowd once, then brought the scythe down. The blade cut the air. Brónmal jolted. Blood sprayed and flowed as the scythe slid across the beast's neck, its life draining out. It did not even groan and went limp after a few seconds.

Bathing his hand in the blood, the priest turned and raised it. The crowd went wild. People jumped and bumped into each other, some looking up tearfully as they thanked the gods.

The Archbishop spoke again. "The spirit of this great Axin belongs to Dubilfen and Filahaich. Its blood, full of vigor and might, is potent. Come now, those that carry children, present yourselves and be blessed! Bathe in the blood and be protected; may the spirit of this beast promote the health and longevity of your children!"

The priest set down the scythe and was handed a twig from a Morohm tree. Pregnant women from all around the crowd lined up before the beast. Many had been impregnated from the first fertility harvest earlier in the year and would soon give birth. Each presented their bellies. The priest sprinkled blood from the Axim's neck onto the women, whispering in prayer as he did. Brónmal frowned.

The Archbishop raised his hands. "Blessed Beinthal, holy people! It is my honor to conclude the second yearly harvest! Go, be with your families and friends! Sing, celebrate, and offer to Daonrex and Filahaich! But do not forget to pray for our protection and fortune in the coming High Winter!

Three bless!"

The crowd dispersed. The nobility disbanded; some went to the church, and some went off to business. Remtaich joined the group going to the church, and Brónmal followed.

Remtaich gripped Brónmal's shoulder. "I am going to speak to the Archbishop. You will keep your words short with a man such as him. I want you to have some respect for holy men."

"Yes, Lord."

"Be silent!"

The Archbishop shook hands with the men of noble families, talking to and blessing them. Remtaich respectfully waited, shaking the Archbishop's hand as he walked over. "Three bless you, Archbishop."

"Remtaich! Three bless. It is good to see a warrior of Mednodorn on this wondrous day. How is your boy?"

Remtaich shoved Brónmal forward. "Getting stronger every day. Show him your hands, boy."

Brónmal raised his torn hands. Destroyed from handling the grips of spears, maces, and swords, his skin was raw and filled with holes. Remtaich forbade Brónmal from wrapping his palms. It was a weakness to shy away from pain. Remtaich wanted him to show courage in the face of pain. Everything hurt to grab, yet his father scorned him if he exhibited pain.

The Archbishop smiled. "You are raising a strong boy. Brónmal, you will be a great successor to your father."

"Thank you, Archbishop," Brónmal squeaked.

"Perhaps his generation will put the filthy Heokolons under a boot?"

Remtaich smiled. "It is a hope of mine. Those filthy Easterlings do not even deserve to be ruled like the Ahamari in the South. We should put them all to the sword."

"Absolutely. I bless all soldiers. You, Brónmal, will be one of the greatest. Three bless you."

Brónmal recoiled as the Archbishop sprinkled Daonrex's blood on him from a bottle in his robes. Remtaich looked down, eyes piercing. "What do you say, boy?"

"Thank you, Archbishop!"

The Archbishop chuckled. "No need to be so hard on him. I can already see his faith is strong in his eyes! His hands are disciplined, and his mind is keen."

"As long as he listens, he will be a great soldier and a man of faith. Come on, Brónmal. We have more training to do. Three bless, Archbishop."

The Archbishop waved. "Three bless!"

Brónmal waved back. "Three bless, Archbishop!"

Remtaich walked out of sight and out of earshot before turning to Brónmal. "You recoil at the touch of Daonrex's holy blood? Are you a demon, boy? A servant of Dubilfen? Should I throw you into the Dornhath pyre with the rest of Beinthal's sin?"

Brónmal gasped. "N-No! Lord, I was surprised! I am no demon!"

"I would feel pride in you and the Archbishop's words if you were not a little heretic and deceiver! I will break Dubilfen's grasp on you. You are going to train until you bleed tonight."

Remtaich grabbed Brónmal, making him squeal. "No, Father!"

"You show me some respect and call me Lord! Come on!"

7

The March to Heonar

The searing sun loomed overhead. Life browned and withered in the fields, forests, and hills of Mednodorn. Rivers and creeks dried up, lakes shrunk, and life became dormant. Brónmal looked at the trees. Insects hibernated in cocoons hung from the dry branches and burrowed in the wilted, brown fields.

Even in thin clothes, Brónmal sweated. The heat bore down hard on his neck, making his breathing sluggish and heavy. He groaned. "Damn! This sun!"

Hacarad chuckled. "A great season to start a war in, huh?"

Brónmal sighed heavily. "Let us just hope it cools off by the time we reach Raothal."

Hacarad glanced back. "Do you think they are burning heretics in sacrifice to Dubilfen back home?"

Brónmal shook his head. "I do not think so. It is not the middle of High Summer yet; Asorabroa is still a few weeks away."

Hacarad shrugged. "Well, we cannot say the North was much better. At least the sun sets here during summer."

Brónmal nodded. "I just hope the soldiers last."

Brónmal turned to the army behind them. Thousands of men marched in column-like formations, following Brónmal and his elite guard. Among them were War Carriages, squeaking and rolling. Many soldiers feared the constructs, keeping their distance as much as possible. Among the ranks were men with Snakebows and pairs with Flamebows. They were hated and shunned by most foot soldiers.

The commanders and peasant soldiers contrasted with each other. Commanders and Brónmal's bodyguards wore full armor, much of which was custom-fitted to them. The peasant soldiers had only standard, ill-fitting armor. Rarely did the armor fit the soldier. Around Mednodorn, many cities had great smithies—factories where blacksmiths slaved away to provide arms and protection. Industry, a new idea. Unlike the first Heokolon War, the legions of modern Mednodorn were equipped. They had full helmets, yet only plates on their shins, chests, and arms. Their backs and areas between plates were covered in tough padding or, rarely, chain mail. Most walked with helmets off, shaven faces red and sweaty from the heat.

Distinct from men like Brónmal, the common soldier wielded axes, maces, spears, and, sometimes, farmers' tools. Even with factories, supplying hundreds of thousands of men was difficult.

Brónmal stood out. His armor was heavy like a steel column with chainmail layered beneath it. It was custom-made and fitted to him. Unlike most Generals, he did not have fancy armor lined with gold and intricate markings. Instead, he settled with an engraved crest on his chest plate. A bird with four wings and a crown, the crest of Beinthal, his home.

His helmet hung from the saddle of his Auhmog. It was domed, with three slits over his mouth, allowing him to breathe. Its visor was a slit that started at the center of his nose and curved downward. It could not open. Instead, the helmet's mask was sealed tight, made to hold together through anything. On his hip hung the sword given to him by Trudumal. Its hilt, golden and encrusted with jewels, sparkled.

"*Show no weakness; do not cower from the heat, and the men will be strong,*" Brónmal thought, recalling his father's lessons. Brónmal sighed. "We will lose men in this heat. They must be suffering."

Hacarad shrugged. "It is the life of a soldier. I once was among them on foot, and so were you."

"I got some accommodations since I was the son of a lord."

"But you still walked, Lord."

"Well, you are right. Three bless them. Loyal to the end, through sweltering heat and biting cold."

Hacarad grimaced. "I hope that they all make it to Raothal."

"We will stop often for water and breaks. We need as many as possible to face the Heokolons."

Hacarad hummed. "I wonder if our fathers lost for a reason. Are we repeating history?"

"*I am not my father. I am not a failure.*" Brónmal thought. He waved dismissively. "We are not them. We are their successors, and we will make them proud. I say we will have the Emperor's head back in Ardmunhaich by the end of the year. The most important thing to take is western Heonar so we can mine for salt."

Hacarad recoiled. "By winter? We are invading an entire empire; it could take years."

Brónmal looked at Hacarad and tilted his head. "You doubt me?"

Hacarad shook his head. "N-No. Of course not, Lord. It just sounds... How do you intend to do it?"

Brónmal smirked. "It's easy. We are going straight for the Emperor. He's a god to them, a mortal man that they worship. If we cut off his head, they are sure to break."

Hacarad furrowed his brow. "Are you sure, Lord?"

Brónmal nodded. "How would we react if the Godspeaker fell? The spirit of their people lies in their emperor."

"What was their emperor's name?"

"Teohapnezal? We just call him Teo, or Teohap."

"I hate their foul language."

Brónmal smiled. "I hate their heathen people."

Hacarad sighed. "All this work for the good of Mednodorn, and we spend all our time in pagan lands with beasts. Have you thought about what we will do after the war?"

Brónmal tilted his head back, staring at the blue sky. "Probably get old, retire... Get fat too, really fat."

Hacarad chuckled. "Buried in women too?"

Brónmal laughed. "Absolutely! Dozens."

Hacarad shook his head with a smile. "No, but what would we really do, Lord?"

Brónmal sighed. "Well, if I am not called back to Ardmunhaich, we must stay and rebuild. We must also convert the Heokolons."

"That sounds easy."

"Right, because we did it peacefully with the Throfi, which has only taken nearly two Aothills."

Hacarad held up a hand and shrugged. "Think of the Ahamari. It's easier with sword and chains."

"Like they deserve."

A commander rode up to the pair. "Supreme General!"

Brónmal stopped his Auhmog. A wave of halt commands went down the entire army. "Yes?"

The man bowed, his Auhmog stirring. "The commanders say the men are tired. They request a break."

Brónmal nodded. "Of course. Tell them to set up the tents for shade or to find trees. Pass around water, and make sure they are fed too."

The commander bowed again. "By your command, Supreme General."

While the man rode away to the rest of the army, Brónmal gestured to a hill. "Let us take a break."

The pair and the elite guard rode their beasts up the hill. Brónmal got off his Auhmog and waved to the guard. "You men can take a break. We do not need protection up here."

They responded in unison. "As you say, Supreme General!"

Brónmal sat under a wilted tree, Hacarad standing beside him. Brónmal looked up, squinting from the sun in his eyes. "What are you doing? Sit with me."

"Yes, Lord."

The pair sat together and watched the army move. It extended beyond the distant hills, thousands of men ready for war. Among them were wagons and families. These were war families. Many took payment to help move armies across the Empire, while others joined the moving army for protection during their travels.

Soldiers and families came together to form living, moving towns. War families cooked for them, washed their clothes, provided medical help, and cleaned up after battles. Priests also joined them. Some were death priests who rode on lonesome wagons destined to bring bodies home.

Brónmal sighed and drank from a flask hung from his belt. "Two months of this wretched heat?"

Hacarad wiped the sweat from his brow. "You act as if you have never been through High Summer before."

"I act like I hate it. The farmers put their animals inside and stay out of the fields, and we are marching."

"And just like High Winter, the farmers starve and suffer. At least we have food. It is not lord-like to complain."

Brónmal scoffed. "I am Supreme General. I have the right to complain. Maybe my new decree as Supreme General is that we march at night?"

"Maybe so. Soon, we will be in the Marcoili forest and in the shade."

"Three know that cannot come soon enough."

Hacarad looked down, eyes narrowed. "What are we going to do with the Algoniva? There's a tribe that lives in the Marcoili forest."

Brónmal frowned. The Algoniva, a non-human species, lived in tribes all over Mednodorn. He clicked his tongue a few times. "They ought to let us through. Strange creatures they are, but they know better than to attack any Mednohail."

"I always wondered about those things. So different from us humans. Do we even bother showing them the Three?"

"They are like animals. Do we bother showing Auhmogs the Three? No, that is the peace of all animals. They are one with the Three and the world, untouched by Dubilfen. Few Algoniva can even speak our language, or even care to. In Beinthal, we chopped down their forests and sent them South. Never was an issue."

Hacarad raised a brow. "By the Three, just like that?"

"They were in the way."

54

"Well, they are more akin to beasts than us. Just like the Throfi."

Brónmal chuckled. "Exactly."

Hacarad grabbed a stick and tossed it down the hill. "Remember when we were boys?"

"Oh, by the Three. I wanted to get rid of you so much, peasant boy."

Hacarad shrugged. "And here I am, shining your armor and sharpening your sword."

Brónmal grinned. "Not all that bad. You get to ride beasts instead of marching, be in nice tents, eat food, and earn a lot of coin, too."

"Oh, who said I was complaining? I would not do it just because you are my friend."

"Is that a bit of disloyalty, I hear?"

"If you count that as *Esadif*, you are thoroughly mistaken. I am just being reasonable."

Brónmal chuckled. "Careful, peasant boy."

"Remember that one time we went into the forest and saw that witch?"

Brónmal leaned his head down. "Oh, by the Three. How often did we prank her before the village baked her in clay?"

Hacarad chuckled. "I think the best was when we released all her animals into the woods."

"She chased after them for hours. Raiding her house was a nice touch."

"That's what she gets for practicing Bogarthdraod. Damned witches and their sin."

Brónmal pointed down to the War Carriages brought with them from Ardmunhaich. "Speaking of which, what do you think of those unholy contraptions?"

Hacarad shook his head. "Surely those must be Aogadraod. Magic in our army? How have we gone so far?"

Brónmal rubbed his chin. "It's an abomination, spitting in the face of the Three. Only Dubilfen could fester such ideas in the minds of holy men. Both the Highlord and the Godspeaker are fine with it."

Hacarad sighed. "If they approve, then it must be holy. Weapons to crush pagans, is that not righteous?"

"How far is too far? How far can we stray from the light in order to gain victory? Would we rather win and submit to evil or lose and be righteous to our dying breath?"

"I know not, Lord. I would never wield one of those unholy contraptions, like that arrow thing. The Snakebow?"

Brónmal nodded. "Snakebow, what a wretched thing. How could anything but a demon of Dubilfen get a bolt to penetrate Heokolon armor like that?"

"Perhaps the inner workings of machines are for thinking men, not warriors like us?"

"Perhaps the inner workings of thinking men should be questioned. How do we know that thinking men are holy men?"

"Food for thought, Lord. I am simply hoping that the Heokolons burn these weapons and die after."

"Well said."

Brónmal whistled to a guard below them. "You there! Grab us some beer. I am thirsty."

"Yes, Supreme General!"

Brónmal rubbed the sweat off his face with a cloth while he waited. The man left and returned with a beer flask, handing it to Brónmal. "Anything else, Supreme General?"

"No, you can return to the others. Grab beer yourselves if you like. I do not care while we are marching."

"Yes, Supreme General. Three bless."

Brónmal turned to Hacarad. "Want some?"

"Absolutely."

Brónmal raised the flask before drinking it. "To a good march, Three bless!"

He handed the flask to Hacarad, who raised it and spoke. "To a won war and an empire broken, Three bless!"

8

The Marcoili Forest

Brónmal watched the army walk into the shadows of the woods. It had been an hour since the sun had set, leaving them only the light of the stars and Narum. Narum, the great ringed moon, cut high into the sky. This month, the moon was full. Its intimidating mass and rings lit up and reflected upon the land.

Hacarad stood beside Brónmal. "The men are nervous."

Brónmal's brow wrinkled. "Why? They fear tribal beasts?"

"Marching into the woods at night has never been good."

Brónmal chuckled. "They will have to get used to it."

"You intend to march into Heonar at night, too?"

"Whatever it takes to crush them."

Hacarad shook his head. "Do not be arrogant, Lord. We must remember that we are going into their land."

"I will burn their land. Do not worry, Hacarad."

The pair grew silent. The ground shook with marching, thousands of men going into the woods with torches and beasts. Brónmal urged his Auhmog down the hill. Hacarad followed, along with their escort. They rode along the line and entered the forest. The air grew cold. The path that the army had followed from Ardmunhaich thinned. Trees enclosed it. Men tripped over their roots, wagons creaking as they hit bumps and holes.

Hacarad grumbled. "I hate this place."

Brónmal glanced back. "Do not scare the men."

"Sorry, Lord. I just wished we did not have to march through here. Why do we not cut down such places?"

"Not a clue. We could use the fuel to make more armor and weapons."

Nervous soldiers faintly whispered over their footsteps and the creaks of wagons. The rest of the forest was silent. Brónmal squinted into the gloomy brush. It was like the forest was hiding, all life inside still out of fear. Good. Everything should fear them.

Hacarad stared into the dark. "Do you think those Algoniva will appear?"

Brónmal sighed. "I hope not. One more thing to bother me if they do. We will need to stop somewhere eventually."

"Make camp in this place?"

"Would you rather walk for the next few days without sleep?"

"You are right, Lord."

"We will walk until first light. I would rather enjoy the coolness of the night for as long as we can."

Hacarad chuckled. "We could have waited until Low Autumn, at least."

"Well, better we spend High Summer marching there and fight during Low and High Autumn than fight during Low and High Winter."

"You think we can conquer them that fast?"

"Of course, Hacarad. We have been preparing for this war for thirty years. I have trained and bled my entire life to get here. The legions hunger. Who can stop us?"

Hacarad frowned. "Lord, have they not been preparing too? The Easterlings must be ready for us."

Brónmal shrugged. "It has been thirty years, and we have not attacked. I am sure they have no idea what is coming for them. The element of surprise. Why would they think we would attack again after the first war was such a disaster?"

Hacarad nodded. "I guess you are right, Lord. I just worry. Three shield us."

Brónmal bowed his head. "Three shield us. We will be fine."

"I could only imagine what their wretched land is like."

Brónmal tilted his head. "My father told me it was mountainous, with spear-like peaks and deep swamps."

Hacarad groaned. "Swamps and mountains? It's going to be a joy to march through there."

Brónmal chuckled. "Three bless us. Hopefully, all of this will be over soon, and we will drink on the steps of the Emperor's palace."

Hacarad nodded. "Hopefully. What do they call their capital?"

Brónmal sighed. "Nasalohotehr, I think. I hate their language more than the Throfi's."

"The first thing we do after beheading the Emperor is rename all their cities and villages."

"Absolutely. That land could use some holy names."

The army descended a hill and went over a bridge spanning a creek. The old bridge groaned. Its wood was rotten, cracking as wagons and beasts went over. Brónmal grimaced. Hopefully, they would not have to rebuild a bridge by the night's end.

"*Stay strong,*" Brónmal thought.

The pair rode over the bridge, heading further into the darkness under the canopy. The path curved and twisted through the trees, past an old, ruined house. Brónmal stopped to gawk.

Hacarad stopped beside him. "What do you reckon happened here?"

Brónmal shook his head. "Owner probably died or fled. The Algoniva know better than to kill innocent Mednohail. No bandit folk out here either, no one to prey on."

Hacarad tilted his head. "Maybe there are monsters in the dark?"

Brónmal chuckled. "I doubt it. Just wildlife. Come on, let us continue."

The pair followed the unending army through the woods. Marching continued for an hour until a commander rode down the line to Brónmal. "Supreme General, hail!"

Brónmal raised his right hand. "Three bless. What's going on?"

"There's a blockade down the road. The Algoniva tribe came out of the woods and stopped us!"

"*Of course they did,*" Brónmal thought and groaned. "What do they want?"

59

"I do not know, Supreme General. They do not speak our language well; it is just that they wanted to speak to a leader."

"I will speak with them."

"This way!"

"*Miserable creatures. I should end them for this interruption,*" Brónmal thought.

The army halted while Brónmal, Hacarad, and their escort rode to the front of the line. At the front, soldiers with torches waited in the dark. Opposite them were a dozen Algoniva, carrying lanterns filled with glowing bugs. Brónmal's eyes widened. He had never seen what the Algoniva of Mednodorn, Mot'Algoniva, looked like. His father told him stories, but they did no justice.

They were massive, standing around seven feet tall and dwarfing the average Throfi man. Their bodies were thick and wide, like barrels. Brónmal could only assume that they weighed around four hundred pounds. Their skin had a moss-like green shade. It was dark but faded, as if the creatures had absorbed the colors of the earth itself. The texture of their skin was bumpy, like a rocky field, and matted with thick dark hair.

With thick noses, large horns, and long, wild hair, they easily intimidated the tiny Mednohail men. They dressed in clothing made from plants. Hide, beads, rocks, bones, and feathers decorated their simple clothes. The females wore colorful headdresses. Brónmal squinted. Despite the difference in clothing, he could barely distinguish between the males and females. Each had a large weapon made of stone and wood, primarily spears and clubs. Brónmal noticed their clubs were taller than he was. Each stone weapon had intricate designs and patterns, with swirling marks on the wooden shafts and sharp geometric patterns on the stone tips.

"*Monsters,*" Brónmal thought, leaning back.

They stared at the army with eyes somewhat too small for their massive skulls. One male stepped forward. "You are leader?"

Brónmal rode forward. "Yes, I am the Supreme General of Mednodorn and the commander of this army. Who am I speaking to?"

The Algoniva gestured to himself. "I am Ma'verd, Hunt-father. You will speak to tribe-father, deep-eyed one. Speaker for Ardolhie, sky-father, and

Hagomi."

Hacarad rode up beside Brónmal. "What do they want?"

Brónmal tilted his head. "I think they want me to speak to their leader?"

Hacarad glared at the Algoniva. "Why should we go with you heathen creatures?"

Ma'verd spoke. "Tribe-father has wisdom. Old knowledge meant for you."

Hacarad glanced at Brónmal. "This sounds like a waste of time. What can we learn from creatures like you?"

Ma'verd recoiled, then spoke. "Not a waste, good for the Empire, good for Mednohail."

"*Good for the Empire?*" Brónmal thought and pursed his lips. "They have my curiosity now. What could the Algoniva know that would benefit us?"

Hacarad chuckled. "How to build stick huts and talk to trees. If you will it, Lord, go and see. Bring the escort."

"Tell the men to make camp. I am going to speak to their leader."

"As you say, Lord."

Hacarad rode off, shouting orders to commanders and getting the army in line. Meanwhile, the escort of guards rode up behind Brónmal.

Brónmal gestured into the woods. "I will go with you."

Ma'verd nodded. "Come."

Brónmal and his escort followed the group of Algoniva into the woods. The primitive creatures stank of herbs and oils, a scent so strong he could smell them from a few feet away. Did they believe in washing? Brónmal was amazed they could speak his language. At least he did not have to slaughter them for standing in the way.

They went up and down hills and through dense foliage until they came to an opening. In the center of the space stood a hill with a creek cut around it. An entire village of huts sat on the hill. Each hut was long, with an arc-shaped roof. The walls of each house were made of logs stacked together, bark layered over to insulate them. The roofs were made from straw shingles, each sewn tightly and layered over one another. Along the roofs were chimneys made from hollowed-out logs. They were stained black. At the top of each was a flap, propped up by a long stick that allowed the flap to be opened or closed. Around the settlement were decorations and effigies made from wood, stone, and bone. At the top of the hill was a larger hut and a set of seven wooden idols in a circle.

"*Interesting,*" Brónmal thought as he looked over the settlement. Where he expected messy piles of raw material to make little nests, he found homes. The Algoniva, though primitive, were not as simple as he thought.

The Algoniva led Brónmal and the escort over a small bridge, through the village, and to the top of the hill. The Algoniva were everywhere. They looked curiously at the humans as if they were aliens. Many came out of their huts to stare, speaking in a strange language when the men passed. At the top, Ma'verd gestured to the large hut across from the pillars. "Tribe-father in there."

Brónmal nodded. He hopped off his Auhmog and looked at his men. "Stay here. If anything happens, do not be afraid to use your swords. I will be out soon."

The men saluted. "Praise the Supreme General!"

Brónmal went into the hut. The smell of flower oil hit him immediately, stinging his nose. The air was thick with smoke. Despite being made of raw materials, the hut was surprisingly warm and well put together. Effigies and strange, pagan decorations hung from the ceiling. Another Mot'Algoniva sat in the hut's center, wrapped in green blankets. It was older, with gray hairs and deep wrinkles.

The Algoniva grumbled as he looked up, speaking with a deeply accented voice. "Welcome to Kerukkoto."

Brónmal stared at the creature. "Are you the leader of this tribe?"

"Yes, in your language, tribe-father. My name is Gu'hag. You are Brónmal?"

Brónmal recoiled and blinked. "How do you know my name?"

Gu'hag gestured across from him. "Sit."

"You do not order me, beast."

Gu'hag chuckled. "We are not so different, Brónmal. Treat me like an equal. Sit or leave without my wisdom."

"Wisdom?"

Gu'hag said nothing and gestured again. Brónmal sighed and sat across from the tribe's leader. "Why am I here?"

"Do not act like I want your kind here. The Mednohail are evil creatures, murderers marching through our land. It is best that you leave here, having learned so that you do not come back for me and my people."

Brónmal squinted. "What do you mean? Who taught your tribe to speak my language?"

"Travelers teach my kinsmen, but I have traveled from tribe to tribe here in Mednodorn and learned through farmers and peasant folk, the bottom of your Empire."

"You speak well for an Algoniva."

"Not perfect. That is not why I brought you here. I want to extinguish the flame in your heart that would have you burn everything."

"What, do you think I will burn down your forest?"

"If told to? Yes. I know who you and your people are. You have murdered before and will again, but even then, you are different. You are among the few men who prize their belief over their leaders."

"*Did it just read my mind?*" Brónmal thought. His heart sank. "What are you saying?"

Gu'hag laughed. "You think you hide it well, do you not? Even your Highlord knows."

"How do you know this? Speak! Or I will kill you for your insolence!"

Gu'hag raised his hand to silence Brónmal. He turned and grabbed a bag, unfolding it to reveal a pile of bones and dried leaves. "The pickings tell me, they show me. I learn much this way."

Brónmal leaned forward. "Witchcraft, what form of Aogadraod is this?"

"Do you not think by yourself? Does faith alone drive you?"

Brónmal's face grew red. Gu'hag waved his hand dismissively. "Calm yourself. I have no one to tell your inner thoughts to but you. Do you want my wisdom or not?"

Brónmal sighed. "If it is worth my time, then speak. Be quick, my patience thins, beast."

"This will not be quick. First, you are unlike the rest of your kind, even the men outside. Your faith is above all else, even the Highlord or the Godspeaker. How could men speak for gods, right?"

Brónmal's right eye twitched. He felt his cheek burn as he thought of his father, who had beaten such questions out of him. "The Godspeaker has every right to speak for the Three."

"No, he does not. And you know in your heart that he does not. I hope that means you will listen to what I say this night. To begin, your leaders hold your people hostage."

"What nonsense is this?"

"You know this well. The Godspeaker does not have Mednodorn's best interests in mind; he only has his own. He holds the hearts and minds of the people like the Godspeakers before him, and just like them, he only cares about power. A servant of Dubilfen, I imagine you would say."

Brónmal's jaw clenched. "This is a sin; you speak out of your place!"

"And do you care? Would you prize sin above your strange gods?"

"What is your point?"

"Why do you think this war is happening? Is it for the good of the Mednohail? No, thousands will die just to get into Heokolon lands. The war you are fighting is for the Godspeaker's power. More land and more people to rule."

"This war is to avenge our fathers and take the land we should rightfully rule."

"And the war before that? There were no fathers to avenge then. The Godspeaker only wants land and justifies it to your Highlord that it's for salt so you may mummify your dead."

Brónmal quivered. His heart pumped, face red with anger and confusion. "Then are we fools?"

"Yes, but there are larger powers at play."

Brónmal leaned forward. "Beyond the Godspeaker?"

Gu'hag chuckled. "There is much hidden from your people. If you want to see truly, we must look at the bones."

"The bones? What sort of witchery is this? What are you planning to do?"

Gu'hag gestured to the pile of bones and leaves from the bag. "You will learn things not meant to be shown to you."

Brónmal squinted at the pile, jaw slack with forbidden curiosity.

Gu'hag continued. "In the rattling, in flame, there were visions of event that will be, even if you do everything you can to stop them. What changes is what you do about them."

"*Three protect my soul*," Brónmal prayed before his eyes locked on the Algoniva chief. "Show me."

Are you sure?"

"Yes, yes. Show me now."

Gu'hag picked up the bones, tossing them between his hands and occasionally throwing them down. "There are many events in the future, but few are good. What to say first? The Heokolons."

Gu'hag poured powder from a bag into his hands. "You will not conquer their empire. They will not be taken by surprise, meeting you at the great river between the two empires. Not even the Emperor's head is yours to take, but you must go anyway. Your men must not know, but there will never be any hope in an iron conquest like Mednodorn did to the Ahamari. Instead, fire."

Gu'hag snapped, lighting up the powder and bones with a crackling pop. A silhouette of a burning city formed from the smoke. "Ardmunhaich will burn, along with the rest of the Empire."

Brónmal's mouth gaped. "Lies!"

A strange fireball appeared over the smoke. "I speak the truth. On the other hand, your people will not perish. Only their ways and cruelty will burn. Come the 150th year, the comet Serkur will usher in the new Aothill, and your people will be reborn."

Brónmal stared at the fireball of sparks. "What about me? What role do I have in this doomed vision?"

"What you do is up to you. You can flee, die in battle, or you can help your people. There will be much you have to let go of. Your hatred, your cruelty, your blindness. There will be no Godspeaker or Highlord in the next age."

"What about the bigger powers? Who are they?"

Gu'hag's eyes narrowed, wrinkles deepening. "The servants of the Breaker of Man."

"The servants of who?"

"Arathmalok, the immortal lord of the Reign."

The name Arathmalok made Brónmal's stomach twist. It was as if some ancestral fear awoke at the very mention of his name, and even Gu'hag sounded uncomfortable. "What about the Reign? What about his servants?"

"The immortal, the one with no belly button, no family, born from darkness, still lives. His servants crawl across the world in fragments, hidden among the faceless and unknown. They wait for Serkur and bring nothing but chaos. The Ebon Armada, an ancient hunt from before the Reign, shall be brought by them. Ancient monsters will emerge from another world and slaughter for glory, leaving the world in ash."

"I have never heard of the Ebon Armada. How can I stop this?"

"Of course, you have not. Very few have. It has been over thirteen Aothills since they have sailed upon our world. There will be no stopping them, only pushing them out of the world."

"What must I do? There must be something I need to do to save my people."

"You can do nothing, or you can try to lead your people out of the chaos and into safety. They need the light once again. If you wish to help them, they must rediscover their faith."

"What about the servants? How do I stop them?"

"You cannot find them. Many are immortal like Arathmalok and can only be defeated if they come out into the light. For now, you must lead your men into Heonar. Do not break your spirit or theirs. It will be needed in the future."

"What do you mean?"

"Every victory you have from here on, even the smallest, is something to be grateful for. Without them, you will not have the will to go on."

Brónmal sat back. "My home is going to burn? The Empire will fall? Impossible, I must stop this. I will stop this."

"Like a forest burning, flowers and new life will replace it. You will be there for this new world if you so choose, but the mistakes of the past must be burned."

66

"The mistakes of the past?"

"Your people have lost their true faith and instead trust men, liars, and deceivers. Those must be burned for them to see again. You will see."

"What else? What else can you tell me?"

Gu'hag shook his head. "I have nothing more for you. I do not know everything that will come to pass, but you have a choice. Do nothing or stay strong in your strange faith and try to stand against fate."

Brónmal nodded. "I will stand against the darkness; nothing can stop the Mednohail."

"Careful of your pride; it is an evil. Now go, leave my forest by morning, and do not return. And speak little of what you have learned here. Just remember that you must act."

9

The Army of Raothal

Brónmal frowned with the weight of his emotions, rubbing his face before staring at his shaking hands. Was the Empire to burn? He would not allow it. He balled his hands into fists. It was a sin to listen to the old chief, yet he walked with a sense of pride. The campaign would not be doomed as long as he led; the Empire would live forever as long as he protected it. He returned to camp and said nothing, leaving the men confused. With the forest now behind them, Brónmal looked ahead. Their campaign was ill-faithed from the start, yet he had courage against doom. Nothing could stop them.

"*I will prove you wrong, primitive wretch,*" Brónmal thought.

His escort rode behind, Hacarad trailing Brónmal. He rode up near Brónmal and spoke. "Lord, are you well?"

Brónmal nodded. "I am fine. Let us just get to Raothal."

"What did the Algoniva talk to you about?"

Brónmal's lowered his head, closing his eyes for a moment. "Nothing, really. They wanted us out of their forest and wished me luck on the coming campaign. Foolish beasts."

"Out of *their* forest? Marcoili Forest has always been Mednohail. It belongs to us."

"It is a waste to discipline them. Maybe after the war."

"I understand, Lord. Are you sure you are well?"

"Yes. Do not ask again."

"As you say, Lord."

Brónmal urged his Auhmog to move faster. Beyond the deep clutches of the Marcoili Forest were the plains of Raothal, stretching for miles and miles. The flat land spanned most of Eastern Mednodorn, only shifting beyond the forest to the West. The land was mostly vacant. Rarely did they come across small farms or little hamlets.

"*What a miserable day. Always miserable,*" Brónmal thought. With few trees, the High Summer sun quickly baked the land and the soldiers. Brónmal wiped his sweat from his brow, sighing. They sometimes stopped to drink water and rest. Between stops, commanders stopped bickering soldiers fighting for shade beneath wagons and solitary trees.

Eventually, a hill appeared in the distance. Brónmal squinted. A vast, leafless tree dominated the hill. Getting closer, he could see silhouettes hanging from the trees. Hacarad rode up next to him. "What is that?"

"No idea..."

The army walked past. Brónmal and Hacarad stared at the tree. It was death. The bodies of heretics and sinners hung from the branches, swaying with the wind. Birds picked at their rotting flesh and screeched at the pair below. The lowest corpses had no shoes. Brónmal assumed travelers had taken what they could since shoes were valuable to peasants.

Hacarad groaned and held his nose. "What a foul smell!"

"The stench of sin never smells good."

"Foul heretics."

"Their spirits belong to Dubilfen now."

"Or they are trapped here."

Brónmal's spine tingled. "Ugh, let us continue. I do not want to deal with the spirits of heretics."

"Well said."

They rode off down the line, leaving the grim death tree behind. Hacarad rode beside Brónmal, drinking from his flask and groaning. "Damned sun! How long do you think is left until we reach Raothal?"

Brónmal shrugged. "A few hours. Probably late noon."

"Will we stop at noon?"

"If the men need it. The faster we get to Raothal, the faster we get out of the sun."

"Of course, Lord."

Brónmal looked around at the endless plains. Life withered under the heat. Grass wilted and browned, trees lost their leaves, and insects hid underground or hibernated in cocoons. Beasts like Crobestir and other herd animals lay in the vast expanses, entering a sort of hibernation. Many animals clumped under trees that still bore leaves, though it was hard to escape the sun. Like in High Winter, the land suffered and died.

So did the soldiers. At noon, men began to faint and fall, forcing the whole army to stop for a break. The sun had beaten many into submission. Commanders ran up and down the troops, screaming for water or medics. While the men rested, Brónmal rode up and down the line. Those resting saluted and shouted. "Three bless, Supreme General!"

Brónmal nodded to them. While he rode, another man charged up the line to him. "Supreme General!"

"What is it?"

"We have company down the line."

"Company?"

"Mudtails. They want to help us."

Brónmal recoiled. He had not seen a Mudtail in a while. Few were ever allowed inside the walls of cities. Even though many Mudtails in Mednodorn believed in the Three, they were not trusted. As non-humans, they would never be equal.

Brónmal gestured down the line. "Take me to them."

They rode down the entire line, passing thousands of men. At the very end was a vast caravan of wagons. Each wagon was large. Instead of a usual Mednohail wagon with a bed and sometimes a cover, Mudtail wagons were houses. They were painted blue and had house-like roofs with shingles. They had multiple stories, floors, and rooms hanging off the wagons' sides. A few had glass windows displaying the caravan's wealth. Beams propped up each extension. To compensate, the wagons had multiple sets of steel wheels. To pull them were dozens of Auhmogs. Umbrellas were attached to the harnesses of each beast, offering them shade. They huffed and drooled from the heat.

Unlike anyone else, Mudtails were nomadic creatures. With no sense of real unity, they were split into groups that traveled from city to city. Each caravan had a unique culture, though all were obsessed with trade and wealth.

An elderly female came out from the caravan. "Three bless, Supreme General. My name is Skalia. I am the Tradequeen of this caravan."

Mudtails were usually a foot shorter than the Mednohail, though age had bent Skalia's back and made her appear smaller. Like most Mudtails, she was mouse-like in appearance. She had large ears and a large snout, her fur white and skin covered in wart-like bumps. Her tail was low-hanging and stained dark from dirt, hence the name for her kind. Since her species could not sweat, she suffered from the heat. She panted, yet it was not enough.

Brónmal nodded to her. "Three bless. It is good to meet you, Skalia."

"Dubilfen has also cursed your men to suffer the heat?"

Brónmal glanced back. "We push on."

"Where do you march to?"

"We march to Raothal. Where do you march to?"

"The Three have blessed us. We are on the way there as well. It would appear you need help."

"*What slimy deal do you want, creature?*" Brónmal thought and narrowed his eyes. He held the Mudtails in low esteem. Like his Father, he had little trust in a non-human race like them. They were greedy and selfish, only caring about their caravans and coins. Many were grumpy but conjured "false personalities" to trick people into making poor trades. They were even willing to do dirty work for coin, like stealing.

Brónmal pursed his lips, then spoke. "And what would your help cost, Tradequeen?"

Skalia's brown eyes narrowed, ears flicking. "You think I am a fool, Supreme General? If I asked for your coin, I would get your sword. My help costs your men to help my caravan get to Raothal."

Hacarad and Brónmal looked at each other and shrugged. Brónmal nodded to Skalia. "Then your help will be much appreciated."

"Grab some of your men. We have gifts to spare."

Brónmal sent a commander down the line to fetch a few soldiers. Within minutes, they gathered by the caravan and stared at the Mudtails with animosity. Mudtails jumped out of the wagons, each with white fur and stained tails. They exchanged flasks of water. Brónmal watched as they handed out strange umbrella-like blankets the men gladly carried back and rested under. It was an insignificant gift to an army so large, yet it was something.

Hacarad looked at the tarps. "Oh, Three bless us. May the men not fight over those."

Brónmal shook his head. "More shade is always better."

Once they were done, the Mudtails immediately jumped into the cool gloom of their wagon homes. Skalia approached Brónmal and bowed. "It was a pleasure buying your help, Supreme General."

"You are welcome. Thank you for the water and shade, as meager as it is. We will be leaving in about ten minutes."

"We will follow you."

Brónmal nodded and rode to the front of the line. Hacarad followed. "I hate Mudtails."

"Strange creatures. At least they worship the Three, unlike those Algoniva."

"True. They are worthy of mercy for that. She did not even ask for coin?"

"Nope. They know better than to barter with soldiers. They just want protection."

Hacarad squinted at the surrounding horizon. "Protection from what?"

Brónmal shrugged. "Animals, outlaws, anything of the sort."

"Whatever, water is water, shade is shade."

Once Brónmal and Hacarad reached the front of the line, the army began to move again. The men groaned from being baked alive in their armor. Brónmal wiped his forehead, praying for the heat to leave. After a few hours of marching, a soldier burst out. "I think I see the city!"

Brónmal squinted. Breaking the flat, endless horizon was the silhouette of a city. As they drew closer, they entered a vast farmland. The fields were vacant of crops, left bone dry beneath the heat of High Summer. As the army moved toward the city, peasant folk and freemen ran out of their houses. They ran to the edge of their fields, cheering joyfully at the army.

In the distance, bells rang. The city came to life, gates opening to the first of three walls. Raothal was much smaller than Ardmunhaich but built in the same tradition, with three walls and a castle built upon a ziggurat in the center. Guards clamored to form a pathway to the city's center for the army.

Hundreds of peasants came to cheer and give praise to the army. Brónmal and Hacarad waved. Their escort surrounded them, forming a barrier between them and the lines of guards keeping the crowds at bay. Men screamed praises. Women wept with joy, and children cheered. Even though Brónmal was not the Godspeaker or the Highlord, he was seen as a beloved, great leader.

Like Ardmunhaich, the walls were divided into classes. The outer wall had peasantry that reeked, was dirty, and stained from work. The second gates opened, and a crowd of freemen greeted the army. Beyond the third gates were noble folk who showered them with gifts such as delicate flowers and jewels. At the very center of the city stood a trio of men near the base of Raothal's castle.

The first was Wetemir, the king of Raothal. Dressed in large robes that stopped just beneath his hips, he had a grand leather belt around his waist. The belt shaped the robe into an hourglass shape, leaving tight pants just below them. He had long brown hair and a short beard to match. A more respected king, Wetemir and his kingdom were responsible for most of the food production for Eastern Mednodorn.

Beside him were the Archbishop, Angamal, and the General of Raothal's army, Drakmanir. The Archbishop wore long green robes from his shoulders down to his feet. He wore no jewelry, only a string belt that kept the robe tight along his hips. The General was dressed in a vest with puffy sleeves and the same tight pants as the king. In addition, he also had a flowing skirt embroidered with golden stitching. On his neck, he wore a necklace of silver, a mark of his nobility.

Brónmal hopped off his Auhmog.

Wetemir approached. "Three bless! Word came early, and I have been eager to meet the new Supreme General. It is an honor; welcome to Raothal."

Brónmal bowed. "Three bless! It is a pleasure, My King."

"I hope the sun has not beaten you too hard?"

Brónmal wiped his brow. "It has been a journey. I hope my men have lodgings for tonight?"

"Indeed, they do. Come, we have much to talk of."

Brónmal nodded. He looked at Hacarad. "Take over command."

Hacarad nodded. "Yes, Lord. As you say."

Brónmal followed the king, Archbishop, and General up the steps of the ziggurat and into the castle.

* * *

Wetemir led the trio into the castle, going through the throne room and into the halls of the vast stone fortress. They went up a stair, eventually entering a room with windows overlooking the West. Brónmal peered out. He could see his army marching in through the walls. Guards stopped the caravan of Mudtails from entering the first gate, keeping them out with the rest of the peasantry.

Brónmal sat down with the other three men. On the table was a map, and cups were laid out before each man. Wetemir grabbed a large jug and poured wine into his cup. "Wine?"

Brónmal nodded. Wetemir passed the jug around, eventually putting it away once everyone got their wine. Brónmal held his cup, staring hard at the map. It showed the Empire and what little was known about the lands of Heonar. "Do I need my commanders for this, My King?"

Wetemir shook his head. "Such discussions will be for later. We wanted to make this short so you can go rest."

Brónmal nodded. "I appreciate it, My King. What do we have to discuss?"

The General, Drakmanir, leaned forward. "We have done all we can to prepare for the coming campaign. We have sent scouts over the Kabhain River, gathered as many men as possible, and prepared our stores for war."

Brónmal sipped his wine. "That is good to hear."

Drakmanir frowned. "Unfortunately, only a few scouts have returned."

"What did they find? Why only a few?"

Wetemir sighed. "Our war is no surprise to the Heokolons. They sent the rest of our scouts back in pieces."

"That damned Algoniva was right?" Brónmal thought, stomach twisting. He clenched his jaw and then spoke. "Are you telling me the Heokolons are across the river now, ready for us? They are aware of our invasion?"

Drakmanir nodded. "We are not sure how many, but we have not engaged them. They wait to speak with you."

"Speak with me?"

Wetemir spoke. "The General of Heonar wants to speak with the new Supreme General. Something about coming to terms."

The Archbishop, Angamal, scoffed. "Coming to terms with a pagan?"

Brónmal gestured to Angamal. "I agree with the Archbishop. Why would we speak to pagans?"

Wetemir shrugged. "There is no reason to. Perhaps an agreement could be found, but we hoped you might learn something about them."

Brónmal cracked his neck left and right, humming for a moment. "I have nothing to say to such heathens. Perhaps I could ask for the bodies of our forefathers back, but I doubt they would honor such a thing. Very well, I will speak to their General, but I know blood will soon be shed. Are the men of Raothal ready?"

Wetemir raised a brow. "With the men of Ardmunhaich standing with them? They are ready to march to the ends of the world for you."

Brónmal smiled. "Good to hear."

10

The Dronmar Towers

Brónmal felt strong. With the twin armies of Raothal and Ardmunhaich behind him, he puffed his chest with confidence. He fought back the doubts, disregarding the words of Gu'hag and his vision. There was no way the Heokolons were ready. Thousands strong, the men sang with pride and courage. They sang of their forefathers who had invaded Heonar thirty years before, words of revenge echoing across the plains.

Hacarad rode beside Brónmal. "I never thought we would be here."

Brónmal glanced at him. "What do you mean?"

"I never thought we would be here, this close to Heonar. Just a few more steps, and we will be avenging our fathers' loss, fixing our past mistakes, conquering for the Empire."

"*You hear that, father? I have almost bested you,*" Brónmal thought. He thinly smiled. "Me neither. I wonder what their land truly looks like. I am sure my father's stories do not do it justice."

"I am sure it is ruined by the sight of pagan homes and wretched heathen altars to false gods."

Brónmal hummed. "What do they believe in?"

Hacarad shrugged. "I think some singular god and the Emperor is also a god? How could a man be a god?"

"*Do you not see the connection, brother?*" Brónmal thought and frowned.

How could a man be a god? How could a man speak for a god? How did Hacarad not see the problem? For the Heokolons, their Emperor was a god, and the Godspeaker was a god for his people.

He opened his mouth, then shook his head against mentioning the connection. "I am not sure. I am not a pagan."

Hacarad shrugged again. "They will learn soon enough. Once we remove their Emperor's head, we will rename their lands with holy names and show them the light."

"Well said."

The army marched for hours through the flat edge of the Eastern lands. Brónmal felt like he would fall off his Auhmog from boredom and heat, his body begging to be done with marching. Eventually, Hacarad rode forward and cried. "There they are!"

In the distance, the great Kabhain River split the two mighty empires. It flowed from the Gisjaf Sea in the North, going into the rocky waters of the Mekden Sea to the South. Fed by meltwater from glaciers and snow, the water was ice cold. It roared, ready to sweep anyone under its brutal currents. Towers dominated the river. There were five, each placed far apart. The army approached the middle one, its adjacent twins so far in the distance that Brónmal could barely make out their figures.

Built in the first Aothill by King Peregrine IV, who formed Mednodorn, the Dronmar towers were mighty bulwarks against the East. Each stood in the middle of the river, with bridges sprouting out to each side of the bank. They were cube-like. Brónmal had never seen such goliath structures outside of a city. Each tower rose high into the sky, touching where the birds flew.

As they approached, Brónmal saw hundreds of soldiers outside the first tower. They waved at the approaching army. Each side of the building had colossal gates facing both empires, large enough to allow hundreds of soldiers to march through at once. Hundreds of archers patrolled the inner bowls of the tower, peering out of narrow windows at the approaching soldiers. An imposing catapult sat on top of the tower. Brónmal looked up. It was ancient, a rare example of its kind.

A man in full armor approached. He was clean-shaven, like most soldiers, a young commander in his twenties. He wore plate armor with a can-shaped helmet hung from his waist and a steel spear in his hand. His reddish-brown hair was short and combed back, brown eyes staring with admiration. He waved and smiled. His teeth were yellow and dirty like a peasant, yet not decayed like one of the nobilities. He spoke with a voice eager with youth. "Three bless!"

Brónmal waved. "Three bless!"

"My name is Clegdamar. I am the commander of the Kabhain forces. Are you the new Supreme General?"

Brónmal nodded. "I am indeed. It is good to meet you, Clegdamar."

"Three bless you, Supreme General. It is an honor to meet such a man in this historic time. I wish I could bring you good news."

"What has happened?"

"The Heokolons await on the other side of the river. They will not let us touch the other shore but dare not attack the towers themselves."

"How many are there?"

"Tens of thousands, we are not sure. It has been a week since they have arrived, but they only seem to want to speak to you."

"*We need more men,*" Brónmal thought, his conviction quivering. It seems the Heokolons were ready for war as well. He gestured over the river. "If they want an audience with me, so be it. Set one up. Are the other towers in danger?"

"Yes, Supreme General. I have split up my men as best I can, but we do not have the forces to defend all five towers if they attacked."

"Lucky I am here. Hacarad!"

Hacarad saluted. "Yes, Supreme General!"

"Talk to the commanders. Split the army between the five towers. I want each tower as well defended as possible, and I want patrols up and down the river. Send scouts to the edges of each sea. I do not want to be caught by surprise."

"Right away, Lord!"

Hacarad rode off while Brónmal and his escort followed Clegdamar. The men around the tower saluted, shouting their praises. The mighty gates facing Mednodorn were opened, revealing a hall. The hall was vast, each corner occupied by great mechanisms that opened and closed the gates. It took multiple soldiers to work them, each pushing with heaving groans. Flanking both sides of the center hall were stairs. They rose into floors above, each level occupied by patrolling archers and sleeping soldiers.

The hall was filled with supply crates, weapons, and waiting soldiers. A sense of impatient dread filled the air. As Brónmal entered, Clegdamar spoke. "Attention!"

The soldiers all stood and saluted. "Praise the Supreme General!"

Brónmal nodded. "Fine-looking soldiers you have."

Clegdamar chuckled. "Best of Raothal patrol here, making sure the Heokolons stay on their side. Now, it's finally time to attack. Many have waited years for the order to go over, and they look forward to serving under you."

"*I am not Trudumal, but I will prove myself,*" Brónmal thought. He smiled. "I am glad to see a strong spirit here."

Clegdamar nodded before turning to his soldiers. "I need five men to go to the Heokolon war camp and tell them we are willing to talk! Who wishes to go?"

A few men stood, Clegdamar pointing to five. Brónmal could see the fear on their faces. None were sure they would return, yet they puffed up their courage before the Supreme General. After a few minutes, the gates to Heonar were opened, and the five were sent out. Brónmal looked out. The great plains extended into Heonar, only stopping at a distant mountain wall. Miles of tents sat in the distance. The Heokolon army was massive, perhaps more significant than his own.

His confidence cracked more. Heokolons believed in perfectionism and were raised from birth for specific jobs. Their soldiers had decades of experience over the single year of a Mednohail soldier. The Mednohail usually had numbers, but if this was not the case today, Brónmal would need a better strategy. They had the towers, and they had Gluvactdraod.

"Three protect us. Daonrex, I humbly beg for your strength this day," Brónmal prayed.

It was an hour before the men returned.

"Supreme General! The Heokolon General will meet with you in an hour on the field! They have a translator!"

Brónmal nodded. "Good. You five are relieved."

Clegdamar went up to Brónmal. "Careful, Supreme General. We have no idea what the Heokolons are like. We did not have negotiations like this during the last war."

Brónmal waved. "It will be fine. I will bring my escort, and if anything goes wrong, we will retreat. Are you ready, men?"

The escort behind him saluted. "Praise the Supreme General!"

Brónmal waited for an hour, watching the twin armies of Mednohail split themselves among the towers. Eventually, he could see a group of dozen men leave the Heokolon camp. It was time. Brónmal rode out into the field, the escort behind him.

After a few minutes, the two groups met. Brónmal wore full plate armor, a sword sheathed on his hip, and a helmet hanging from his saddle. The Heokolon General was dressed in gold-colored armor. It was far more complex, with intricate designs and wave-like patterns. He rode a strange beast. A golden helmet hung from its saddle. It had a face-like visor and a blade-like horn rising from the forehead. Alongside it was a glaive, a polearm with a long shaft and a curved glass blade. It dangled with the helm.

Brónmal recoiled. His father's stories were correct. The General was the only man without a helmet, showing off his Heokolon features. His skin was a pale, greenish color. His eyes were golden, and he had no hair, like all Heokolons. Unlike other peoples, the teeth of Heokolons were square, like those of an herbivore. They were around the same height, the General only an inch taller than Brónmal.

"*Savage, your golden facade cannot hide your wretchedness,*" Brónmal thought.

A pair of Heokolon servants set out a table and two chairs. Together, the Generals hopped off their beasts and sat. A Heokolon in robes emerged from the Heokolon escort. "Greetings, Supreme General. I am Tahitul, and this is General Temkemeletl."

"I am Brónmal. I feel blessed to have this opportunity."

Temkemeletl stared at Brónmal, golden eyes piercing and unmoving. Brónmal stared back. Hatred filled the air. Tahitul nodded and spoke. "We brought you here to discuss terms."

Brónmal raised a brow. "What are these terms?"

Tahitul and Temkemeletl exchanged conversation, Brónmal glancing between them. He truly hated their language. Tahitul spoke again. "We know of your desire to invade our lands, which is why we are here today. The General here has proposed that we agree on a land exchange."

"Land exchange? What do you mean?"

Tahitul and Temkemeletl spoke again before Tahitul responded. "None of us want to lose thousands of young men to a meaningless war. We know you truly want this side of the river for salt, especially near the Mekden Sea. We would be willing to let you mine here if you gave us parts of Raothal to farm on."

"*Is this a joke?*" Brónmal thought and scoffed. "I am not going to give you Mednohail land, pagan. Our lands are sacred, and no heathen will ever have them."

Tahitul translated. Temkemeletl scowled, brow wrinkling in anger when he responded, Tahitul translation back. "Our lands are sacred as well, yet we would be willing to come to peace in exchange for mercy on our men and yours."

"I would never let heathens live on my land."

"And if they converted?"

"Would they convert? Your god must mean something to you."

"You are right. So, is there no agreement we can have?"

Brónmal shook his head. "I knew I was wasting my time to come here. I will not sit here and barter for land, pretending I am not here to take your Emperor's head home for the Highlord and Godspeaker. I will not have to worry about land when all of it will be mine."

Tahitul recoiled, slowly translating to Temkemeletl, whose face grew slightly yellower with each word. Brónmal gawked, surprised to see how the greenish hue of Heokolon skin reacted to the blood rush of anger. Midway through the translation, Temkemeletl stood and slammed the table, shouting in Heokolon and turning to leave.

"*I am in your head,*" Brónmal thought and laughed. "What did he say?"

Tahitul turned. "He said he will enslave you and make you watch as he burns down your home."

Brónmal stood. "And I will hang his head from my saddle and have him watch as I conquer all of Heonar."

Temkemeletl spat and mounted his beast. He shouted and urged the creature away. His escort followed, Brónmal chuckling when they left. He stood and mounted his Auhmog, riding toward the gates of the central Dronmar tower. As the gates opened, he drew his sword and pointed it upward. "We will have war!"

The soldiers within shouted. "For Mednodorn!"

11

The Kabhain Battle

Brónmal rode into the tower with his escort behind him. "Close the gates!"

"*I will crush every single Heokolon. I cannot fail here,*" he thought. The clinking of chains and gears echoed as the tremendous gates facing Heonar closed. Hacarad rode up to Brónmal. "What happened, Lord?"

"There will be no peace with pagans. Alert the other towers and prepare for the siege! I want archers in the windows, the Flamebows above the gates, and all men ready to march East. Now!"

Hacarad saluted. "Right away! You heard him! Move!"

Hacarad barked orders at the other commanders. They sent riders to the other towers while archers and men with Snakebows ran into the tower's higher levels. Brónmal felt as if he had sinned. He was forced to use the Flamebows and Snakebows. It gave an advantage, but at what cost?

Once Hacarad finished giving orders, Brónmal shouted to him. "With me, Hacarad!"

Hacarad came to his side as Brónmal dismounted and scaled the tower to the top. From above, they could see the entire Heokolon war camp. It stirred. Soldiers poured out from camp like ants from an enraged ant hill and marched on the towers. Thousands of men split between each building. The wrath of the East had awoken.

Hacarad leaned over the battlement. "By the Three, there are thousands more than we thought."

Brónmal approached the edge of the tower. "We have the advantage with the towers and our magic."

"What if they break through?"

"They will not break through. We will whittle down their army and then charge."

"Charge into thousands of trained Heokolons?"

"Yes!"

Hacarad shook his head. "You are insane; we cannot possibly win!"

Brónmal turned. "You question me, Hacarad? I am the Supreme General; if I say we charge, we charge! We have the advantage. We have the support of the towers and our new weapons. The Heokolons have never seen what we are about to use on them!"

Hacarad looked down "O-Of course, Lord. I will stand by you through anything."

"Better to die than retreat like our forefathers."

"We will avenge them."

"*How dare you doubt me, brother? I will show you as I will show father,*" Brónmal thought.

The pair watched the Heokolon formations split among the towers. Each soldier was dressed in glimmering, golden plate armor underlaid with chainmail. Their armor plates were carved and decorated, each piece shaped in sharp and blade-like angles. Every man had a glass weapon. Heokolon glass. Strong like metal, each glaive, spear, and sword the Heokolons carried was sharper than anything made in Mednodorn. Their helmets displayed Heokolon perfection. They had blade-like protrusions that started by their ears and met at the crowns of their heads. With full-face visors, each soldier was faceless, only peering out through two eye slits. Between the soldiers were giant, strange crossbows on wheels. Five went toward each building. Brónmal pointed. "What are those?"

Hacarad squinted. "Seems we were not the only ones who brought machines."

Brónmal shook his head. "Men are pushing them. No foul magics like us."

Hacarad chuckled. "Who knew sin would give us an advantage?"

The Heokolons marched toward the five towers, pushing their siege weapons with them until their army was just out of bow range.

Hacarad snorted. "Look, they think they are safe."

Brónmal smiled. "From bows. But not Snakebows."

A man came up from the stairs below. "Supreme General! The Heokolons are here. What do we do?"

Brónmal glanced back. "Prepare the men to shoot on my mark."

"Yes, Supreme General!" the man turned and shouted down the stairs. "Aim!"

The command relayed down. Meanwhile, Brónmal watched as the Heokolons moved formations and wheeled their siege machines forward.

"*Here I stand on the brink of war, the exhale before the fall. Am I ready to plunge into battle, to lead as those before me?*" Brónmal thought.

Hacarad looked at Brónmal. "Well?"

Brónmal shook his head. "Just nervous. Are you ready?"

Hacarad nodded. "Always."

Brónmal pointed at the man behind them. "Shoot!"

The man shouted. "Loose!"

Hundreds of whines from Snakebows filled the air, bolts shooting out from the slits of the tower and flying out to the Heokolons. Unlike arrows, the bolts penetrated Heokolon armor and stuck, turning the Easterlings into bloody pin cushions as the hail came down. The Heokolons burst into a panic. Across the river, commanders in the other towers ordered their men to shoot. Within moments, the Heokolon army fell into momentary chaos while their commanders tried to keep the formations together.

Brónmal shouted. "Keep firing!"

The hail of bolts never ended as the Heokolons put their dying formations together. They formed a wall of shields. The unprotected men on the crossbows died, replaced by soldier after soldier while they pushed the siege weapons closer.

Hacarad leaned forward. "What are they doing?"

Brónmal shook his head. "Something... Prepare the men below to march forward!"

The man behind them shouted the order to the commanders below. The crossbows drew closer. They stopped at the edge of the bridges, shield-wall formations following. A loud set of clicks echoed before all five siege weapons shot massive bolts into the tower's gates. Debris splintered everywhere. The bolts were attached with chains, the metal rattling as they hit the ground.

Brónmal shouted. "They are breaking in! Prepare to march forward!"

Hacarad grabbed Brónmal. "Wait! Are you sure you want to face the Heokolons head-on?"

Brónmal swiped away his hand. "We have the advantage here!"

Heokolons turned the wheels on the siege weapons, retracting the chains to pull the doors open. The gates cracked and groaned, slowly giving in to the siege weapon.

Brónmal ran down the stairs. "Come on, Hacarad!"

They descended in a circle, each stair following the walls down as they passed bedrooms, kitchens, and soldiers. Each level had window slits. Archers occupied each slit, firing nonstop. Brónmal shouted at each level. "Keep firing! Keep firing!"

Once the pair arrived at the ground level, Brónmal pointed and barked commands. "I want a single line of shields in the front with Flamebows and War Carriages behind! Protect the Flamebows and War Carriages at all costs! Burn them if the filthy pagans get their claws on them! When we march forward, I want the shields to move and the Flamebows to scorch the heathens!"

The army moved and switched formations while the gates cracked. Brónmal put on his helmet. His stomach sank, and his hands shook. The battle was just outside the gates, so close yet far away. He closed his eyes.

"Three, give us strength; shield my people and the Empire from the heathen hordes. I will stand as a saint, a divine sword acting as your vessel, to save this world from sin," Brónmal prayed.

Hacarad stood beside him. "I feel blessed by the Three this day."

"We all are blessed. May we drive these wretched pagans back and have their emperor's head before winter."

The two grew silent as the top of the gate broke off and flooded the hall with sunlight. A loud crack rang out as the rest of the gate snapped open, revealing the Heokolon horde outside. A cry came from both sides as they marched forward.

Brónmal charged ahead with his escort behind. "Kill them all! For the Three! For Mednodorn!"

The two armies met in the middle of the bridge between the tower and the East. Soldiers carrying shields retreated into the formation, the Flamebows marching forward in their place. Searing, tar-like goo spewed over the Heokolons. They stumbled back and shielded themselves as goo covered and cooked them alive. They shrieked and ran, diving into the river to be boiled in the water instead.

Broken, the Heokolons retreated backward while the Mednohail baptized them with flame. Brónmal rode with the army as they marched onto the other side. The fire of the Flamebows flickered and went out as they exhausted their fuel, the War Carriages replacing them.

The Heokolons charged forward with renewed vigor as the Flamebows retreated, only to be broken again by the War Carriages. They were unstoppable. Rolling over bodies, bolts shot out of the little slits and openings of the war machines every few seconds. The Heokolons piled onto them. While they did, Mednohail soldiers stabbed them with spears and beat them back with maces.

Brónmal raised his sword in the air. "Push forward! Burn their camp!"

The army spread into various formations, men with unspent Flamebows leading with War Carriages behind. Brónmal looked across the battlefield. Cinders filled the air. The smell of cooked flesh made his stomach turn. Bodies lay everywhere. Despite the hard push, the Mednohail foot soldiers fell quickly as they neared trained Heokolon warriors.

Hacarad shouted. "The others are not advancing!"

Beyond their push, the other towers had yet to do the same. Instead, the Heokolons pushed forward into the Towers, only held back by sheer numbers and Flamebows.

Brónmal waved his sword. "It does not matter! We will burn the camps and starve them! Keep pushing forward!"

The men zealously charged to their deaths by Heokolon glaive, spear, and sword. Blood soaked the ground. Ill-protected, the glass weapons of the Heokolons tore through the Mednohail. Numbers did little. Every chance the Mednohail got, they brutally beat the Heokolons to death with maces. They ran Heokolon warriors through with spears, only to be cut into pieces.

It did not take long for the last Flamebows to flicker and die out. Once they were pushed back, the War Carriages came next. The Heokolons charged them. Men fell to defend the war weapons, unable to as the Heokolons broke into the tops of the carriages and slaughtered the men inside.

Brónmal shouted. "Burn the carriages! Burn them!"

More men died struggling to carry torches to the War Carriages as the Heokolons surrounded them. Brónmal pointed with his sword, shouting to Hacarad. "We need to help them!"

Hacarad reached out. "It's too dangerous, Lord!"

Brónmal urged forward. "Come on!"

Hacarad and the escort chased after Brónmal, charging into the fray. Brónmal swung his sword, trying to stab between the gaps in the plate armor of the Easterlings. Slashing did little. He ran into a group of Heokolons, screaming with his sword in the air.

Hacarad cried. "Lord! No!"

One swung a glaive out. It slid across his armor without penetrating. He smacked it away and stabbed back. The Heokolons surrounded him. Their glaives and spears raised, snaking in the air toward him.

"*Three, protect me!*" Brónmal thought.

Hacarad crashed into a Heokolon and wildly stabbed at the rest. Brónmal lurched forward to help. His escort joined, helping to throw torches onto the War Carriages.

Hacarad stumbled back as frenzied Mednohail ran past them to protect their Supreme General. "Lord! We need to retreat!"

Brónmal looked around. Their army fell apart. For every Heokolon crushed under Mednohail mace, they lost ten men. Their numbers were nothing without their sadistic weapons of sin. Brónmal waved. "Retreat! Retreat over the water!"

The escort surrounded the pair while they ran back, with the rest of the army following. Men died to buy time for others, but the Heokolon war machine did not stop, marching forward through the towers.

Brónmal screamed. "Where are my commanders!? Tell the other towers we are retreating to Raothal! Send a messenger to the Empire! We need the Nine Armies!"

They ran through the central tower to the other side, looking down the river at the other buildings. Each had fallen. The twin armies of Ardmunahich and Raothal could not withstand the Heokolon onslaught, running back into the countryside in terror.

Brónmal pointed and screamed. "Get back to Raothal! Defend the retreat! Go, GO!"

A few soldiers remained behind, laying down their lives to stop the Heokolons as much as they could. It did little. Brónmal ran into the flat fields of Raothal, looking back once. He had failed. All that was left was to recover and push the Heokolons out of the Empire.

Hacarad stood beside him, panting and falling to his knees. He tore off his helmet, huffing as tears rolled down his cheeks. "We failed, Lord. We failed..."

This was the power of the East, the very monster that broke men like his father. Brónmal and those around him were no different. Arrogance had defeated them.

"*I failed, Father, I failed,*" Brónmal thought.

12

The Siege of Raothal

"Archers, to the walls! Keep their ladders off! Where are the Flamebows?" Brónmal shouted.

"They are still refueling, Lord!" Hacarad cried out in response.

Brónmal groaned. "Tell them to hurry!"

Hacarad sprinted off. Brónmal went into a tower and climbed up to the adjacent walls. It had been days since the retreat to the city. The land outside the city burned. Over the rolling hills and withered plains, great fires scorched the land and blackened the sky. The Heokolons torched farms and homes, leaving nothing. The flames, made worse by High Summer, heated the air and rained down cinders.

Patrols circled the city, slaughtering anyone who approached, closing the city off from the Empire. On a distant hill sat the Heokolon camp. It stirred constantly, never resting like a hive of wasps. Every day, more soldiers and supplies came from the East, invigorating the war camp.

Brónmal squinted. In the distance, the Easterlings began to rise into commotion. The Heokolon camp surged forward with men. The swarm of warriors marched on with ladders. Another attack.

Brónmal shouted to his men. "Prepare for battle! Get the Flamebows up here!"

Hacarad arrived from one of the towers with a group of men with Flamebows. "They are ready, Lord!"

Brónmal pointed to each Flamebow team. "Go around the wall, burn all Easterlings that dare climb up!"

The Flamebow teams ran along the wall. Hacarad joined Brónmal by his side, gazing at the approaching Heokolon terror. "Perhaps this was a mistake?"

Brónmal rubbed his face. "What? Retreating to Raothal or this entire invasion?"

"The entire invasion."

"We just have to wait for the other seven armies to arrive."

Hacarad shook his head. "So we can push them back and die in Heonar instead of Mednodorn?"

"It would be an honor. More honorable than dying here or dying in retreat."

Hacarad sighed. "We already retreated."

Brónmal dismissively waved. "No, we did not retreat. We advanced backward."

Hacarad chuckled. "Advanced... Backward?"

Brónmal nodded with a thin smile. "All of it is planned. Now, we need to make it through the coming few weeks."

"Three bless us. Hopefully, the walls hold."

"Have courage. They will."

The Heokolons attacked the walls. The Mednohail archers opened fire, raining bolts and arrows down on Heokolon's shields.

"*Daonrex, safeguard my soldiers and deliver us unto victory,*" Brónmal prayed, closing his eyes and tilting his head to the heavens.

Among the Easterlings were men carrying shields large enough to protect ten soldiers at a time. Archers hid behind them. Once they were close, they lifted the shields and unleashed arrows at the men on the wall. The arrows flew from longbows as tall as the men, easily penetrating Mednohail armor.

Brónmal screamed. "Shoot them! Shoot the archers!"

The two sides exchanged arrows and bolts, men dying and falling off the wall while the Heokolons hid behind their shields. From the formations came ladders. The ladders came from the army's rear and passed between the Easterling formations to the front. They raised the ladders, soldiers climbing them in daring dashes to get onto the wall.

Brónmal pointed. "Flamebows! Burn the ladders!"

The Flamebow teams approached the edge of the walls, Heokolon bowmen firing at them. The climbers looked up in horror. Flame spewed, roasting the soldiers alive and turning the ladders into char. More ladders and soldiers replaced them. Men rushed to push the ladders off. Arrows felled them, allowing a few Heokolon warriors to climb onto the battlements.

The men shouted. "They are on the walls!"

The Heokolon warriors cleaved down man after man before being over-whelmed. A Heokolon in golden armor lined with ornamental designs hopped onto the wall, glaive in hand. Like the wind, he effortlessly cut through the defenders. Dozens fell before he reached Brónmal, pausing momentarily to stare.

Brónmal drew his sword, eyes narrowing behind his helmet. They ap-proached each other, the Heokolon growling out something in his foul language. Brónmal spoke back, spitting his words out. "You have come to die, heathen!"

Both swung their weapons. Glass and steel sparked. The weapons rang, the two combatants slicing at one another. Brónmal stumbled back. The Heokolon was too fast, his light glaive blazing through his defense. With a shrieking clink, Brónmal's sword flew from his hand.

The Heokolon raised his glaive. A mace slammed through his head, sending him off the wall to reveal Hacarad behind him. "Brónmal! Are you hurt?"

Brónmal's heart skipped. "I... I am fine. Three bless. I am glad you got here in time."

Hacarad grabbed Brónmal's sword and handed it to him. "Always, Lord! Come on. The Heokolons are attacking the gate."

They ran across the wall to a duo of towers connected by a vast gate. Along the battlements were holes and slits. Archers fired out of them, drawing arrows from baskets placed along the wall. Peasants ran along the ramparts. They replaced the empty baskets of arrows with full ones.

Metal grates lined the wall. Pairs of men hoisted iron pots along the ramparts. They filled them with sand or oil and held them over firepits until scorching. As teams, they poured the burning sand and oil through the grates onto the attackers below. The sand slipped through gaps in armor. Men screamed and broke formation as it was poured on them, thrashing as if covered in ants. The oil was far crueler. It made ladders slippery, causing Heokolons to fall to their deaths as they were boiled.

Brónmal approached an archer. "What is going on here?"

"They are rushing the gate, Supreme General! They have bags of something they are trying to hook on the gate!"

Brónmal leaned over the battlement, watching the Heokolons stack bags onto the gate. Soldiers escorted them, shielding them from arrows. He squinted, then turned. "We need fire! Light the arrows! Go!"

Two men disappeared into a tower and returned with a brazier. They wrapped arrows in oil-soaked rags, lit them, and fired them over the walls.

Brónmal pointed. "Shoot the bags!"

Arrows rained down on the men carrying bags. The escorting soldiers shielded them, keeping the fire arrows at bay. Brónmal barked. "Keep shooting! Shoot the bags!"

An arrow slipped by the shields. The ground shook as the bags detonated into a fiery explosion, blasting the escort into pieces. Brónmal dove for cover. The walls vibrated as the tremendous explosion sent shockwaves throughout the city. The fire curled over the battlements. Heat tickled Brónmal's armor. The archers still standing around him screamed as they were scorched. They ran, diving off the walls in burning panic.

Ears ringing, Brónmal stood. "Hacarad!"

Hacarad stumbled out of a tower with not a scratch on him. "Over here, Lord!"

Brónmal peered over the battlements, looking down at the gates below. They were still intact. Embers covered them, though the explosion had weakened the gates. Brónmal looked to Hacarad. "Get men and reinforce the gate! I do not want the Heokolons to break through."

"Yes, Lord!"

Brónmal went along the walls, barking orders for hours while the Med-nohail fended off the Heokolons. As the sun began to set, the Easterlings withdrew. Each wave and attack had failed. The Mednohail picked up their comrades' bodies and carried them into the inner city, tossing the corpses of Heokolons over the walls.

The attack was brutal. Each day, they lost more and more men. At least rations would last longer. The men gathered for soup, leaving patrols along the walls in case the Heokolons attacked again. Brónmal walked among the exhausted men, waving at those who greeted him.

In the distance, he could hear screams. Drawing toward the sound, Brónmal stumbled upon the medical tents. Men lay everywhere, coughing and moaning as nurses and physicians ran among them. Brónmal stopped and stared. Blood splattered the ground, the smell of decay lingering from infected wounds and punctured guts.

Young, old, strong, weak, they all were broken. A few wept, others prayed, and a few were dead. Brónmal's gaze drifted to one of the injured. A young boy, no older than eighteen, sat and held himself. He wept. "I want my mother. I want my mother."

In one tent, a man screamed. "Hold him down!"

A blood-curdling cry erupted from the tent. Another man screamed as he was carried into a different tent by a group of three men. He thrashed. His right leg, snapped in half, dangled and flopped as he fought them. "No! I do not want to lose my leg! Please! Anything else!"

Brónmal recoiled. Amputation, leeches, stitches, infection, blood. The survivors of war were never pretty. Few would return home. Only those who survived the infections and blood loss were left disfigured and broken. He grimaced. Sometimes, death was a mercy. He walked away from the sight of the broken and wandered into a calm street, gazing down at the ground. He frowned. Dark thoughts haunted him.

"*Will we hold out? Have I failed? Do you all even trust me?*" Brónmal thought. How could they trust him? He had failed at the very gate to the East, far earlier than people like his father did in the first war. He felt numb. A failure, an unworthy successor to the previous Supreme General. He could imagine his father laughing, proven right about his worthless son. What went wrong at the Dronmar Towers? Brónmal's men had advanced and pushed the Heokolons back, yet the other towers did not do the same. Angrily, he toyed with the scenario, trying to determine if he could have won. The gates would have broken regardless, so what then?

From the dark came Drakmanir. "Three bless, Supreme General."

"Three bless, Drakmanir."

Drakmanir gestured to him. "Are you busy?"

"No, why?"

"I wish to speak to you, Supreme General."

Brónmal followed the man, leaving the army behind as they wandered into the inner streets. "What is it?"

"Eventful day."

Brónmal nodded. "We killed many."

Drakmanir sighed. "We lost many."

"We just need to keep the Heokolons off the walls. I am having the men move oil closer to the walls to refuel the Flamebows faster."

"Good to hear. Did you expect the Heokolons to put up such a fight?"

Brónmal closed his eyes, nose flaring. "Not like this. I expected to march straight into their lands, but we need far more men. The other seven armies are on the way. We just need to hold out."

"I wanted to ask if you could hold out that long. If the Heokolons do not kill us, fighting in the heat of High Summer will."

"We will make it."

"And what about their bags of fire they are trying to get to the gates? If they cannot carry them there, soon they will throw them."

Brónmal paused and stared. "Are you questioning whether or not I can defend Raothal from these pagans?"

Drakmanir turned to him. "I am, Supreme General. And no one will believe you if you were to tell them. I have the utmost confidence in our men but not in you. You are new. Even I would struggle to command so many, which is why I am only General of one province."

"*Esadif? How dare you spout your sinful thoughts to me?*" Brónmal thought. He turned red. "I ought to have your head, but I will assume there's more to this than belittling my abilities?"

"There is. I want you to be aware, not arrogant. The Heokolons did not defeat men like your father for no reason. Your father and the men of his time did not fail to cross the river separating our lands. They failed at the Khagoreti Mountains."

"So, what advice do you have?"

"Be wise. We will not live long if we passively defend. We are not fighting fools. They observe and learn. And for the love of the Three, do not meet them on the battlefield like a fool and die."

Brónmal clenched his jaw. "I understand. Now get out of my sight."

Drakmanir bowed. "Three bless, Supreme General."

The man walked away. Hacarad emerged from a distant alley, bowing to Brónmal. "Three bless, Lord."

Brónmal waved dismissively. "Did you hear that?"

"I did. I see there are some doubts about our success here."

"Do you doubt me, Hacarad?"

Hacarad shook his head. "Absolutely not, Lord. I have seen you do many things, and defending a city is not anywhere near difficult for you."

Brónmal scoffed. "I do not need your praise. I need to understand what that man was saying."

Hacarad shrugged. "I believe something like viewing this war from a different lens. We are in a new age with strange, heretical machines and new sinful ideas. I guess brute force might not work this time."

Brónmal hummed. "What was different today?"

"The bags, Lord. They shook the walls and burned us."

Brónmal gasped. "Ah! The bags. What if we made something like that and launched them at the Heokolons?"

"How, Lord?"

"The oil from the Flamebows."

"What about it?"

"Perhaps if we put the oil in barrels, we can launch the barrels at the Heokolons and shower their formations in flame."

Hacarad looked up at the walls. "Do you think it will work, Lord?"

"It's just an idea. We must prepare something before the next attack."

"I am with you, Lord."

Brónmal pointed. "Gather some men. We need to test this!"

"Very well, Lord!"

13

The Nine Armies

The earth shook with another explosion. Men screamed as Heokolon fire burned them and sent pieces of debris everywhere. The gates weakened, soon to break. Brónmal shouted and pointed. "Launch the barrels! Launch the barrels!"

Catapults creaked as they flung flaming barrels into the Heokolon horde beyond the walls. Fires consumed them, yet the formations did not break. Brónmal stared out over the Eastern horde. The bodies kept piling up, the dead increasing by the day. After nearly a month of siege, the Mednohail had simply started collecting their dead and burning them nightly - dire times left little room for custom. The men, sleepless, fought on the edge of their strength. They fought like wild animals, fighting tooth and nail to live another day. The Heokolons were determined to raze the city. Brónmal would not have it.

Brónmal pointed. "You squad! To the gates! Reinforce them! Do not let the Heokolons pass!"

A squadron of men ran to the gates. With the constant defense needed for all sides of the city, the remnants of Raothal's and Ardmunhaich's armies were spread thin. Brónmal's armor was scratched. Heokolon blood splattered him, and dirt and grime were caked in the crevices of his armor. Arrows stuck out of his shoulder pauldrons and chest plate, barely stopped from penetrating. Though death had almost claimed him many times, he fought alongside his men.

Hacarad ran up to Brónmal. "Lord! The Heokolons are swarming the Southern gates!"

Brónmal turned. "Grab reinforcements! Form formations by the gates in case they break! The heathens cannot get into the city! Make sure everyone who cannot fight is evacuated to the second wall!"

Hacarad saluted. "Yes, Lord!"

Brónmal ran down the battlements, gathering men while he sprinted. "On me, men! The Easterlings are trying to break in! Join me! For the Three!"

Those who could, joined him. Brónmal barked commands. They ran along the walls. As they ran from the eastern part of the city to the southern, Brónmal looked over the walls. Thousands of Heokolons circled the cities. The golden horde was impatient. The Easterlings stirred, anxious to breach the city, while their comrades climbed ladders and shot arrows over the walls. Dozens of men followed Brónmal as he ran. They descended a stair in front of the southern gate, joining others. Soldiers stacked logs and beams against the gates while peasants carried arrows and boiling oil to the ramparts above.

Brónmal shouted. "Crescent formation! I want this gate surrounded!"

The men formed into a half-moon formation, all facing the gate. Brónmal raised his bloody sword. "Men of Raothal, men of Ardmunhaich, good men of the Empire! Out there await the pagan hordes, those that would burn our temples and desecrate our love for the gods!"

The men booed and jeered. Brónmal continued. "I will never allow such wretched beasts into the Empire, into our city! Who will join me in repelling the fist of Heonar?"

The men cheered. Hacarad went up beside Brónmal. "You ready, Lord?"

Veins popping, face red, Brónmal nodded. "As ready as I could ever be. They will not stop until the city burns, and I refuse to let that happen."

"I stand beside you, Lord, as I always have."

"And I stand by you, brother. Let us make a stand for the Three."

"For the Three."

They faced the gates, waiting. Once mighty and stalwart, the massive gates had been charred and splintered. They barely hung off their hinges. Only the logs and beams placed by soldiers held them up. Minutes crawled by while archers fired on the invaders outside, keeping as many at bay as possible. Brónmal nervously swallowed. When? When would it happen?

"Three save us, guide our weapons true," Brónmal prayed.

An archer shouted. "Take cover!"

Brónmal braced. The gates imploded. Splinters and flaming debris rained down while the walls shook. The bridge between the two towers guarding the gate fell, swallowing the archers on it. None survived as they were burned and crushed. Brónmal stared, mouth agape. A hand stuck out of the rocks, twitching before becoming still. Brónmal panted before he looked over the debris. Raising his sword, he shouted. "Stand ready, men! Slaughter anything that passes through that hole!"

The Mednohail stepped forward, lowering their spears to form a wall of death. There would be no way in without blood. The air became filled with shouting and footsteps. The first of the Heokolons charged over, their glass weapons shimmering in the light as they plunged through the smoke to the other side.

Spears stabbed straight through the first wave, leaving the Heokolons dead. More came. The Easterlings pushed into the spears. Their glaives and swords cut through the defenders, who died even as more Mednohail soldiers replaced the fallen. The faithful zealots of Mednodorn seemed countless, though Brónmal knew they were thinning out fast.

Brónmal shouted. "Keep fighting! Hold them back! Hacarad!"

Hacarad cried out. "Yes, Lord?"

"Get oil! Hurry! Get six barrels!"

"Right away, Lord!"

Brónmal faced the incoming Heokolons. The horde beyond bottlenecked, kept at bay by the wall of spears. Every moment, Mednohail soldiers died. Each was replaced, the two armies stepping on the dead while clashing. After a few minutes, Hacarad and a few soldiers returned with barrels of oil. "Here, Lord!"

Brónmal pointed. "Spill four on the debris! Go!"

Hacarad raised his sword, commanding a few men to roll the barrels to the debris. Brónmal waved onward. "Advance! Protect them at all costs!"

The formation marched forward with unified steps, thrusting spears back and forth to keep the Heokolons away. Once part of the formation stood on the debris, Brónmal raised a fist. "Hold here! Go, Hacarad!"

Hacarad helped the men while they poured oil across the debris. Once it was soaked, Hacarad screamed. "We are done, Lord!"

Brónmal waved. "Retreat! Retreat!"

The Heokolons ran over the debris, cutting through the reversing formation. Brónmal ran, grabbing the last two barrels with a few men. "Light them! Light them now!"

Sparks flickering, the men struggled to light the wicker fuses attached to the barrels. Hacarad cleaved at and kept the impending Heokolons back. "Now or never, Lord!"

A flame caught. Brónmal pushed the barrel with a few other men. "Go! Go!"

They went straight into the fray, Mednohail surrounding and dying for them. They got the barrel to the debris, turning to run. Brónmal waved. "Take cover!"

The wicker burned, entering the oil-filled barrel. Brónmal dove. The air became searing hot as flames engulfed the Heokolons and the front of the Mednohail formation. Fire devoured the debris. A hellish blaze separated the two armies, burning everything to ash. The air reeked with burnt flesh and oil. Like living, flaming pillars, Heokolon and Mednohail soldiers ran around as fire consumed them. They screeched, clawing at themselves and rolling on the ground. Mednohail soldiers caught their comrades and killed them, allowing the Heokolons to burn and suffer - no mercy for the East.

Brónmal turned, gazing at the screaming, smoldering Heokolons. This was it, the time they needed. "Retreat to the inner city! Retreat! Grab everything, go!"

The formation fell apart. Soldiers ran everywhere, spreading the command. Archers evacuated the walls, carrying down sacks and barrels of arrows. Foot soldiers helped carry pallets of rocks while the heavy iron cauldrons were abandoned. Together with peasants, other soldiers moved supplies and wounded comrades into the second wall. Men with Flamebows torched what they could not save, leaving nothing for the Easterlings. All around the city, the twin armies retreated. Easterlings swarmed through the Southern gate once the flames at the gate died.

Hacarad and Brónmal led their army further into the city, sealing the gates from the impending horde. Brónmal's heart sank with a sense of defeat. They were running out of time. How could they be saved if they were all dead? Brónmal removed his helmet. He sighed, rubbing his unshaven, dirty face. He stopped, staring at his hand. His fingers were stained with blood and dirt, his hand unable to remain still as it quivered. For a moment, his head was empty. He could hear everything. The melody of his heart quickly beating, the whine in his ear from all the explosions, his exhausted breathing. The High Summer heat bore down. Drops of sweat ran down his forehead, dripping off his nose and chin and falling to the ground. Like all the soldiers, he was slowly baking alive in his armor.

Hacarad approached with a waterskin. "Are you okay, Lord?"

Brónmal blinked back to his senses. He drank from the waterskin and wiped the sweat from his red face. "No, this is getting worse."

Hacarad waved dismissively. "This is one city, Lord. See how long it has taken them to even breach the first gate? If we do not burn the last of their army within the next month, the rest of Mednodorn will crush them."

Brónmal groaned. "More come every day. How could we last against the endless swarms of Heonar?"

"Have faith, Lord. Maybe we are not meant to last but are left to kill as many as we can. How could they hope to take this province if we leave their army broken here?"

Brónmal leaned his head back, inhaling deeply. The scent of burnt flesh and death nearly made him gag. He put his helmet on, then nodded. "Perhaps we are meant to die here, but you give me courage, Hacarad. Let us take as many of those filthy pagans with us as we can."

"To battle, Lord?"

"To battle!"

Brónmal raised his sword and shouted to his men. "Archers, to the wall!

Keep their ladders off! Reinforce the gates. Get more barrels! We will not falter!"

The soldiers cheered. Brónmal's confidence filled them with zealous bravery. They were not afraid to die. Instead, they were eager to lay down their lives for their homeland and their Supreme General. Brónmal looked over them.

"In the eyes of the Three, we are immortal. Our spirits never die but are judged. May you judge me well, Daonrex. Judge me better than my father," Brónmal thought.

Hours crawled by. Every moment was consumed with battle. The Heokolon horde was frenzied with the promise of victory. One wall down, thousands dead, and no help on the horizon for their enemies. Every moment, Brónmal ran, screaming until his throat hurt.

Day turned into night. Unlike the weeks before, the Heokolons did not retreat to rethink their attacks. They kept coming forward, throwing up more ladders onto the wall. Heokolons carried sacks of oil into the city, their explosive power kept at bay with bolts from Snakebows. Heokolons dared the ladders, only to be incinerated by vicious Flamebows. In the third wall, homes and buildings burned, filling the air with ash. Heokolons ran around with torches, making sure the Mednohail of Raothal would have nothing left.

An archer shouted. "They brought their siege weapons! Supreme General!"

Brónmal ran over. "What is it?"

"Look!"

Brónmal peered over the battlements. He could barely see the giant crossbows in the dark. The Heokolons wheeled them toward the gate, Brónmal's stomach dropping. "Grab more barrels! Shoot at them! Throw anything you can to stop them! Get Hacarad!"

Archers turned their bows and Snakebows to the siege weapons. Brónmal ran to the gate and pointed. "Down there! Shoot everything at the ones pushing the siege weapons!"

The archers turned their bows, crossbows, and Snakebows toward the siege weapons. Brónmal helped, grabbing rocks and throwing them at the Heokolons - anything to stop them. A group of men came with three barrels, approaching the edge of the battlement.

"This was all that's left, Supreme General!"

Brónmal looked at the three barrels. "It will make do! Light them and throw them over!"

The men lit the wicker fuses, lifting and tossing the barrels over. Brónmal watched. They exploded upon impact, turning the siege weapons into splinters. It would not be enough, but it bought more time. Brónmal turned. "Get men to reinforce the gates! I want a formation ready at all four! They will not breach the inner city!"

The men sprinted to carry out his orders. Brónmal climbed down the wall and to the city below. People ran everywhere. Peasants and soldiers came together, moving supplies and dealing with the wounded. Those who did not help cowered between buildings and in alleys. Many prayed, others wept. Even in war, they would never be allowed into the innermost wall, their lives damned if the second wall was breached.

A woman sat in the middle of the chaos. She was still, holding onto the body of a bloodied, dead man. A soldier. He had fallen from the walls, Heokolon arrows sticking out of his chest. In the chaos and destruction, she was like a still frame. No wailing, no hysteria, just silent tears.

Brónmal stumbled past. How long could they keep this up? How long could he keep running? He had not slept in three days. His mouth was dry, and his tongue stuck to the roof of his mouth. Blood, sweat, and dirt caked him in a shell of grime. His legs burned, his feet ached, and his forearms scalded from squeezing his sword.

He stumbled and sat on a box, looking around. His ears whined, vision blurred. He only saw shapes as people ran past, the distant cries of dying men becoming muffled.

"*We are fools,*" he thought. Was this what they wanted? They wished for war, and this is what the Mednohail received. Would the Heokolons have attacked, anyway? His mind spun from exhaustion.

"*Show no weakness. Have strength, and it will be given to you by the Three,*" Brónmal thought. His father's lessons echoed in his mind. Only death could stop a man of true faith. His thoughts stilled. He looked up, eyes fixating on a man running at him.

Hacarad approached. "Lord! We have run out of oil barrels."

Brónmal looked up. "Do we still have any oil?"

"Barely, Lord."

"Then give the rest to the Flamebows! We need to keep those ladders off the walls."

"Of course, Lord. Are you well?"

"I am fine! It does not matter. Just carry out my orders!"

Hacarad nodded and ran off. Brónmal cupped his face with his hands, sweat dripping onto the mud below. Brónmal looked up. "Fetch me water!"

A man brought a waterskin. Brónmal drowned his face in it, spilling water everywhere while he sucked it up. The cold water cooled his burning, red face and seeped into his hot, sweaty armor. It was like being bathed in bliss. He dropped the waterskin, standing and stumbling forward. "Keep fighting, men! Keep fighting!"

The hours crawled on through the night. The Mednohail kept the giant crossbows away as well as they could, pouring flaming oil and throwing rocks at them. Narum, the ringed moon, crossed the sky, setting as the sun peaked over the horizon.

The gates to the second wall weakened, siege weapons slowly peeling them from their hinges. The walls faltered, dozens of Heokolon warriors cleaving down the archers. Soldiers ran everywhere. They frantically tried to defend, falling as the Heokolons slowly cracked the waning defenses. The Mednohail were running out of supplies and blood. Their spirits waned.

A man sprinted toward Brónmal. "Supreme General! Supreme General!"

Brónmal turned. "What is it?"

"There's something on the horizon. Come look!"

Brónmal followed the man. They ran through the houses and alleys of the inner city, shielding their heads while Heokolon arrows rained from above. Climbing up a tower, they stepped out onto the battlements on the other side of the city. Brónmal squinted. "What is it?"

The man pointed. "Flags! Someone is coming!"

Brónmal waited, peering at the horizon until he could see the silhouettes of an army. Thousands of men. He recoiled. No, there were hundreds of thousands. The hammer of Mednodorn had arrived. The armies from nearly every province had come, waving the flags of their home realms. The sun rose over them, their steel spears gleaming in the light.

Brónmal stumbled back. "We are saved. Our prayers have been answered! The legions are here!"

"Supreme General?"

Brónmal grabbed the man and shook him. "We are saved! Tell the men to keep fighting! Mednodorn has come to save us!"

The man sprinted away. Brónmal ran into the streets, joyfully screaming at the bloodied soldiers around him. "Keep fighting! Keep fighting! The Empire has come to save us! Mednodorn is here!"

The army burst into cheers. A new, fearless spirit filled them. As morale returned, the men daringly clashed with the Heokolons on the walls. They gave their lives to kill them, pushing the remainder off the battlements and burning the ladders. With a renewed will, the rest of the twin armies gathered. They held fast, waiting to charge out of the Eastern gate.

Hacarad joined Brónmal by his side. "It is a glorious day, Lord!"

Brónmal nodded. "The Three have answered our prayers! The vengeance of our forefathers has come!"

Minutes passed before the Heokolons began to shout in fear.

An archer appeared over the wall. "They are retreating!"

Brónmal raised his sword. "Open the gates!"

The gates creaked open, cracking to reveal the formations of Heokolons retreating from the city. Brónmal pointed his sword. "Charge!"

A unified cry echoed as the soldiers charged after Brónmal. "For the Three!"

Like a spear, the Mednohail cut through the retreating Heokolons, their formations shattering to pieces as they fell to the zealous fanatics. Relentless, the Mednohail kept pushing until the Heokolons were out of the city. In the plains, Brónmal gazed upon the glory of Mednodorn.

Like an unstoppable tsunami, the Nine Armies merged and flooded across the Heokolons. The Easterlings fled back to the river. The Mednohail chased, surrounding and trapping a few formations. Like a snake, they crushed them. There was no hope for those left behind. The Mednohail had won.

Watching the Heokolons retreat, Brónmal shouted. "The Three have blessed us! Victory!"

14

The Burnt Plains of Raothal

The plains were destroyed. Ruined farmsteads littered the land, smoldering and charred. The Heokolons destroyed everything in their retreat. Brónmal eyed the plains from his Auhmog, frowning at the sorrowful defilement of Raothal. So many innocent dead, and so many homes lost. Brónmal's new burden weighed heavily. He was the first Supreme General to let the Heokolons cross into the Empire.

"*I am a disgrace, an unworthy man,*" Brónmal thought, face creased into a frown.

The ground shook. The endless legion of Mednohail marched across the land, sweeping through the ruins. More would come from the furthest ends of the Empire. Brónmal looked ahead, feeling some solace and strength as he gazed upon the thousands. The Heokolons could not withstand the Mednohail tide. First, they would retake the Kahbain Tributary. Then, they would burn Heonar. Thoughts of what the old chieftain in the forest said came to him. They would never get to behead the Emperor. There was not even a point to the invasion, only that he had to do it to save Mednodorn. How could he save his people if the Empire would burn?

Hacarad spoke. "Damn Easterlings."

Brónmal glanced over. "What?"

"Damn Easterlings. Look at how much they have destroyed. I cannot wait to march into their lands."

Brónmal smirked. "Me neither. I am glad to be out of that city after a month. Fighting in the heat was hell. Low Autumn is coming soon."

Hacarad nodded. "And may we be at their capital by Low Winter."

"Well said."

"*If we make it there*," Brónmal thought. He was exhausted. His eyes had dark bags beneath them, and he sat limply on his Auhmog. It felt like he could barely hold on. His muscles had almost given up. As he rode, he blinked in and out, sleeping for small periods of time. His body woke him up whenever he began to slide off the saddle or fall over. An ability he learned at Baradun; it kept him alive.

A group of men approached on Auhmogs, each wearing decorated armor. The other eight of the Nine Generals. Among them was the new General of Beinthal and the successor to Brónmal, Cosalmir. They had their helmets off, faces wrinkled with discontent.

Drakmanir saluted. "Three bless, Supreme General."

Brónmal nodded. "Three bless, Drakmanir."

Crangramal, General of the Southwestern province of Reinthal, looked Brónmal over. He was a small and stout man. His body was round, like a barrel, with a square block-like face. Like many Southerners, he had a thick, bony brow. One of his ears was missing, one of his more famous features. He spoke. "Luckily, we arrived on time with a third of the Empire to save you, Supreme General."

Hacarad spat. "Watch your tongue."

The General of the Southern province of Gaothal, Domganmir, snorted. Known throughout the Empire as lazy, he was the half-failure ruler who commanded the puppet emperor of the Ahamari. Brónmal hated him. Domganmir spent more time at feasts and orgies than doing his job. He was fat, his cheeks bulbous like his fingers. He huffed and wheezed, breathing through a patchy, dirty beard. He sneered, teeth black and decayed from sugar. "Or what? You are going to shake us with your brilliant strategies of wasting a province's worth of soldiers?"

Brónmal's brow wrinkled, jaw clenched. "And what would you have done, Domganmir? Sat in your estate growing fat while the Ahamari grow restless?

I kept the might of Heonar at bay for a month, and you can barely control a people we have ruled since the Second Aothill."

Hacarad snorted. "A shame. All your predecessors had it easy."

Domganmir recoiled. "I certainly would have done better than you. At least men like your father kept the Easterlings over the Kabhain!"

The General of the Northeastern province of Munsthal, Talcemal, laughed. He was a thin man and one of the few Generals that Brónmal tolerated. He was literate, well-versed, and known for his obsession with scrolls, books, and anything written. Munsthal, Mednodorn's capital for universities and libraries, was the home and birthplace of many scholars and priests. Brónmal expected nothing less from a man from there. Talcemal, with a long and skinny body, had a well-shaven face and blinked constantly. He could not see far away, though it never seemed to hinder his ability as a General. He gestured at Brónmal. "At least he marched into their lands before being pushed back!"

Brónmal raised his voice. "And if I were like my father, you would all be gutted for Esadif. I will not tolerate these traitorous words from fools who were not there! Men like you have softened the Empire, weak and lazy! Three decades of peace have made you soft!"

The Generals around him grew silent. Brónmal pointed to Eastward. "I have no use for lazy Generals and commanders. If you think I am incompetent, leave. Otherwise, I will cut the tongue out of the next man who speaks."

None of the Generals responded. Brónmal looked among them, then gestured to Hacarad. "Come, I have no time for this."

"*Worthless scum. I ought to take all their tongues, perhaps even their heads. Father would never tolerate such insolence,*" Brónmal thought.

The pair rode away from the group, Brónmal groaning. Hacarad glanced back. "Fools, they know nothing. We would all die if they led the first march into Heonar."

Brónmal waved at him. "It was our arrogance that sent us into retreat. Not again. We will not underestimate the Heokolons, especially with the Nine Armies behind us."

Hacarad shook his head. "Perhaps we were too eager marching in with so few."

Brónmal sighed. "We lived, so we learn. At least we can march forward again and not go home like my father."

"They mention your father with such respect."

"If only they knew what sort of wretched man he was to his shameful son. I will show him. I have gotten much further than he ever did."

"Do you hate him, truly?"

Brónmal leaned his head, closing his eyes. "Could I ever confess to such a sin?"

"Have you not confessed sin to me before?"

Brónmal lowered his head. "I truly hate that wretched man. He took his dishonor from Heonar back home and never let it go. Why not force your son to carry your dishonor?"

"What do you mean?"

"You know what he did. I broke bones for him and suffered to make him proud, yet he never was. Now, I lead the entire Empire to finish a war he started, so what does that make him? Nothing."

"He truly was wretched and saying that to me is not a sin. You are far greater than he ever was, and I am glad to stand by you."

Brónmal nodded. "I appreciate that, Hacarad. I am glad I have a friend and brother to stand by me at the gates of death. What monstrous things have Dubilfen prepared for us in the East?"

Hacarad shook his head. "Who knows? Their weapons of glass are certainly cruel."

"If we bring unholy weapons of our own, who knows what they have? First, we need to cross the mountains."

Hacarad squinted. "The Khagoreti Mountains. I have heard wretched things from those who survived that battle."

"My father told me there were men who used unholy witchcraft to fly and attack with wicked black fire."

"Such Aogadraod. Are our living weapons so sinful in the face of such men?"

"To channel forbidden divinity into an object is one thing, but to cast it out from your body? Is that not to take Dubilfen truly within your spirit and heart?"

Hacarad frowned. "Some places in the world are truly lost."

Brónmal nodded. "We will guide them to the light. Do not worry."

Hacarad bowed his head. "First, the Emperor."

"What do you think it will be like to sit on the steps of his palace?"

"Well, with a good drink, we can ignore the smell of fire while we burn down their pagan heritage."

Brónmal grinned. "Oh, I look forward to renaming their land. I heard their land touches the sea far in the East."

Hacarad hummed. "Would that be the end of the world?"

Brónmal chuckled. "I hope so. If we can convert the North, I hope there are not more places to convert in this world."

Hacarad scoffed. "Lazy?"

Brónmal sighed. "Very. Once this business in Heonar is over, I want to be just like my Generals."

"Fat and lazy?"

"Fat and lazy on my estate."

"Think I could get an estate?"

"With enough Heokolon slaves, I will build you one."

"Why thank you, Lord."

"You are welcome."

Hacarad glanced back at the Generals. "They should show more respect."

Brónmal sighed. "How could they respect me after such a failure? That was the first time the Easterlings ever crossed the Kabhain into Raothal."

Hacarad frowned. "Well, you kept the entire army of Heonar at bay for over a month. You were the one who pushed into their forces at the Dronmar towers when all the others did not. The men of Ardmunhaich respect you, and I imagine the other province armies will, too."

"You are too kind, brother. I am unworthy of this position but have far too much to prove to simply give up."

Hacarad scoffed. "I will not hear such words. You and I were raised better than that. We do not give up or shirk the duty given to us. It is the will of the Three to do with what they give us. You were given this position for a reason."

"*A gift from the gods? Could it really be?*" Brónmal thought. He nodded slowly. "You are right, Hacarad. If the Highlord and Godspeaker thought I deserved it, I must be wrong thinking otherwise."

"I have seen you become the leader you are now. Do not let the fools play with your mind. What have they ever done? They were not the ones tasked to protect the Godspeaker in the North, and they were not the ones given the position of Supreme General. That says something."

Brónmal chuckled. "Imagine if Domganmir was the Supreme General."

Hacarad laughed. "Then there would not be a war! Just feasts for all the soldiers."

Brónmal smiled. "That does not sound bad. Better than marching all day."

Hacarad shrugged. "I guess you are right."

Brónmal glanced at Hacarad. "Thank you, brother. I would not be here without you."

15

The Broken Towers

The towers awaited. The great bulwarks of Raothal were turned against them. As Mednodorn's iron tide approached, the Heokolons retreated in fear. They slammed the gates to the West shut and filled the tower with archers. It was futile. What could such warriors do against an endless legion?

Brónmal and Hacarad led the march. There were so many soldiers that a dust cloud followed them. This time, Brónmal did not feel nervous. He looked forward to stepping on Heokolon soil, marching into their ancient homeland with the banner of conquest.

Brónmal drew his sword and raised it in the air. It glimmered, jewels sparkling in the light of High Summer. The shining idol of Mednodorn's wrath.

Brónmal shouted. "Death to Easterlings!"

Nearly a million strong, the Mednohail chanted in unison. "Death to Easterlings!"

"Louder!" Commanders shouted.

"Death to Easterlings!"

"Louder!"

"Death to Easterlings!"

"*The power of Mednodorn at my hands. Who can stop me?*" Brónmal thought.

Hacarad chuckled. "What a feeling."

Brónmal smiled. "I wonder how the Heokolons feel right now?"

"Like they are about to die. Three have blessed us with Mednodorn's full might, and I am glad to be here to see it."

Brónmal squinted at the towers. He saw the Heokolons peeking out of the windows of the great central tower, terrified of the impending iron flood. "The Heokolons locked up the towers. How do you think we should deal with that?"

Hacarad hummed. "I was thinking about this. We could blow them up with oil like they did to us. Or find a way to cross the river."

Brónmal squinted at the river. "Crossing the river could take days. Oil could take hours. The less time we waste, the better."

"But if we blow up the doors, the towers have nothing left to block passage."

"We do not need the passages blocked. Go tell the men to prepare barrels of oil."

"Yes, Lord."

Hacarad rode into the army, leaving Brónmal to lead them closer to the towers. Once they were near, Brónmal raised his fist. "Halt!"

The army stopped. Brónmal stared at the tower before them. Both sides said nothing. Only the sounds of flags flapping and gears shifting could be heard over the wind. After staring at the building for a minute, Brónmal began to ride along the lines. He gazed at the sea of soldiers, the men staring back in anxious anticipation.

Meanwhile, the other Generals rode up to him. Before they could speak, he waved his hand. "Yes, I have a plan. We will bomb the gates of the middle tower and push in. Once that is done, we will send parts of the army around to capture the other towers and allow all the men to march over."

Drakmanir raised a hand. "What about the gates? Will blowing them up not render the towers useless?"

Brónmal nodded. "And what use do we have for the Dronmar towers when we rule all the East? There's nothing the Heokolons can do to push us back."

The Generals looked at each other. Brónmal's eyes narrowed. "What? Does anyone have a better plan? I will have dinner on Heokolon soil by the end of the night. That, I promise."

Though they said nothing, Brónmal could see the doubt and disapproval in the Generals' eyes. It enraged him. Jaw clenched; he bit his tongue. Hacarad rode back with a group of men carrying barrels of oil. They set them down, sweating and exhausted. Hacarad saluted. "As requested, Lord."

Brónmal gestured to the men. "Which of you are brave? Which would sacrifice themselves for their Supreme General and the Three?"

All the men raised their hands. Brónmal smiled. "Beyond us lie the gates to Heonar, fortified and unyielding. The Heokolons took hours to breach them, but we will do it faster. I ask you men to lead the charge and plant these barrels at the central tower. Once placed, we will shoot fire arrows into them until they explode."

One man saluted. "For the Supreme General!"

The others saluted and shouted the same. Brónmal smiled, filled with pride as he looked at his other Generals. If the plan worked, he would rub it in their faces. Or maybe the plan's success would do that for him? He shook the thought from his mind and pointed to the central tower. "I want a formation of men shielding those carrying the barrels. Plant them and retreat. I want archers covering them, keeping the Heokolons ducking and hiding."

Hacarad nodded. "Yes, Lord!"

He turned his Auhmog and rode off, shouting orders at commanders who relayed Brónmal's will down the line. Brónmal watched the formations shift. Hundreds of men gathered to march to the central tower, shielding a dozen barrel carriers in the center. A horde of archers gathered behind them. They carried crossbows, bows, and Snakebows, each ready to rain thousands of arrows upon the Heokolons.

The formation waited, commanders in each squadron staring at Brónmal. He raised his sword and shouted, "March forward! For the Three!"

"March!" The commanders cried.

Marching forward, the soldiers raised their shields against Heokolon arrows. Brónmal raised his sword, shouting to his line of archers. "Loose!"

The two sides exchanged hundreds of arrows. There were so many that the Heokolons could barely shoot back. Like a waterfall of arrows, most bounced off the tower and fell to the ground below. Now and then, a stray arrow found a Heokolon through a slit in the tower, weakening them more. Meanwhile, the formation marched to the tower gates. The defenders threw stones and shot at them with little effect.

Once the formation arrived at the gates, Brónmal waved. "Hold!"

The lines of archers held their attack. The formation remained closed, only letting out one barrel holder at a time. Each man planted the barrels at the gates, a few dying as Heokolon arrows pierced them. Once the barrels were placed, they retreated. With a unified cry, the formation backed away. From a distance, Brónmal could see Heokolons running out to the other side across the river. He chuckled, then shouted. "Bring out the braziers! Light them up!"

Men brought out flaming braziers, helping the archers exchange their arrows for ones wrapped in soaked clothes. They lit them, waiting for Brónmal's command. When the entire line was ready, Brónmal shouted. "Loose!"

A hail of flaming arrows filled the sky. Flame and smoke filled the air. The ground shook, the gates bursting open with splinters and cinder. Brónmal blinked as the shockwave went through his chest, shaking his bones. In the distance, he heard cries of terror from the Heokolons.

Brónmal turned to his army. "March forward! Take the tower!"

A column of soldiers marched toward the tower. Brónmal and Hacarad rode forward with an escort, watching as the Heokolons formed a wall of shields and spears at the tower's entrance. The two forces collided. They pushed into one another, the Mednohail heaving forward with crushing force. Vicious and zealous, the frenzied men broke formation, swarming over their comrades to reach the Heokolons. Outnumbered, the Heokolon defense collapsed within minutes. The Mednohail flooded into the tower, slaughtering every Heokolon they encountered.

The rest of the army continued marching to the other side, splitting into three formations and marching toward the other four towers. Brónmal led the central split toward the Heokolon camp. He swept his sword ahead. "Forward, men! Burn their tents! Take everything you can!"

Hacarad laughed as they rode onto a hill. "Look!"

Brónmal stared ahead, watching the rest of the Heokolon army retreat East, leaving the camp behind. "They are running."

Hacarad smiled. "We have broken their army."

"The battle is not won yet. We still need the towers."

Hacarad stared down both lengths of the river. "I doubt the Heokolons can hold, Lord."

The men cheered as they rushed into the camp. They tore apart everything, burning the tents and looting crate after crate of supplies. In the distance, Brónmal could see the routed Heokolons run from the other towers, formations of soldiers chasing them down. There was no defense left. Brónmal looked up, letting out a relieved, exhausted sigh.

"I thank you, Daonrex, for this victory. Praise to you, praise to the Three," Brónmal prayed, looking upward.

Hacarad chuckled. "Looks like we got here so fast they could not assemble a defense."

"Good thing. They will regroup in the East. They must have more for us."

"And we will break whatever they throw at us."

Brónmal sighed. "Shows those foolish Generals a thing or two."

"They will never accept your victory here. They will just say it was their men who won."

"It is the men who won, but I will have more victories in the future. Perhaps I will have their heads for such insolence."

Hacarad shrugged. "It is best to keep them alive until after the war."

Brónmal groaned. "Yes, yes, of course. Shall I gather the men back together?"

Hacarad shook his head. "No, Lord. Let them have their fun. They need it after the first march."

"Very well. It will be nice to eat dinner on Heokolon soil tonight."

"I feel like eating bird tonight."

Brónmal smiled. "Bird does sound good."

Hacarad nodded. "And a beer."

"Oh, do not forget the beer."

16

The Day Mom Left

Remtaich's voice thundered through the estate. "Brónmal! Where are you, boy!"

Brónmal's attention shifted from the dull scriptures before him. He heard his mother speak, followed by Remtaich's booming voice. "Be silent, woman!"

The sound of Remtaich's footsteps reverberated toward Brónmal's room. To give the impression of being occupied, Brónmal looked down at his scriptures. Remtaich slammed open the door. "What are you doing, boy!"

"Reading, Lord! Reading the holy scriptures!"

Remtaich's eyes narrowed. "You should be done reading those."

He grabbed Brónmal, making him scream as he dragged him out. "I will not tolerate laziness, boy!"

"Lord, I have not been lazy! I have read them carefully. I wish to learn them as deeply as I can!"

Remtaich dragged Brónmal downstairs to an altar dedicated to Daonrex, Remtaich's holy patriarch. "Lies, in His holy house? Aolfrao, deceit, how could I be cursed with a wicked child?"

"I am not wicked, Lord! I love the Three!"

Brónmal's mom, Arderva, ran into the room. She was shorter than Remtaich, with flowing brown curls for hair and soft, doe-like eyes. "Remtaich, stop! Believe the boy!"

Remtaich struck her across the cheek. "Stay out of this, woman!"

Arderva screamed and covered her cheek. "Stop! He said he was reading the scriptures! Make him go back and read again!"

"I already did! Begone! I am going to train him until the wicked spirit leaves him!"

Brónmal screamed when dragged out. "Mama!"

Remtaich took him to a mud pit beneath a tree. Around it was a training dummy, a target, and training weapons. Here, Brónmal trained through rain, snow, and hail. He trained until he bled.

Remtaich threw Brónmal to his knees, tossing a sword at his feet. "Pick it up, boy."

Shaking, Brónmal grabbed the sword and stood. Remtaich pointed to the practice dummy. "Attack it. Offensive stance, you are to slaughter it a thousand times."

Lowering his head, Brónmal attacked the dummy. He struck it repeatedly, approaching it with aggressive footing and swift, decisive strikes. Remtaich stared like a vulture, silent and cruel-eyed. Brónmal hit the dummy until his muscles grew tired, his form weakening. Remtaich smacked him. "Keep your form straight, boy! What happens if you grow weak in front of an enemy?"

"I die, Lord!"

"You die! Heokolons do not show mercy! Throfi do not show mercy! Ahamari do not show mercy! Heretics do not show mercy! You will have no mercy either!"

Brónmal straightened his tired form up. He kept striking, the splintering wooden handle slowly rubbing his hands raw. His muscles ached, and his form weakened again.

Remtaich slapped him again. "Straighten your stance! You will not falter until you drop! Outlast your weakness. Outlast the heathen!"

Raising the sword, Brónmal's eyes watered. He kept striking. Tears rolled down his cheeks, sweat covering his body.

Remtaich barked. "Strike harder! Cleave through the dummy. Break the sword if you must!"

Brónmal kept striking. He hit repeatedly until Arderva came out. "Remtaich! Stop this! You are breaking the boy!"

Remtaich turned. "And that is what I intend! I will break him over and over again until I cannot!"

"You are pushing too hard, Remtaich! Enough!"

"You will not disobey me, woman! Get back in the house!"

Arderva spat on the ground. "I will not have your failures be his burden! He is far from a man and will be far better than you!"

Remtaich approached her. "What did you just say?"

Arderva slapped Remtaich. "He is not you!"

Remtaich stumbled back, holding his cheek with widened eyes. Arderva walked past him, grabbed Brónmal, and took him inside. She brought him to his room, closed the door, and hugged him. "It's okay, my little Brónmal. It's okay."

Brónmal fell into the hug, speaking with a weeping voice. "Mama... I am tired. I do not want to train more."

"You do not have to. You can stay in here. I will stay and protect you."

"I do not want to go out. I do not want to go out."

"You do not need to. Just stay here with me."

The two grew silent. Brónmal clung to her and cried, hands aching and raw from the training sword. After a while, Remtaich's voice echoed through the house. "Arderva! Get down here!"

Arderva slowly let go of Brónmal. "I need to go talk to him."

Brónmal shook his head. "Do not go! He will hurt you."

"I will be fine. Stay in here. Read your scriptures."

"No!"

"Stay, Brónmal. I will be fine."

Arderva left the room, closing the door behind her. Brónmal went after her a few moments later, sneaking downstairs. He crept until he saw Arderva, Remtaich, and three guards in armor.

Remtaich pointed at her. "I have always wondered why Brónmal was such a little demon. Who knew that Aolfrao and Esadif came from my wife and entered my son?"

Arderva held her mouth and looked between the guards. "R-Remtaich!

121

What are you talking about?"

"You struck me and instilled evil ideas and thoughts into my son's head. I am raising him to become a proud warrior of Mednodorn, a faithful servant of the Three. And what do you do? You make him weak."

"He's just a boy! You push him as if he was one of your grown soldiers, the ones you failed in Heonar!"

"You speak out of your place! I intend to solve this today. I was thinking of bringing you to the Archbishop for healing. Perhaps he could have cleansed you of these evil ways? Now I see I am wrong."

"Remtaich! What are you saying?"

"I will not allow my beautiful son to turn into a lazy and wicked person like you. If you are in the way, then I will remove you."

"You would not!"

"Silence before you bewitch us with your words! You belong to Dubilfen! Take her!"

The guards stepped forward. Arderva slapped one, struggling as they grabbed her and dragged her out. Brónmal hopped out of his hiding place. "Mama!"

Remtaich grabbed him. "Stay back, boy! We are removing evil from this house. Do not let her touch you, or she will bewitch you."

Brónmal reached out while Arderva screamed. "I love you, Brónmal! Stay strong!"

The men dragged her out, leaving Remtaich and Brónmal. Brónmal turned and hit his father as hard as possible, fists collapsing against the old veteran's body. "You monster! I hate you!"

Remtaich let out a thunderous shout. "Silence! You do not know what's best for you! I should beat you for your words, but this is enough. If you had discipline, this would not have happened. This is your fault! Now get out of my sight!"

"*My fault?*" Brónmal thought and stumbled back. He hyperventilated, letting out a pained scream and running away. He ran to his room, slammed the door, and jumped onto his bed. Hatred stirred in his head. He wanted to kill Remtaich and save his mom, but he had no power. There was nothing he could do. He wept for hours, raging and grief stirring as he collapsed repeatedly.

His fault? No. Brónmal's thoughts focused over the hours, a searing hatred forming in his mind. His mother was right. He was the better man. He would outdo his father. That would be his revenge. He wanted to plunge a sword through Remtaich's heart but now was not the time. Brónmal would grow and wait.

"*I will find glory. I will achieve more than he ever did. I will do it for you, Mother,*" Brónmal thought.

17

The March into Heonar

Brónmal raised his glass to Hacarad, who sat across from him. "To burning Heonar."

Hacarad raised his glass. "To burning Heonar."

They sipped from their glasses. Inside the tent, under the shade, the pair were cool, protected from the fading High Summer heat. Brónmal had enough of the heat. He wanted the coolness and the gentle breezes of Low and High Autumn. The front of the tent was open, allowing them a wide view of the lands before them.

Brónmal put the glass down with a contented sigh, looking across the war camp. One million soldiers. In the distance, smoke from a razed village rose into the sky. Bands of ravenous Mednohail ran rampant across the land, burning every town west of the Khagoreti Mountains. In the East, Brónmal could see the silhouette of the mountain range.

He had done it. He had gotten farther than his father. Brónmal was drinking in the very fields where men like his father failed.

"*I am here, mom. I finally did it,*" Brónmal thought.

Hacarad sighed. "Quite an achievement, is it not?"

"To be here, relaxing?"

"Indeed. It seems you have finally outdone your father."

"I outdid him a long time ago. He got to be a commander, not anywhere near a province General. Now, as Supreme General, he is nothing to me."

Hacarad tilted his head. "He still bothers you, does he not?"

Brónmal's face deepened into a frown. "He does. He always will. As long as I have scars from him, I will have a hole in my heart."

"Was your mother good to you?"

Brónmal's gaze fell. His mother's smile flashed through his head, seizing his mind with memories of her warm hug and gentle love. He shook his head. "She was. He had her taken away for speaking against him to protect me."

"What happened to her?"

"I do not know. I assume they killed my mother for sinning. If she lived, I imagined she would have come back."

Hacarad shrunk into his seat. "I am sorry, Lord. I did not mean to bring her up."

"You are forgiven. It has been long since those days, and I have healed as much as possible. I just worry that I may never fully heal."

"Perhaps it is important to have those scars. To remember and be better."

"*Is it a sin to take vengeance? To hurt him like he did to her?*" Brónmal thought. He was silent for a moment, then spoke. "My scars do not make me better. They only compel hatred out of me and the will to be better than my father. Maybe one day I will return and have his head, and maybe then there will be peace."

Hacarad shook his head. "I doubt that, Lord. It will only feed the cycle. Do not conquer Heonar to spite your father. Conquer Heonar for your people, for your Highlord and Godspeaker. Conquer Heonar for the Three."

Brónmal's head fell slightly. "You are right. It is better to do out of passion than hate, right?"

"I do not know many things, Lord, but I would agree with that."

They grew silent. Brónmal drank, thoughts settling on the coming darkness. Gu'hag's prophecy rested on him again. They were not destined to succeed. Could he prove the prophecy wrong? He pondered and glanced over. "Hacarad?"

"Yes, Lord?"

"Do you think we will be able to conquer all of Heonar?"

"Absolutely, Lord."

"And if we do not? Arrogance has backfired already. What if they are smarter than we are?"

"Are you losing faith, Lord?"

Brónmal shook his head. "No, I am thinking ahead, unlike the men of the first war."

Hacarad leaned forward. "Well, I doubt the Heokolons could survive against a million soldiers. They would run out before we ever would. But... If we failed, we could settle on conquering what we need."

Brónmal sighed. "We mummify our dead with salt. I know the Godspeaker justified this invasion to the church to get the salt from Heonar."

"Salt? Where is this salt?"

"As far as I know, west of the Khagoreti Mountains. This entire plain between the Kabhain and the Khagoreti Mountains is rich with it, enough to last for Aothills. If all else fails, we got what we needed already."

Hacarad leaned forward and scooped up a handful of dirt. "Interesting. So, does the very land around us have salt?"

"As far as I understand. There should be pockets, like ore. All we must do is hold onto it. This land is as valuable as gold."

Hacarad let the dirt flow out of his palm and onto the ground. "Why worry so much about this? There is not an empire in the world that can stop us."

"*Are we all so arrogant? I have proven we can fail,*" Brónmal thought, jaw clenched. "Do we tell ourselves that, or are we sure? Breaking Throfi tribes or disciplining the already conquered Ahamari is one thing. How long has it been since Mednodorn has faced an actual battle against something as grand as Heonar?"

"Are you giving compliments to the heathens?"

"I am saying that we need to be wise. They might be pagans, but they are not fools. We are working against an enemy who wants to defeat us as much as we want to defeat them."

Hacarad chuckled. Brónmal narrowed his eyes at him. "Why are you chuckling?"

He shrugged and replied. "Perhaps this is why we are sitting here drinking instead of your father so many years ago. You are better, and you think. I am glad to be by your side."

Brónmal relaxed into a thin smile. "Thank you, Hacarad. I will try to win this for us."

Hacarad raised his cup. "More!"

The man who came to attend to them was a Heokolon slave. His skin had multiple lash wounds and dark bruises, accentuating its light green hue. With golden eyes, he stared with an empty gaze as he came over and poured more drink for the pair. Like the rest of his people, he had no hair and strange, square teeth. Brónmal stared at him, then waved him away once their drinks were full again.

He sipped his drink and spoke. "Where did we get that one from?"

Hacarad glanced back. "Local village, I suppose."

Brónmal chuckled. "We will have a surplus of those soon. Plenty for the salt mines."

Hacarad shrugged. "First, we must give them proper names and teach them the correct belief."

Brónmal tilted his head. "I am glad that's not my job."

Hacarad nodded. "Me neither. I am fine with cutting them to pieces."

Brónmal took another sip of his drink. "We are only an hour's walk from Raothal's border, and I already miss the Empire."

"You have anyone at home you miss?"

"Nope. I am barely in one place for more than a week, anyway. You?"

"There was this girl last time I visited Eidthal."

Brónmal leaned forward and stared at him. "Really?"

Hacarad closed his eyes and nodded. "Yep. Pretty farmer's girl. Beautiful, muscular legs on her."

Brónmal laughed. "Oh, look at you. A girl in every province."

Hacarad waved dismissively. "It's one girl."

"What's her name?

"Caialaya. Her hair was soft too, like the feathers of a baby bird."

"I bet she gave you quite the time."

"Hours. Amazing what those farmer girls can do. Far better than the nobility and their lazy brats."

Brónmal snorted. "Oh, come on, at least they smell good and comb their hair."

"You can get used to the smell of a farmer."

Brónmal gagged. "You are foul, you know that, right?"

Hacarad shrugged. "I have taste. Dark skin from years under the sun and powerful bodies."

"Well, you take all the farmer girls, and I take the noble ones. Maybe I should marry myself to the daughter of a king?"

"I would avoid royalty."

"Really?"

"Nothing but drama. A quarter of the men in the army here are hardened from dealing with troubles across the Empire. You marry royalty; you deal with royalty problems."

"And you want to settle down to a quiet life?"

"Absolutely. Maybe somewhere on the edge of the Empire, far from the nonsense going around. Do not get me wrong; spreading the light of the Three and fighting are all me now, but when am I old? Knees only last so long."

"You are absolutely right. Cheers to old age?"

"Cheers to old age!"

The two clinked their drinks together and drank. Brónmal narrowed his eyes as a soldier ran up to them. "Supreme General!"

Brónmal sighed. "What is it?"

"We captured a slave!"

Brónmal shook his head. "What of it?"

"She can speak Mednohail, Supreme General. We wondered if you would like to have her."

Brónmal blinked and raised his brow before waving. "Bring her in and then leave."

The soldier bowed. "Yes, Supreme General!"

Hacarad scoffed. "A Heokolon that knows our tongue? There's no such thing."

Brónmal shrugged. "They live only a few feet from the Empire. Who knows?"

Hacarad sipped his drink. "I am hardly a wiseman. Let the Heokolon prove itself."

A scuffle echoed outside the tent before a frail Heokolon woman was tossed before them. She had been beaten. Blood and mud covered her as if the soldiers had dragged her through the camp to Brónmal's feet. As she fell, she stayed on her knees with her head bowed. The woman was hairless like any Heokolon, with skin that was a lighter green than that of the other slave.

"*Disgusting fiend. Where did they find you?*" Brónmal thought. He leaned forward. "You understand me, heathen?"

The girl, voice quivering, whispered, "Yes."

Brónmal and Hacarad looked at each other before Brónmal spoke again. "Do you know who I am, girl?"

The girl responded in an accent that disgusted Brónmal. "No, I do not. Only that you are a lord."

Brónmal chuckled. "You do speak our language. I am Brónmal, Supreme General of Mednodorn. You will address me as Lord."

The girl nodded. "Yes, Lord."

Hacarad smiled. "What a strange sight. It's as if a wild animal learned how to speak. What should we do with her?"

Brónmal shrugged. "Toss her to the men?"

Hacarad pursed his lips. "No, how many women have they been through already? This one is special. This one speaks the holy tongue."

Brónmal nodded. "You are right. What is your name, girl?"

The girl responded. "Azratanoa, Lord."

Brónmal stuttered. "A-Azratano- Azra. You are now named Azra until we find a Mednohail name for you. Understood?"

"Y-Yes, Lord."

Hacarad chuckled. "At least it learns fast. What a curiosity. What use would we have for it?"

Brónmal hummed. "A new cupbearer? Guards!"

Two of Brónmal's escorts entered the tent and bowed. "Yes, Supreme General?"

Brónmal pointed to the slave in the corner of the tent. "Get rid of that. Go kill it outside the camp."

The men went in and grabbed the slave. He gasped. As he was dragged out, he began to kick and scream, leaving the terrified slave girl with the pair.

Hacarad raised a brow. "Are we just going to waste that one? What about those salt mines you were talking about?"

Brónmal shrugged. "There will be plenty. We will send every slave we capture back here. Soon, these lands will be covered in salt mines and Mednohail settlements."

Hacarad shrugged. "What's one dead Heokolon anyway?"

Brónmal lowered his gaze to the girl. "Azra, silly name. You will bring me my drinks and be my slave. Remember, worse things can happen to you than what will happen to that man."

"Yes, Lord."

Hacarad narrowed his eyes. "We could use it as a translator."

Brónmal tilted his head. "Do we need one? I intend to cut down Heonar, not negotiate."

Hacarad nodded. "I agree, but you never know when you need to talk with the enemy."

Brónmal shrugged. "I guess you might be right. Slave! Stand in the corner, bring us drink when we need it."

"Y-Yes, Lord!"

The girl, golden eyes wide with fear, jumped to her feet. She went to the corner of the tent, standing by a table with a full jug of Mednohail beer. She stood straight, hands balled in fists as she trembled.

Hacarad raised his drink. "What do we say cheers to now?"

Brónmal hummed. "I am not sure. Do we need a reason to do cheers?"

Hacarad chuckled. "At this point? I guess not."

Brónmal raised a finger. "Oh, wait, I got it."

Hacarad tilted his head. "What is it?"

Brónmal raised his drink. "Cheers to conquest!"

Hacarad chuckled. "Cheers to conquerors!"

18

The Khagoreti Mountains

Brónmal stared upward, mouth slack. The Khagoreti Mountains. They stood like an immortal wall against the West. Tall and skinny, they separated into massive pillars adorned with green and wreathed in unending mist. Rarely, massive plateaus rose out from the pillars. Forests grew out of them. They were dense, jungle-like, with strange trees. Brónmal could not describe them as independent, singular plants. Instead, they were bunches of saplings that grew up and wove together over time, forming a tree.

From the base of the mountains, the Mednohail could hear the cries of birds no Mednohail had ever heard. Alien animals hid in the ferns and bushes. Some were bipedal predators. Most were thick and heavy herbivores that plowed through the undergrowth. Above them, birds with sets of four wings circled in the sky while strange lemur-like creatures with groups of six to eight arms hid in the leaves.

Hacarad and Brónmal approached a stone staircase. The stones, ancient and worn, were clean and taken care of. Someone had swept the old and worn rocks and cut back the growth on both sides. Carved from red stone, each step had a small bowl-like dent in the middle, showing Aothills of use. Brónmal had never seen such a fine stairway placed in what he thought to be the middle of nowhere. The steps disappeared high into the mountains.

Hacarad took the first step onto the stone stairs. "This is farther than any

Mednohail has ever gone in these cursed lands."

Brónmal knelt and touched the stones. "The first step into the Heokolon Empire. What a holy day this is."

"What evils do you think await us?"

"Untold evils. What else could we expect from a pagan, untamed land? No better than the Throfi."

"We will cut down those evils, Lord."

"As we will do to all who face us." Brónmal raised his hand and gestured forward. "March!"

The pair stepped aside as the unending legions of the Nine Armies marched past. Brónmal allowed a few hundred to go first before merging into the formations with his escort. Engineers deconstructed the War Carriages and carried them up the stairs for reconstruction and, later, for battle. They took out papers and stones containing energy to animate the carriages. After that, the carriages were taken apart, screw by screw, panel by panel. Once apart, the engineers packaged them together onto wagons and gave the signal that they were ready to leave.

They ascended.

"*Three shield us,*" Brónmal prayed.

Unknown beasts and birds sang and cried far in the deep brush. Forest enclosed them. The men grew cautious as they tired, the ascent seemingly endless. Like a jungle, the air became thick and humid, with a layer of moisture on each step. Looking at the plants around them, Brónmal saw they had water beads all over them. Insects were everywhere.

The stone path leveled momentarily, coming to the side of a pillar-like mountain. To the left was an unscalable wall, and to the right was a sheer drop into a valley. In the valley below was a swamp. Brónmal approached the edge. He felt the winds gust against him, cool and moist, speckles of water hitting his face. Below, above the swamp at the root of the valley, were birds. Most had one or two sets of wings, gliding gracefully on wind gusts. Brónmal saw white birds, brown birds, and multi-colored birds that looked as if they were adorned with rainbows.

Hacarad looked down. "By the Three, what a drop. Will we lose more to the Heokolons or these damned mountains?"

Brónmal frowned. "Be careful, men! Move with caution!"

Now and then, they came to crossroads that descended or ascended the mountains. The roads had signs, though they needed help to read the strange Heokolon letters. Brónmal examined one of the signs. Mednohail and Heokolons had different writing styles: Mednohail used separate letters, while Heokolons wrote words in long, vertical strings. He was unsure whether they should read the words top to bottom or left to right. They were nothing like the scriptures he had grown up with.

He frowned. "What a strange language."

Hacarad shook his head. "Savage and complex. We will introduce them to a better way."

Brónmal sighed. "We need to read this." He turned and snapped at one of his bodyguards. "Fetch my slave, Azra!"

The bodyguard ran off. Hacarad scratched his chin as he traced his fingers along the strings of Heokolon words. "They are painted on. I wonder if that slave even knows where to go?"

"All we need to do is go east, from what I understand."

"We need to find a map, at least."

Brónmal frowned. "I have told the men to search for them. We will find one eventually."

Eventually, the bodyguard came back with Azra. Neck wrapped in an iron collar; she was dragged along with a chain. Brónmal took the chain and pointed at the sign. "Which way do we need to go?"

Azra nervously approached and read the sign. After a moment, she pointed to the right path in the crossroad. "That way is a town called Charoka. That is the right way, Lord."

Brónmal looked at the path. "Like I said, Hacarad, east."

Azra rubbed her finger on part of the sign. "The letters are worn, Lord."

Brónmal tugged her chain. "Silence. Take her back with the rest of the slaves."

He handed Azra back to the bodyguard, who dragged her along to the line of slaves further back in the army. Hacarad crossed his arms. "I swear by all the Three, if that thing leads us in the wrong direction, I will cast it off the mountains myself."

Brónmal nodded. "Agreed. Come, we must continue."

They continued along, eventually reaching a small plateau in the mountains. Shouts came from ahead of the line, drawing Hacarad and Brónmal forward.

A soldier shouted. "Buildings in the brush!"

A commander barked. "Send a squad to investigate."

Brónmal and Hacarad approached, looking into the deep jungle. Buildings were among the trees, overgrown and abandoned. The buildings themselves were square and built on top of each other. Their roofs sloped down all four walls, with ornamental extensions that jutted upward from the corners. Clothes and ornaments hung from the roofs and ceilings, faded and torn from time. The jungle had consumed the buildings.

Brónmal waved. "Belay that order! There is nothing here for us."

The commander nodded. "You heard the Supreme General! Back in formation!"

The army continued forward once it reestablished the formation. The stone path went upward into a staircase. On either side was a broad hill overgrown with trees, bushes, ferns, and other plants. Songs of birds and cries from strange animals echoed. Brónmal heard chirping. He gritted his teeth, each chirp making him clench harder and harder.

"*If I find you, I will crush you,*" Brónmal thought.

Hacarad squinted. "I hate this place."

Brónmal chuckled. "Missing home already?"

"Who does not? How could these heathens live here? There is no space, no calm plains like those of home."

"Who knows? I would not want to live here."

Soldiers shouted ahead. "In the bushes!"

Another commander barked. "Go investigate!"

Brónmal peered ahead. "What are they riled up about?"

Hacarad shrugged. "Probably an animal."

The two stared. Soldiers went into the jungle. Most had spears and maces, leaving them nothing to cut through the thick undergrowth.

Brónmal sighed. "I could go for a drink at this rate."

Hacarad nodded. "How many hours of marching do we have left?"

Brónmal's head hung down. "Probably until night. We do not even know where we are going."

Hacarad leaned his head back. "Oh, by the Three, this land is gonna ki-"

He turned and pushed Brónmal, an arrow whizzing past them. They looked at each other, eyes wide. "Ambush!" Brónmal shouted.

Men drew their maces, nocked their arrows, cocked their Snakebows, and spread out. Arrows flew from all sides. Heokolon soldiers jumped from the overgrowth, glass weapons cleaving through unprepared men. Commanders shouted in panic while the thinned-out army was cut down from all sides.

Brónmal pointed to one of his escorts. "My helmet! Now!"

He grabbed his helmet from one of his escorts and put it on. Drawing his sword, Brónmal moved forward with Hacarad and his escort. Brónmal pointed at those with Flamebows. "Do not burn them! You will burn us all alive in this damned forest!"

Together, Hacarad and the escort helped Brónmal cut down Heokolon after Heokolon. The arrows kept coming. Some hit Brónmal in the chest. The hits hurt but did not penetrate his armor. His soldiers were not so lucky. With low-quality iron plates, the Heokolon bows easily penetrated the armor of the common foot soldier.

Even as hundreds died and dropped, the Mednohail were endless. Where one died, ten came to avenge. The legions spread out into the jungle, cutting down the ambush.

A soldier cried out. "Aogadraod! Watch out!"

Men dressed in red loincloths appeared. From their hands and feet came a blackish-purple mist that seemed fuzzy. The energy projected from their feet allowed them to fly over soldiers. They blasted man after man with bolts from their fists, burning through flesh. Each bolt was concussive, smashing soldiers into the ground. Men screamed, ribs cracking and shields shattering as they were blasted.

Hacarad cried out in horror. "Witchcraft!"

"*Is there no end to their pagan evil?*" Brónmal thought. He pointed. "Kill the magic users! They will be the end of us!"

The men wielding magic easily killed foot soldier after foot soldier, arrows and bolts taking them down from afar. Hacarad sliced one down, turning to Brónmal. "Watch out!"

Brónmal turned. A purple bolt collided with his chest plate. The world spun as he flew down the mountainside. He rolled through the undergrowth before hitting a tree, the world going black. Brónmal blinked. Everything was fuzzy through the slits in his helmet. His ears rang. His head had been rung like a bell.

Then pain. His chest burned. He shrieked and swatted at his chest, rolling in the undergrowth. "Get it off! Get it off!"

The heat subsided, allowing Brónmal to come to his senses. He tore off his helmet and looked at his chest. He was alive, and his armor had survived. The impact had dented his chest plate, which undoubtedly bruised his chest. Despite the charred dent, his chest remained unscorched by the flames. He looked up.

"I thank you, Daonrex. I am not worthy, and I bow before your divine shield," he prayed.

Hacarad ran up to him. "My Lord! Are you okay?"

Brónmal grunted. "I am fine, I am fine."

"The Heokolons are retreating, Lord."

"Send men to cut them down. If they get too far, have the men come back. We need to go back to that village and set up camp somewhere. See that the wounded are taken care of."

"What of your wounds?"

"I think I am fine. My chest might be a little bruised, but that is all. It does not matter. Fulfill my orders!"

Hacarad nodded and ran off. "Send squads after them! Hunt them down!"

The Heokolons disappeared into the jungle, leaving the confused and terrified army to tend to their wounded. Men were sent out to hunt down the ambush party, though they eventually returned. The legions descended the mountain, finding every little nook to set up tents. Mostly, the wounded got tents, leaving the rest of the men in the elements beneath small tarps.

Wet, muddy, cold, they wrapped themselves in dirty blankets. Many lay under trees, a few digging up the ground beneath large roots and sleeping beneath. Among them, bugs. Insects were everywhere, soldiers swatting the air and itching red, irritated bites on their skin. A few coughed, sickness festering among the ranks.

Horrid conditions. Brónmal gave orders until all was right, though he could not stop himself from shaking. He felt the dent in his armor. He would have to have it fixed, though the attempt on his life left him unnerved. Would he die in this land?

19

The Monks of Khagoreti

Hacarad crossed his arms. "So, we must climb through a valley, up a slope, just to get to a staircase that can fit what? Two men at a time? Just to burn a monastery."

Brónmal and the eight Generals of Mednodorn looked at each other. Palagrad, the General of the Southeastern province Faothal, leaned forward. He had a thick, bony brow like any Southerner and a completely bald head. Raised on the shore bordering the rocky and dangerous Mekden Sea, Palagrad was known for his lack of fear and strange stride. It was as if he was always on a boat, though it had been years since he had been on any ship. On his neck was an anchor-shaped scar that had been burned in with an iron, a tradition among experienced Mekden sailors. "And why can we not simply march around?"

Domganmir, the General of the Southern province Gaothal, waved his hands. Puffing and wheezing, he pointed at Palagrad. "How long have we disciplined the Ahamari together, Palagrad? Shortcuts are not our way."

"And wasting our time is not either!" Palagrad scoffed.

Brónmal slammed the table. "I grow tired of this bickering! We burn the monastery because it is in our way. Our torturers tell me that these monasteries are few and far between in this land. We destroy this one and will not have these monks bothering us for a long time."

Cosalmir, the successor to Brónmal in Beinthal, nodded. Like any Northerner, he had a slight reddish hue to his brown hair. Stocky in the shoulders and wide in his legs, Cosalmir was known for his strength. As a new General, he was not trusted or respected by anyone other than the other Northerners like Brónmal, Hacarad, and Baufrius. He spoke with a dialect that Brónmal knew came from the eastern part of Beinthal. "I will gladly stand by my Supreme General in burning this monastery. We burn the pagans. We burn their Aogadraod. Less witchery we must destroy once we conquer this land."

Cangramal, the General of the Southwestern province Reinthal, sighed. Though he was like any Southerner, his face was covered in scars. A survivor of many assassination attempts, he was the cruel and tyrannical backup to Domganmir. The Ahamari hated him, and he bore the scars of their hatred with pride. "You Northerners are fools. These are not simple Throfi tribes we are conquering. We are marching to the very capital of Heonar!"

Brónmal's brow wrinkled. "And that march will be easier without warrior magi destroying our men and flying away!"

Maomarad, General of the Western province of Peresthal, stood. A warden of the West, Maomarad was the main shield against the Western land of Etutakur. Descended from a family who had guarded Peregrine's Wall for Aothills, he was little respected. Many believed the position of protecting the Wall had become easy as the Western lands became more dormant over the decade. He spoke in a Western dialect with many older words, a dialect that some had trouble understanding. "If none do this, I will gladly have my men burn the monastery alone! I have never stood for such cowardice to turn down a chance to kill heathens."

"Watch your words!" Palagrad spat. "I will not be called a coward by a weak Westerner. How long has it been since the Stygian Men climbed Peregrine's Wall in the West?"

Maomarad went up to Palagrad. "And what would a warden of the South have to say about cowardice? Is there honor in ruling the broken?"

"*Worthless fools. By the Three, why have I been cursed to deal with all of you?*" Brónmal thought. He rubbed his face before shouting. "Silence! We do not need the nine to burn this monastery. I will take those who volunteer. It will be enough. We march at noon!"

The eight looked at Brónmal and then saluted. "Praise the Supreme General."

Brónmal pointed to the tent's exit. "Fetch me volunteers, and get out of my sight!"

The eight left, leaving Hacarad behind. "Never gets easier."

Brónmal massaged the bridge of his nose. "Do we really need eight Generals? Can we return them to master their reserves and take the legions for ourselves?"

Hacarad chuckled. "If only it were so simple. They argue now, and once they are side by side on the battlefield, they are more loyal than a dog."

Brónmal sighed. "A dog causes me less headache. This monastery is vital."

Hacarad shrugged. "It is merely a tough climb. We will lose hundreds just to get up there."

"And hundreds more if we let them pester us. How many did they kill in a simple ambush with only a dozen of those warrior magi? How close did I come to death?"

"Too close. Three bless, maybe you are right. I will stand by you either way."

"Then we will march at noon. Ready to climb a mountain?"

"Always."

* * *

Even with a fraction of the nine armies, the legions were in the tens of thousands. Relentless, the soldiers of the West marched up the mountain valleys and between the monolithic peaks. Most of the soldiers were Northerners. Amongst them were volunteers from the rest of the Empire, men hungry with bloodlust.

Brónmal groaned. The dent in the chest plate had been hammered out, though the plate's fit on him was ruined. It pressed in weird spots and felt loose. Scratches and marks covered it, small holes seen where Heokolon arrows had hit him. He would have to get it fixed.

"Those damned buffoons. How can we win this war if they can barely agree on one thing?" Brónmal thought and frowned. "Would the Godspeaker be angry if I sent the heads of my Generals back with the head of the Emperor?"

140

Hacarad bit his lip. "Not sure. If you alone had control of the Nine Armies, would that make you the Highlord?"

"Not sure. Such an idea would be a sin."

"Then we will hold our tongues."

The mountain path curved, twisted, rose, and fell along valleys and dips. The path descended only once, climbing the rest of the way upward to a distant, high-up plateau. Through the brush, Brónmal caught glimpses of a remote monastery. The structure had levels, shrinking as it went up. Each was square, with triangular windows. The top of the building was a pyramid with sloping edges that protruded at the corners, much like the village the Mednohail had found.

They drew near until they came to the base of the plateau. Two statues depicting strange animals guarded the steps that led upward. This was it, the narrow path. There was only so little space on either side. Beyond a few feet of brush were sheer drops, making the army bottleneck.

Brónmal and Hacarad drew their swords. The army split into formations, marching up the stone path with shields and Snakebows ready. The escort tightened around Brónmal. They passed two statues at the beginning of the path. Both statues depicted beasts, each resting a paw on a stone lantern in front of them, a flame flickering within them. As they marched up, they passed under stone arches. Each stone arch was lined with Heokolon script.

"*Three protect us, Daonrex shield me,*" Brónmal thought.

Hacarad looked up the stone stairs. "Where are they?"

Brónmal narrowed his eyes. "Quiet, they are bound to be ready for us."

Arrows hissed over the footsteps.

A soldier shouted. "They are in the trees!"

From trees, bushes, and rocks, camouflaged Heokolons shot arrows at the army. Men fell and tumbled off the mountainside. The formation at the front clashed with another wall of Heokolon glass blades. The Mednohail flooded forward. The soldiers climbed over their dead comrades and attacked the Heokolons with maces and spears.

Brónmal pushed forward with Hacarad and their escort, occasionally absorbing an arrow. They quickly slaughtered any Heokolon that dared charge them. Brónmal stared at the chaos. They were facing no army but rather a small resistance. They reached a giant arch that marked the beginning of the plateau, pushing through until they got to a wide-open field. Houses, training areas, and sacred sites covered the plateau, all built around a central monastery. On the eastern side were the houses, each square with sloped roofs and ornamental protrusions at their corners, much like the ruined village the army had found. Outside each house were gardens and animals, and laundry hung above along the streets. This was no simple living space but a fully functioning village. The western part of the plateau had a vast field of training dummies, strange poles, targets, and pits of sand. On the opposite end of the plateau was a cliff.

The men rushed forward, meeting the Heokolon resistance. Among the Easterlings were their warrior magi. With strange, purple energy, they blasted through the Mednohail. Brónmal looked around. Beyond the defenders were monks in robes, defenseless. They ran in fear, cowering and hiding as the Mednohail flooded into the village. Some fought, hitting the soldiers with brooms and wooden rakes before being cut down.

"Duck!" Hacarad shouted.

Brónmal ducked as a purple bolt shot past his head into a foot soldier behind him. A monk landed beside the escort. Effortlessly, he dodged the blows and stabs of the bodyguards, shooting out purple bolts from his hands and feet. It was like fighting a butterfly.

While the man easily beat Brónmal's bodyguards, Brónmal watched as he thinned. He had mass, flesh, and muscle when he landed. The more he fought, the skinnier he got until his bones were visible. It was as if his magic sucked the life out of him. The warrior monk withered and slowed. Brónmal swung his sword, the man jumping over the strike and spinning through the air. He landed, grunting as Hacarad grabbed him and pushed his blade through the warrior's neck. The monk fell, gurgling and rolling before growing still. The two stared at each other. They panted, Brónmal's eyes wide beneath his helmet. After a pause, Brónmal gestured and shouted. "They are weakening! Forward!"

The plateau became filled with Mednohail, alive and dead. They overwhelmed the Heokolon soldiers, leaving the warrior monks to fend for themselves. It took dozens of men to feel each monk. One by one, every warrior monk was cut down and filled with arrows. Mad with blood, the soldiers spread across the plateau, breaking into the village homes and structures and slaughtering defenseless monks with no mercy.

The bulk of the force flooded toward the monastery. The doors were closed. Filled with bloodlust, the men shouted for axes and began to cut down the doors, chipping them away slowly. It took over twenty minutes to get them to weaken. Men with shields started to charge and crash into them, eventually cracking them open. They flooded in.

There was no resistance left in the monastery. Only a group of monks were left in the center, raising their hands and screaming in fear. Brónmal shouted over his men. "Leave them to me! Pillage the rest of the monastery!"

The men did as they were told. They ran to the upper parts of the monastery, leaving Brónmal, Hacarad, and their escorts to approach the group of monks. The monks begged, reaching their hands out and crying in Heokolon. At the center of them was an old, wrinkled Heokolon.

Brónmal drew his sword and pointed it at the man. He raised his hands, yet he did not flinch. The other monks crawled away in fear. Brónmal looked the old man over. Hairless like all Heokolons, his face was deeply wrinkled with darker shades of brown intermixing with the light hue of green that Heokolons had. His cheeks sagged, lips wrinkled, and his ears were large and thick. He stared with slightly faded, gold eyes, not a shred of fear.

"*You are no warriors,*" Brónmal thought.

Hacarad drew his sword. "What do we do with them, Lord?"

Brónmal squinted. "They might have information for us."

Hacarad spat. "What can we learn from these heathens? We should kill them now!"

Brónmal waved at him and then pointed out of the monastery doors. "Quiet! Get me the translator!"

A bodyguard nodded and ran off. "Yes, Lord!"

Hacarad looked at the bodyguard as he disappeared before gazing at Brónmal. "What are you doing, Lord?"

Brónmal stared at Hacarad. "I wish to learn about them. Perhaps they have something useful for us, perhaps not. What could they tell us about their people, their lands, about breaking their Emperor?"

Hacarad shook his head. "It is a waste of time. We should purge them, as we should with this entire unholy place."

"Enough!" Brónmal snapped. "I will hear no more of this. I will burn this place down once I am done."

Hacarad bowed his head. "As you say, Lord."

20

The Burning Monastery

T he wild Mednohail calmed as the battle ended. Despite only having a hundred defenders, the Heokolons killed nearly a thousand. Men carried the bodies away. They left the Heokolons, flies, and birds already swarming to their bodies. Crazed for loot, they trashed the village around the monastery, taking everything. Animals, jewels, clothes, artifacts, and food disappeared, while others smashed pots, plates, and furniture.

Only Brónmal, Hacarad, their escort, and the monks remained in the monastery. Azra sat between the two groups. She was skinny, beaten, and tortured by the Mednohail. With an empty gaze, she awaited Brónmal's command, her hollow expression a reflection of enslavement under the Mednohail.

Brónmal stared at the oldest monk. "Why did you not fight back?"

The girl translated for the monk, then translated again as the old man spoke. "I am far too old, and these young disciples have not learned enough about Anhanka to defend themselves."

Brónmal squinted. "What is this Anhanka?"

The man listened to the translator. "Anhanka is the magic taught to us by the First Emperor, Otevtecprov, known to many as Otev."

Brónmal tilted his head. "Why do the men who use it thin when they fight us? It is as if their life leaves them."

"Anhanka demands both the energy of the world and one's own energy.

Like a candle, we burn out. It demands balance, or else it will destroy you, as Otev taught us."

Brónmal nodded. "I have heard of Otev. He founded your religion, Nepasni. What was the name of your god?"

"Vishilburkaili, or Vishil. We are all children of Vishil, even you. Vishil is everything, from the energy that allows us to use Anhanka to the earth and the sky."

"*How dare you?*" Brónmal thought and scowled. "You would do best not to offend me by saying I am a child of a pagan god."

The old man recoiled when the translator translated. He spoke again. "What is the point of keeping us alive? Do you seek to learn?"

"I want to know what to do with you. My squire here says we should throw you off the mountain, but perhaps we should enslave you. Or even better, punish you in the way we punish all who commit Aogadraod. There will be no room for witchcraft once this Empire is Mednohail."

The old man chuckled. "You cannot conquer Heonar. What happens is not for me to tell. Do what you will with us. We are not afraid. If you put us to death, I only ask that you let me die like those before me."

Brónmal tilted his head. "The Heokolons are not afraid of death?"

The old man nodded upon translation. "It is one of the six truths of the Chekor, the flower of truths."

"*Do you believe in sin as well? Perhaps we are not so different?*" Brónmal thought. He looked at Hacarad, who shook his head with crossed arms. Brónmal leaned forward, eyes narrowing. "What is this, Chekor?"

"Why do you want to know?"

"So, I can better exterminate it. It makes it easier if I understand how heathens think."

"And why should you exterminate it?"

"There is no room for sin in this world. My job is to destroy it and lead everyone into the light. It is my Daodamath, my divine purpose."

The old man chuckled. "So, the Mednohail believe in a determined destiny? Is that what you believe? Is that what he told you?"

"What do you mean, he?"

"You know who."

"*Gu'hag? How do you know if that creature?*" Brónmal thought. He looked at Hacarad, who furrowed his brow and tilted his head. Brónmal shook his head, then kept speaking. And what do the Heokolons believe? This Chekor?"

"Since you are so curious, the Chekor is the flower of truths. I do not fear death because it is Chekor's fourth truth, called Zidro. Zidro is death. We understand it is an unstoppable force in the universe. It is neither good nor bad. There is no reason to fear it, only to accept it and live well."

"What are the other truths?"

"The first is Cetorvenna, perfection. It means we must always seek perfection and order, which is why our warriors train for a decade before even seeing battle. It is in constant battle with Cazatonia, chaos. While perfection is a constant immortal force, so are chaos and disorder. The two forever battle."

The old man paused, thinking about his following words. "I told you of Zidro, death. Its adversary, the third truth, is Zidra, life. The universe always seeks to create life and end it."

Brónmal squinted. "What are the last two?"

"The fifth is Seletorvu, the great web. Seletorvu signifies all things are connected, and all things are Vishil. Even you and I are connected. The last truth is Ceborca, which represents all primordial forces in the universe, even the truths of the Chekor."

Hacarad shook his head. "What a silly belief. Ten years to make a soldier? We make ours within a year."

Brónmal waved at the translator, stopping her from translating Hacarad's words. He gestured to the elderly monk. "I have come to my decision. I will have you and your monks here dead, but I allow you to choose how to go."

The old man nodded upon translation. "The others can go how they wish. I wish to go like all those who have lived in this monastery. I wish to burn my life energies."

Brónmal tilted his head. "And how will that be done?"

"These monks here will help me."

Brónmal waved. "Very well."

* * *

The escort, Hacarad, and Brónmal sat and watched the monk prepare. The old man sat cross-legged at the plateau's edge, looking at a great valley. Brónmal stared in confusion. The monks fed the man alien fruits and foods Brónmal had never seen before. The man drank strange elixirs that, from a distance, gave off a range of odors. Some smelled foul, some smelled of alcohol, and some were sweet. The more the old man drank, the more still he became.

Eventually, the monks stopped feeding him, allowing him to assume meditation. They got on their knees in a circle around him. Each grabbed another's hands, purple energy foaming around their fingers.

Hacarad leaned over and whispered to Brónmal. "Why do we allow this?"

Brónmal whispered back. "To see how they think, to learn. We will put the rest to the sword and burn the monastery."

Hacarad furrowed his brow. "And what if they are trying to kill us?"

Brónmal shook his head. "They would have tried already. Do you fear death, Hacarad? Not even the Heokolons do."

"No, Lord. I do not."

"Then watch."

The monks hummed in unison, the purple energy siphoning from their hands into the old man. His veins expanded and darkened, fingers shaking. Brónmal's eyes widened. It seemed as if the pores in the monk's skin bled the strange, purple energy of Anhanka. Brónmal felt the heat even from far away.

"What is this unholy ritual? What infernal power does Dubilfen give you, fiends?" Brónmal thought.

Then, the energies merged and went up like flames. The monk's skin fell apart like ash, yet he did not scream. Disturbingly, he was calm and silent. The energy consumed his body, leaving only a dark visage in the purple flames slowly fading. Brónmal saw his skin wither, then his muscle, then his skeleton until the purple flames took all the ash and carried them away with the wind.

After only a few minutes, nothing remained. All that remained were the monks. Without speaking, they stood and approached the edge of the plateau.

Hacarad stood. "Ki–"

Brónmal grabbed him and shook his head. One by one, the monks threw themselves off the plateau, joining the old man of their own free will. As the last toppled off the edge, the monastery was silent.

Brónmal stood and walked toward the stairs, leaving the plateau, gesturing to Hacarad. "Have them burn the monastery. I want nothing left."

Hacarad nodded and went to a few dozen soldiers piling bodies. "Burn it! Burn it all!"

After a minute, Hacarad joined Brónmal. They marched down the blood-stained steps leading back to the army's camp. There was so much blood that a small river flowed between their feet. The pair said nothing to each other. Brónmal looked back once, gazing upon a vast smokestack.

The monastery burned, taking ages worth of history with it.

21

Meeting Hacarad

Brónmal slowly turned the knob of his door and squinted out into the hall. The sun had not risen yet. All was still. Not a servant or his father stirred. Perfect. He opened the door and crept out, wincing. Bruises covered his arms, legs, and chest, his muscles aching.

He had enough. He would have another hard training or studying day if he did not escape now. Just one day. He needed one day. Brónmal snuck on the balls of his feet, moving like a fox toward the stairs. He eyed each hall before he took it. No servants, no father.

Step by step, he descended onto the first floor. A ray of early morning sunlight beamed through the estate's expensive glass windows. Was he too late? He could not use the front door. No, the guard would see him. Creeping through the kitchen, Brónmal passed the servants' quarter and went toward the greenhouse.

It was High Spring, and the greenhouse flourished. Flowers and fruits filled the planters, providing thick foliage for Brónmal to keep his head under. He got to the door, grabbed the door handle, and whispered, "Three, hide me."

The birds had just woken, filling the air with whistling songs and harmonic cries. Brónmal stayed low. Only one guard was out on patrol, lingering around the front gate. The stone wall surrounding the estate was far too high for even a grown man to scale. Yet, there was one spot. Brónmal took off toward the back of the estate, looking behind him every ten steps.

An old tree loomed over one corner of the estate wall. Brónmal went to it. He grabbed its old bark and clawed his way up to a branch, climbing up high until he reached the edge of the wall and leaped over.

His feet stung as he hit the ground, his legs nearly folding from the force. He was free.

"*Three, thank you,*" he thought.

The forest of Beinthal awaited him. The trees were tall and old, born from the far roots of the distant Fjandgarth mountains of the North. The foliage was low, overshadowed by the high-up canopies. Brónmal ran as fast as he could, heart pounding. Wind flowed through his brown hair, and a sense of wild joy turned his mind into a storm of excitement.

He ran far, leaving the estate behind until he grew tired. The sun rose steadily into the sky with morning. The forest came to life. Birds flew all about, insects landed on High Spring flowers, and forest critters ran everywhere. Most prepared, storing food or fattening up for High Summer. They paid no mind to Brónmal. If he got too close, they scurried away and continued their business.

Brónmal needed a sword. Even a broken boy needed his myths, fantasy, and fun. He picked up a stick, the greatest sword known to man. Alone, he fought the invisible hordes, jumping from boulder to boulder, fighting among trees. He imagined fighting monsters, Heokolons, heretics, and all the dreadful nightmares of the Mednohail people. He was his people's salvation. Brónmal was judge and executioner, a divine hand of justice carrying out the will of the Three in his imagination.

Finding a more curved branch, Brónmal had a bow. He shot down winged beasts, switching to his sword to fight those he drew close to him. The war lasted for an hour until the sound of the river met his ear. Brónmal dropped the sticks. Running through the woods, he got out of the brush and found it. The trees leaned over the river, shading the slow-moving water. Approaching the edge, Brónmal touched the water. It was freezing. The water flowed from the icy peaks of Fjandgarth and the glacial-fed waters of the Gisjaf Sea.

Brónmal shied away and followed the river. On the way, he found a thicker piece of driftwood. This, in his mind, was a great sword. He walked and walked until the bushes rustled beside him. Startled, Brónmal faced the bushes with his weapon out. "Who goes there?!"

Nothing. Brónmal squinted and spoke again. "I am Brónmal, servant of Daonrex and the divine shield! Face me, and I will destroy you!"

A boy, no older than him, stepped out with a stick. The two collided, smacking sticks back and forth. Brónmal easily evaded and parried. He ducked under a blow, swinging straight into the boy's stomach.

The boy let out a groan and stumbled back. "Ow! That was too hard!"

Brónmal recoiled. "Y-You attacked me!"

"I was just playing. You are really great with a stick."

Brónmal stared, walking around the boy. "Who are you?"

"Name's Hacarad. What's yours?"

"Brónmal. Next time, you should ask before attacking someone!"

Hacarad chuckled. "I am the defender of this river! It is my right to attack whoever trespasses."

Brónmal shook his head. "This land belongs to the king of Eidthal and the High Bishop!"

Hacarad scratched his head. "I am just imagining. I do not really own the river. I just live near here in Angmere."

Brónmal tilted his head. "Angmere, the village?"

Hacarad nodded. "Yeah."

"Are you a peasant boy?"

"Who are you?"

"I am the son of Remtaich."

Hacarad gasped and stepped back. "Y-You are a lord! I am sorry, I am sorry! I did not mean to attack you. I will just leave. No one needs to know."

Hacarad started to leave. Remtaich's lessons echoed in Brónmal's head, discussions of superiority and disgust toward the lower classes. He shook the thoughts away. Brónmal reached out before Hacarad started to leave. "W-Wait! It's okay. I forgive you. I am not like my father. You can stay."

Hacarad bowed his head. "Thank you, Lord."

Brónmal waved dismissively. "You do not have to call me Lord. Just call me Brónmal."

Hacarad nodded. "I knew your teeth were a little too nice for a peasant. You must know swordsmanship, right?"

Brónmal nodded. "My father trains me daily and wants me to be a soldier."

Hacarad gasped. "I want to be a soldier, too. Could you teach me some stuff?"

Brónmal blinked. "Uh... S–Sure. Grab your stick."

The two raised their sticks to each other. Brónmal pointed. "Stand like me. If you stand that way, you are easy to tip and hit. You want to hold it right here. Your hand is too far out, so it is weak, and you are open."

They clashed, Brónmal quickly blowing through Hacarad's defenses and tapping him. "Good, but again, do not be so wide and open. Tight defense is a good defense, and do not get nervous."

The two played and fought for an hour until Hacarad was a far better swordsman than ever. He was nothing compared to Brónmal. But, for once, Brónmal felt a sense of happiness. Hacarad had an eager, confident, and zealous spirit like Brónmal once had. His father had cast so much fear and hardship that Brónmal rarely smiled.

Hacarad chuckled. "I cannot believe I was playing with the son of a lord. Three bless, it's an honor."

Brónmal smiled. "I was told not to speak with peasants, but maybe my father was wrong."

Hacarad frowned. "Why not speak with peasants?"

Brónmal fell over his words. "Well... My father thinks peasants are pawns, dirty and dumb. Those who cannot even read the holy words of scripture are not worthy but to serve in his eyes."

Hacarad scoffed. "Reading? Who needs that? I am as faithful and strong as anyone else! Is it not faith in the Three above all else?"

Brónmal nodded. "Of course, I can see that your faith is strong. I think I like you, Hacarad."

"I like you too, Brónmal!"

"Do you want to be friends?"

"Of course! I can introduce you to my friends, too, and maybe you can introduce me to your friends?"

"*What would father think?*" Brónmal thought. His anxiety took hold as thoughts of what would happen to him when he went home flooded his mind. He frowned and looked away. "I do not really have any friends," he said.

Hacarad's smile fell. "Well, that's okay. I can help you get friends, and maybe you can teach us all to be soldiers?"

Brónmal's cheer came back. "I can do that."

"Deal! Let us go do something fun!"

"Like what?"

"Something with swords! We can explore the forest; pretend we are adventurers looking for lost treasure?"

"I like that idea!"

"Come on!"

22

Into the Swamps

Deeper, ever deeper into the heart of Heonar. Every step forward meant danger. The army had made it through the Khagoreti Mountains with little resistance. The Heokolons rarely tried to ambush them. The Easterlings used hit-and-run tactics, burning food and supplies at night and leaving quickly. It left the men on edge. Did the trees speak Heokolon? Was there a figure just now? Were they being stalked?

Low Autumn was underway, relieving them from the heat of High Summer. Thousands had died from the journey across the Khagoreti Mountains. Heatstroke took many, though the Heokolons had thinned their numbers. Worse still, sicknesses spread through the ranks. Sleeping in mud, bothered by insects, bunched together, the army was a breeding ground for disease. Those too weak to march were left behind. There were still nearly a million soldiers left. In formations as wide as three, the army took a long time to pass through anywhere. They trampled the land, ready to swarm out at any moment and flood over the enemy.

Hacarad sighed. "We are finally leaving these damned mountains behind."

Brónmal squinted ahead. "We must be descending. The air is not thin anymore."

Hacarad inhaled deeply. "Thank the Three. I have had enough of mountains for one lifetime."

Brónmal chuckled. "At least they are beautiful."

Hacarad shrugged. "As beautiful as a tree with termites. Maybe I will be happier once the termites are gone."

"Well said."

The mountains and uneven terrain made it hard to transport the army. Using War Carriages and wagons was impossible, forcing people and beasts to carry most supplies. The moving village of war families suffered as well. They were the ones who supplied, took care of, and fed the soldiers. Without wagons to transport them, they were forced to carry and pull supplies all day. It was backbreaking.

"*Curse this place*," Brónmal thought.

The stairs went down. They twisted and turned until they rode along a ledge. A vast valley separated them from more distant mountains. Like all Khagoreti mountains, they too were pillar-like, with rare plateaus. The valley echoed with metallic clanks and thousands of footsteps, shouting and talking reverberating through the trees. Brónmal stopped and looked out over the valley from the ledge. They had made it. He had passed the immortal Heokolon mountains that stood as a bulwark against the West. Even if they failed here, he would be a hero.

"*I will not fail like you, father*," he thought. He would prove Gu'hag wrong. The Emperor's head was his, and Heonar was Brónmal's gift to the Mednohail people. He envisioned walking down the streets of Ardmunhaich, holding the Emperor's head with pride as the people wept with joy.

Then, the stench of rotten fumes made him recoil, his thoughts leaving him. Below was a swamp. Even from high up, the wretched swamp stink reached him, turning his stomach and making him detest the coming march.

Hacarad groaned. "The smell! Dubilfen has cursed us!"

Brónmal shook his head. "Is it any worse than the smell of corpses? We will be through it."

Hacarad looked over the drop into the valley. "It will take us days to get through there."

Brónmal nodded. "It takes us days to get through anything. Best to just keep going."

Hacarad tilted his head and squinted. "I see smoke."

Brónmal perked up. "I see it, too."

Far down the steps were distant smokestacks, their sources hidden by the dense trees of the awaiting swamp. Brónmal waved back. "Cosalmir!"

Cosalmir, the new General of Beinthal, rode up to Brónmal. "Yes, Supreme General?"

Brónmal leaned toward him. "I trust you more than the Generals behind me. There's something ahead. I want you to send your forces down there ahead of us."

"Yes, Supreme General. As you say."

Brónmal rode back toward the army. "Halt!"

The army halted. Cosalmir mustered a force of soldiers and sent them down. Impatiently, the endless legion waited, ready to move at a moment's notice while they watched the hills. An hour passed before five soldiers returned and bowed to Brónmal. "There's a village ahead, Supreme General!"

Brónmal squinted at the distant smoke. "Were there any defenses? Soldiers?"

"No, Supreme General. There were only a few village guards, and they surrendered when they saw how many of us there were."

Brónmal nodded. "Then let us speak with them and see if there's a quicker way out of this swamp. Grab my translator! Watch the tree line! I want the entire village surrounded! Be prepared for an ambush!"

They grabbed Azra from the stock of slaves dragged along with the army. Once she was with Brónmal and the escort, the entire army continued the march toward the village. Men spread out into the hill below and above, cutting through the brush and searching for any Heokolon soldiers. Their boots squished in the mud as they entered the swamp. Soldiers surrounded the village. No one in, no one out. The formations formed into a wall of shields and spears as they looked out into the swamp, ready for any attack.

The village was small. Unlike the sturdy clay houses of the Khagoreti mountains, the swamp village had homes built on stilts and made primarily of wood and branches. In Heokolon fashion, each hut had ornamental pieces that stuck out from the corners of each roof, with Heokolon ribbons, clothes, and ornaments decorating them.

Brónmal stared at the village folk. The entire village came outside, completely at the mercy of the Mednohail soldiers. The soldiers waited, weapons ready to massacre. Brónmal grabbed Azra. "Ask for the village elders."

Azra spoke. The crowd parted to let a Heokolon man of Brónmal's age approach. Dressed in orange robes that were tucked in, so they stopped at his knees, he looked like any other Heokolon to Brónmal. His muddy and wet boots reached his knees and curled into forks at their toes. Around his neck was a chain necklace. From it hung a golden ring with a gold ball at its center. He waved, his words translated by Azra. "First Emperor protect you, great leader."

Brónmal got off his Auhmog and approached. "Three bless, Easterling."

"You Westerners will find nothing of value here. I beg that you simply pass through."

Brónmal stared at all the Heokolons that the soldiers were keeping back. "I would watch your words and do not presume to think you understand my wishes. If I had wanted to hurt anyone here, this village would be burning already."

"What is it you seek?"

Brónmal gestured out into the swamp. "My men are marching toward the home of your Emperor. We seek the quickest way out of this swamp. You will tell me, and if you misguide us, I will return for your head. The rest of your people will be captured and sold as slaves in Mednodorn."

The man frowned. "You seek only directions?"

"That is right. Give them to me, and we will leave without anyone harmed or taken."

"There are many ways out of the swamp to get to Nasalohotehr, but it is up to you which way you wish to take."

Nasalohotehr, home of the First Emperor of Heonar. Brónmal had heard the name before and hated it. Perhaps he could rename it? Maybe they would use his name? Brónmal tilted his head. "Many ways? Explain."

"You can go north and take the mountains. That is the safest way, though the longest. To the south, the swamps bend around the mountains to the

East and extend into plains. It is far, and you will meet many soldiers."

"Is there another way?"

"There is, straight through to the east. It is an old way, something from the Reign."

"*What unholy path would still exist from that time?*" Brónmal thought, his spine tingling. He narrowed his eyes. "The Reign?"

"It is a cursed path, used by the servants of that dark time for transportation. We do not use it. It cuts through the mountains and is the quickest way to go east."

"What do you mean, cursed?"

"The path is hundreds of years old, yet it never ages. The plants do not dare grow on it, the soil recedes away from it, and the trees that bend over it are gnarled and dying. Some go there, but we never hear from them."

"What happens to those who cross it?"

"We do not know. I wish for the safety of my people, and I have told you the best ways."

Brónmal nodded. "You get my blessing to live. If you have misled me, no one will ever know this place existed, understood?"

The man raised his hands and nodded. Brónmal turned and faced his Generals and Hacarad. "We go east into the swamp! The Easterlings will not expect us to take that way!"

The men cheered. Brónmal turned and pointed to the village leader. "You will take my men to the beginning of this path."

The man nodded. He led the army out of the village and into the swamp. Hacarad rode up beside Brónmal. "What is this about a cursed path?"

Brónmal shrugged. "Pagan superstition? He mentioned the Reign, but how could that affect us now?"

"Brónmal... How could we trust a pagan, let alone a path from a damned time?"

"We cannot, but he said it was the fastest way. It is just a path, and we have thousands. I will destroy whatever stops us, for what can possibly stand in the way of Mednodorn?"

"I trust your confidence, Supreme General. If you say it, we will do it."

"The Three protect us. Can the Easterlings say the same?"

"One day, they will."

"One day. If we want that day, we march east."

"Well said, Lord."

The village leader led them to the village border. A lone stone path cut straight into the swamp beyond. It was flawless, untouched by age and nature. The Heokolon gestured and spoke, Azra translating. "This is the ancient path."

Brónmal approached the path. His hairs stood straight. It was as if everything in his body cried out against walking forward. He frowned. The Three would protect him. No wretched road would turn him away from his victory. His thoughts wandered to the village.

"*I cannot let these Easterlings go in peace,*" he thought. It would go against his training, what his father taught. No Easterling deserved mercy. It was the will of the Three, his divine duty to the Godspeaker.

He turned to the man, drawing his sword. The man stumbled back, crying out in Heokolon. Brónmal plunged the blade into the man's throat. He squirmed, gargling before he grew still. Azra screamed and stumbled back in horror, covering her mouth with her hands as tears rolled down her cheeks. Retracting his blade, Brónmal pointed to the village. "Burn it to the ground. Kill everyone; I want nothing left."

Hacarad nodded. "Yes, Lord!"

Soldiers followed Hacarad as they went into the village. Screams of terror filled the air as soldiers tore apart the settlement. Men with Flamebows burnt down the swamp huts while foot soldiers cut down men, women, and children. Insatiable, the Mednohail plundered every valuable, leaving nothing behind.

Brónmal turned to the ancient path. He stepped forward against his fear, leaving the destruction behind as he ventured into the darkness beyond.

"Three protect me. Shield me from evil as I enter the lair of the damned," he prayed.

23

The Old Witch

Mud. Nothing but mud. The trees loomed overhead. Though all the branches that hung over the path were dead, they were dense enough to block all sunlight. Their roots grew away from the path as if petrified of the stone. The path was cursed. Brónmal's feet tingled with every step, goosebumps forming on his skin. So distant from the temples of home and the warmth of Daonrex, Brónmal felt as if Dubilfen himself embraced him with his cold, damning grasp. There were no seasons here, no stars or sun, just an oppressive weight that slowly crushed his spirit.

"*This was foolish,*" he thought.

The insects and the soil receded away from the path, as if touching it would kill them. Or worse. Despite hundreds of thousands of men following Brónmal, the army was dead silent. Only the sound of their gear rattled over the stillness.

Hacarad whispered. "This place is cursed."

Brónmal peered into the surrounding fog. "Nothing is natural here. Keep an eye out. If I must, I will burn this place and hack up this path myself."

A gust of wind blew through them. Brónmal shivered as if all the warmth of his life had been sucked out of him. He looked around, withdrawing any notion of voicing more opinions in this evil place. They marched deeper into the swamp. Brónmal could see nothing in the fog.

There were no forks on the road, no crossroads, just a straight path. Despite this, Brónmal felt as if they marched in circles. Now and then, he swore they passed the same tree or the same rock. He paused. Brónmal stared into the fog momentarily and saw soldiers marching in the distance. He could not see whether they were Mednohail, Heokolon, or something else. Brónmal pointed. "Hacarad, are those soldiers?"

Hacarad peered into the fog. "What? Where? I see nothing."

Brónmal furrowed his brow. "They are gone. I do not see anything."

Hacarad turned his head. "Are you trying to scare me or just imagining things?"

Brónmal shook his head and kept walking. "Imagining things."

Further into the mist meant further into absurdity. Brónmal saw glimpses of other armies marching, ghostly visages of Heokolons, and black shapes of tendrils and limbs in the murky waters. While the water lapped against the muddy soil elsewhere, it was entirely still where the path touched it.

Brónmal looked into the dark depths. He saw hands reaching out from the depths. They were bloated and rotten, grasping at him as if they wanted to pull him under. Their fingers never poked through the water's surface, unable to escape, as if pushing against a layer of glass. Brónmal silently pointed. Hacarad looked down at the water and then leaned back in horror. The pair exchanged glances, then kept walking.

Brónmal shouted behind. "Stay clear of the water!"

Commanders relayed his order back along the line. Over the silence, Brónmal heard echoes of their voices before the swamp became quiet once again. The men fearfully clung to the right edge of the path. Ahead, Brónmal saw a flicker of light and pointed. "Do you see that?"

Hacarad nodded. "Light. From what?"

Brónmal drew his sword, and Hacarad and the escort did the same. They slowly walked toward the light. Out of the mist came a wagon. It was alone, with no beast to pull it and no guard to protect it. Part of the wagon was on fire. The flame flickered and danced, never consuming the cart or being extinguished. Hacarad approached, stomping at the flame a few times. It danced around his foot, refusing to be put out.

Brónmal waved. "Stop, stop, do not disturb it. Let us carry on."

They sheathed their swords and kept walking. The endless path twisted and twisted until another shape came into view. A house. It was a low building, like a shack, with a grass-covered roof that touched the ground. It had a stone wall, with one door and one window. A glimpse of light came from the window.

Hacarad pointed up. "Aogadraod. Witches' things."

Fetishes and idols made from bones, hair, feathers, and other grotesque objects hung from the trees above them. Bloody ears were everywhere. They were in the trees and bushes, pierced by branches with no flies around them. Brónmal pointed to the door. "Is someone still here?"

Hacarad approached the door. "Let us see."

Brónmal followed Hacarad. The door slid open as the two drew near, a figure peering out from the shadows. To Brónmal's surprise, a tiny old lady stood at the door. She was hideous, so ancient that her cheeks hung beneath her jaw, and her eyes sunk into her skull as if she were dead. Her hair was wispy, like that of a skeleton. Dark robes covered her whole body, though they could see her skeletal hands. Her veins were black, pulsing back and forth.

She spoke, voice whisper-like. "The Supreme General of Ardmunhaich and his squire. It is an honor."

Her Mednohail was fluent, though she spoke with an accent Brónmal had never heard before. It was not Ahamari, Throfi, or even Heokolon, but something else entirely. She trilled her Rs and spoke in her throat rather than on the tip of her tongue. Her dialect came closest to Western Mednohail, like General Maomarad, though far removed from any accent in Peresthal. Brónmal squinted. "You know us?"

"Brónmal and Hacarad, of course. Do you wish for tea?"

Hacarad rested his hand on the hilt of his sword. "Who are you, witch?"

The old woman recoiled. "Witch?"

Brónmal pointed up. "These fetishes are the mark of one who does Bogarthdraod."

The old woman shook her head. "They are decoration. There is no Bogarthdraod in this land, only Anhanka. Do you come only to pester an

163

old woman with questions? Come in, make yourselves comfortable."

Brónmal and Hacarad looked at each other when the old woman retreated inside and opened the door to let them in. Hacarad shrugged and followed her.

Brónmal pointed to his men. "Guard the door. Break it down if you hear anything happen."

A putrid stench of rotten brews and moldy herbs hit his nose on the way in. The shack's roof was low, fitting more for the tiny woman than the two Mednohail soldiers. Fetishes and strange objects decorated the hut, hanging from ceilings, pinned to walls, and sitting on bookshelves. A sensation of dread curdled in Brónmal's stomach. The path cast fear into his body, yet this home felt like he had found the core of the swamp's evil. A hand rested on the hilt of his sword. He eyed every inch of the room.

"Daonrex, shield me from this darkness, and I will flood this damned place with your light," Brónmal prayed.

At the far end of the shack was a fireplace, a small flame flickering in it. Brónmal stared at it, sure he did not see a chimney from the outside. He remembered the light in the window, though it was impossible for it to be from the small flame. Brow furrowed, he looked around, searching for the impossible light source. The old woman sat on a chair, gesturing to two chairs across from her. "Sit, sit. Tea will be ready soon."

The pair sat and stared. She waited silently, eventually whispering a few words. "You want my name, do you not?"

Brónmal nodded. "Since you know ours."

"I am Rosura."

"*Who are you really, witch?*" Brónmal thought, narrowing his eyes. Rosura was not a name in any language he knew. It felt familiar, like western Mednohail, though nothing came close to it.

Hacarad leaned forward. "You live in a strange place, Rosura."

"I live where there is peace, Hacarad. None bother me out here, not a Heokolon, Mednohail, or any other people."

Brónmal tilted his head. "You seem awfully friendly to us."

Rosura chuckled. "I know the ways of the Mednohail, savage men with no mercy. What choice does an old woman like me have but hospitality?"

Hacarad spoke. "You think us savages?"

Rosura smiled. "No, not you two. I am still alive. That is why I bring you in for tea. To talk and share wisdom. What news is there in the West?"

Brónmal pursed his lips. "In Mednodorn? What news do you seek?"

"What happens beyond Peregrine's Wall? With the Stygian Men?"

Brónmal frowned. Servants of the Breaker of Man, Arathmalok, the Stygian Men, lived in the cursed land of Etutakur. The wall, built by King Peregrine the First Aothill after the Reign, had been silent for nearly six hundred years. Patrolled by four families, General Maomarad had spoken of recent activity beyond the wall, though many dismissed him and the idea that Etutakur could bring any threat to the Empire. Brónmal often agreed. How could broken tribes of magically corrupted men ever hope to face Mednodorn?

Brónmal shook his head. "Nothing has happened. The Stygian Men do not stir. They have been dormant, as they have for the last four Aothills."

Rosura spoke after a pause. "It's good to hear those cursed fiends are kept at bay. My Master would not want them to surge over the wall just yet."

"W-What do you mean?" Hacarad stuttered.

Rosura chuckled. "My Master. He is coming soon. I see it in the way the birds fly. I heard it in the whispers of the water. The Old Ones awaken."

Brónmal spat. "Who is your master?"

"Mednohail have always been the fools. I remember when my Master enslaved your people. Good servants to the Ahamari you were! Such back-breaking work you could endure. No wonder most of your empire is farmers, slaves, and factory workers. Even now, you work to the bone. Do you not know the futility, Brónmal? I know what the old chief told you in that forest."

Brónmal recoiled. "Be silent! What sort of witchery is this? How could one such as you know these things?"

Hacarad growled. "Bogarthdraod. Filthy witchery. I have cooked many witches in clay before, those who could see the future, those who could heal, those who could curse."

Rosura shook her head. "I am no lowly practitioner of Bogarthdraod - peasant's magic. Arathmalok would not grant his servants such superstitious and weak-willed magic. I practice Asharnak, the craft of the Accursed, the Chosen."

Hacarad drew his sword. "I will slaughter you, witch!"

The woman raised her hand as Hacarad swung. A black mist came from her fingers, forming into demonic, shadowy claws. The claws ripped the blade from Hacarad's hand, throwing it across the room and knocking Hacarad onto his back. Brónmal shouted. "Men! With me!"

Rosura chuckled. "They cannot hear you. It is just us here, on this island in the void."

The shack fell apart. The walls and ceiling came down around them, revealing a dark void sky. A black sea surrounded them, leaving them alone on a small island. Figures, horrific aberrations, stood in the distance, their hollow eyes piercing Brónmal. They were gangling and slender, their bodies seemingly constructed from shadowy, poorly held-together strings. The string moved, wriggling like worms. Few moved, though when they did, they moved like shadows, only facing one direction or the other.

Brónmal stared at them, his heart slowing. He felt his veins go cold. His spirit left. He felt the invisible warm shield the Three gave him flickering and fading. There was no hope in this void, no divine hands, no glory.

Rosura spoke again. "Calm yourself. I would have drowned you in the darkness if I had wanted to kill you. Do you want to learn about your future? Learn your fortune?"

Hacarad pointed. "Be silent before your forked tongue casts a curse on us!"

Rosura raised her hand and squeezed it into a fist. Black tendrils formed around Hacarad's mouth, clutching it closed and silencing him. Hacarad grabbed his mouth, eyes wide in panic as he fell and writhed on the floor. Screams silent; Brónmal only heard his panicked breathing from his nose. Paralyzed, Brónmal stood still, head numb, unable to will himself forward and rescue Hacarad.

"*I am sorry, brother,*" Brónmal thought.

She pointed to Brónmal. "Now, now, young one. Listen to your elders, or I will punish you the same."

Brónmal raised his hands. "I listen, evil one."

"My Master waits in this void beyond all worlds. He awaits with his true kind, the Deothers, makers of reality. Your gods are false, but my Master is true. You will learn to worship him and know his divinity is the only truth. He will not be born until the next Aothill when the comet Serkur ushers in the Second Reign."

Brónmal's nose wrinkled. "I have heard this nonsense before! I will destroy Heonar, then march home and stop the Ebon Armada!"

"There is no stopping us now. The Skinbook is almost complete. Once we finish the Skinbook, we will flood Mednodorn with the Stygian men, and the Ebon Armada will destroy all resistance. Once this is done, we will rebuild Arathmalok's empire, using your people as slaves. Such a strong spirit. Such strong faith. I admire it. You will serve well. I admire struggle, and perhaps you deserve a taste of true power. A church of black stone awaits in the fog. It will only appear for a moment, but if you wish to try to stop us, bring your blade to the church. Kill if you think you can."

"I take up your challenge, and I will burn your heathen church to its foundations for the Three."

Rosura smiled. "I cannot wait to see the idols of your false gods be undone."

"Release us, demon of Dubilfen! Release us from this void!"

Brónmal fell back. He blinked and found himself in the shack, gazing at the ceiling above. Hacarad sat beside him. With a loud gasp, Hacarad held his throat and stared at Brónmal, chest rising up and down as he savored fresh air. Brónmal's heart pumped again, his body warming as he felt his will come back. He sat up, staring at his hands and rubbing his face, shocked to be back in the world.

Confused, Brónmal looked around the shack. The witch was gone. The door was now wide open, the fireplace extinguished, and the fetishes in the shack gone. An escort entered. "My lords, are you okay?"

Brónmal and Hacarad locked eyes, wordless and horrified.

24

The Black Church

"Brónmal, why do you refuse to utter anything of what that witch said?" Hacarad pestered. "Of what that Algoniva said in Mednodorn?"

"It is for me to know," Brónmal grumbled.

"What do you know? What is this Ebon Armada, and what of the Stygian men? What shakes your spirit and faith so much that you do not dare utter it to even me?"

Brónmal turned and snapped at his friend. "Lower your tone, Hacarad. I am still the Supreme General, and I demand your silence. What I know is for me to know, and what I keep secret, I keep secret for the good of the Empire, the Three, and the men."

"At least, speak of this black church? What do you know?"

"*If only I could confess what the darkness holds for us, brother,*" Brónmal thought, his gaze falling to the ground. He sighed and looked up again. "I know nothing. Only that enemies of the Three dwell there, and we will burn it on the way to killing the Emperor."

"Where is it?"

"I do not know. She said in the fog, so I assume somewhere along this cursed path."

Hacarad squinted into the fog. "Should I spread the word?"

"Tell the men they should go to it and burn it if they see it."

Hacarad went to the line commanders and passed the order down to the thousands behind. Brónmal watched him disappear down the line and into the fog beyond.

"Mother, what would you think? Is it a sin to hold my silence? I must burn Heonar, for me, for Mednodorn. It is my destiny," Brónmal thought.

The armies kept marching forward, wary and watching. Brónmal squinted into the fog. Seemingly endless, the path twisted for hours, perhaps days? The swamp had so little light that he could not tell if it was night or day.

"Curse this place," he thought. He wished to chop down these trees, burn this place, and destroy it until nothing was left but soil. If he could, he would have the ground salted so that nothing would ever grow again.

Perhaps one day, when Mednodorn ruled Heonar and good, faithful Mednohail lived in this land, they would turn the swamp into a peaceful farmland, he thought. There was so much space, so much to farm, plenty to chop down. He imagined the fog, the water, and the trees, all gone and replaced with a field of gentle, ripe crops.

Brónmal paused now and then, peering into the mist. Hacarad came back and joined him at his side. Brónmal sighed. "Will we ever escape this place?"

Hacarad nodded. "Three willing. I miss the light. I miss the plains and hills of Mednodorn."

"I hate these heathen lands. How could anyone live here? No wonder the Empire's glory is centered in Mednodorn, the greatest of lands."

"Our home is truly blessed. I have never seen so many mountains, so many swamps, not like this place."

"I miss fields of crops, the breeze of the plains, the gentle rains, the cities embraced by walls."

Hacarad sighed. "Perhaps it is not good to think of home, Lord. It will weaken our spirit."

Brónmal nodded. "You are right, brother."

"May I see home again?" he thought. He remembered the ripening fields of Low and High Autumn, the peasants at work, the animals fattening themselves in the fields, and the preparation of firewood and food for the arrival of winter. Yearning for home, he wanted to see at least the plains of

Raothal and the freedom of their vastness.

Hacarad spoke. "Lord, I see something!"

Brónmal stopped and looked into the mist. "Where?"

Hacarad pointed. "There!"

Brónmal squinted and saw the silhouette of a building. "With me, men!"

The escort, Hacarad, and part of the army ran across the swamp. Their footsteps squelched and splashed, mud slowing them down while they climbed over roots and ducked under branches. Brónmal sunk knee-deep into the watery depths, water filling his armor as he clawed forward. It was cold. He grunted, groaning as he felt more and more water fill his steel shoes and greaves.

The silhouette seemed to move. It stayed the same distance away no matter how fast Brónmal ran. He glanced back. Hacarad was gone. The escort had disappeared as well. Alone, the fog had stolen everyone away. Brónmal did not surrender. He clawed forward, stumbling until he fell to his knees and looked up.

By a strange miracle, the black church stood before him. It was unlike any holy structure Brónmal had ever seen. It was a mass of black stone, standing as a brutalistic cube of darkness. On its sides were smaller cubes that had sloped roofs. There were only thin slits for windows. No idols, statues, or other symbols of man marked the structure. It was soulless. The oppressive immortal walls crushed all spirit. No plants grew on or near the building. The trees grew away from it, revealing the night sky above. Not even the soil dared to touch the tyrant structure. Only rocks touched the unholy structure, and they, too, seemed unwilling to do so.

Brónmal looked behind him. A few soldiers had made it through the fog, muddy and panting. The rest were lost. Not even their voices were heard beyond the tree line. Three of his escorts, a few soldiers, and a man with a Flamebow awaited his command. Brónmal squinted. "Where is everyone else?"

One of the soldiers spoke. "Lost in the mist, Supreme General. My comrades were right behind me, but when I turned, they were gone."

Brónmal clenched his jaw. "Three bless them. May they return to the others. You men are brave, I hope?"

They all saluted. "Yes, Supreme General!"

Brónmal pointed to the ominous black structure. "We face an unknown enemy in that building. They are not Throfi, Ahamari, or even Heokolon. We must slaughter them and destroy this structure! Then our march continues."

"For Mednodorn!"

"Draw weapons. We do not know what lies ahead."

Brónmal drew his sword and approached the black church. A double door marked the entrance. It was at least three times higher than him and wholly made of metal. Brónmal was unsure if it had been scorched black or whether the metal itself was black. He grabbed a simple, black handle and pulled. The door was heavy. The soldiers came to his aid, the door groaning loudly as it opened. Inside was pitch black.

Brónmal gestured to the men. "Who has a torch? Anyone?"

"I do, Lord!"

Brónmal pointed to the man with the Flamebow. The man was no soldier like the rest. He was bent, a beard sticking out from under his helm with streaks of gray through it. Perhaps the Mednohail were taking all that they could get nowadays? He stuttered. "L-Light the torch."

The man uttered no words of affirmation or respect and merely lit the torch. Brónmal took it, glared at the man, then marched inside. There was nothing within. The hall they entered was darker than any night Brónmal had ever endured. At first, there were walls, but then they disappeared. No matter where they went, they did not find the walls again. What evil was this place? Surely, it was not this large.

Then, the men began to itch. They whispered, muttered, scratched at their armor, and shivered. Brónmal could hear their teeth click. Then he, too, began to itch. It felt like there were bugs under his armor, small insects crawling around his ears and whispering. They uttered words that he could not fathom. They were unlike any language he had ever heard.

"*Get out of my head, get out of my head, get out of my head!*" he thought, swatting at the sides of his helmet as he felt the insects.

One of the soldiers stumbled as blood started to pour from his nose. "I... I need to leave! Let me out! No!"

He sprinted into the darkness. Brónmal reached out and barked. "Stand your ground!"

The man disappeared before any of them could do anything. Brónmal panted, lowered his hand, and turned to the others. "Stay together!"

The floor began to feel strange. It went from feeling like stone to sand to slippery mud that tried to swallow their boots. One by one, the men began to stop, moaning and crying. Brónmal groaned when he felt his veins burn.

He dropped the torch at the sound of a hoarse, gasping voice. "Lodhur..."

Brónmal shouted. "Who goes there!"

"Lodhur... Bring the page, complete the book."

The man with the Flamebow, seemingly unaffected by the strange sensations that maddened the others, marched into the darkness. Brónmal pointed at him. "You stay here!"

The man disappeared into the darkness. Brónmal grabbed the torch and threw it after him, the darkness receding with a hiss. They had walked in circles. The interior of the structure was cube-like and soulless like the exterior. At the far end was a stone table, emptiness consuming most of the structure. The floor was all stone.

At the table were two figures. One was the man with the Flamebow, helmet now removed to reveal the face of a withered man. It was as if he had aged far faster than what was natural. He had all his hair, though it had streaks of gray. His skin was youthful and spotless yet wrinkled like an old man. He kneeled, presenting a red page. The page did not fold or move like paper but flopped like leather. It had golden letters that had been carved into the page.

The other figure was far more hideous. It was like a man made from a vase. Covering him was clay that slowly fell off, revealing a body made from ash. He inhaled, and all the parts that withered off him returned. He groaned, body sealed fully by clay. Slowly, the clay fell off once more. He had no eyes, staring with hollow sockets. Shirtless, the withering man wore a long, black robe that started at his hips and ended at his ankles. The robe was covered in faded, golden designs. Holes filled it, and a metal belt held it up. The buckle of the belt was diamond-shaped, the metal so rusted that any design it once had was gone.

His voice gasped as if it was dying. "Well done, Lodhur."

Lodhur bowed. "The final page, Chosen One."

Brónmal looked around. The men around him had gone mad. Some ran around, silently screaming and clawing off their armor as if burned. Others lay on the ground, weeping and holding themselves. A few stood still as if paralyzed, their mouths hanging open. Brónmal pointed at the bearded man. "You! Who are you? Traitor to the Empire!"

The bearded man looked over. "I am Lodhur, a man free from the tyranny of the Godspeaker and the Highlord!"

"You are no soldier! How did you sneak into my ranks? How long have you been a snake?"

"For a very long time. We do not need to fight, Brónmal. Soon, you will bow before your true god."

The withering man took the page and placed it into a red book. It was the Skinbook the witch spoke of. A howling groan came from the book as it was completed, the structure rumbling. The burning in Brónmal's veins intensified. He felt the unforgiving darkness the witch had cast him in gradually clawing at his mind. Figments and specks of the shadowy Deothers appeared in the corners and dark places of the church. They stared, appearing and fading away.

"*Daonrex, give me strength!*" Brónmal thought. He charged with his sword, swinging at the ashen man.

The man turned and waved at him. "Prostrate yourself."

Brónmal fell. Darkness came and swept him up, blinding him. He felt himself hit the floor, helpless. He groaned, eyes closing. It felt as if his eyelids were made of steel, impossible to open as he gritted his teeth.

The man spoke, voice hissing and wheezing. "You are strong, Brónmal. You always have been. But there is no need for strength in the coming age, only obedience."

Brónmal groaned. "Who are you?"

"I am Astrophel, the first of the Chosen, once known to your people as the first Accursed."

Brónmal forced his eyes open, weakly blinking, and found himself floating in an infinite darkness. His eyes closed again, and he cried out, "Men! Slaughter this demon!"

"You are alone, Brónmal. Abandoned by mother, abandoned by father, abandoned by the Highlord, Godspeaker, and false gods."

"What do you want?"

"Nothing from you. You have a destiny to fulfill, failure to accomplish, and a home to return to, so you may watch it burn. This book is only the beginning. It is very powerful, created at the beginning of the Reign by the great Arathmalok from the skin of his first servant's family. We will use it to bring the Second Reign."

"Why?"

"For peace, of course. You infidel mongrels, you do nothing but fight. There is no progress, no unity. You are animals, nothing more. You are fortunate that animals can be domesticated, enslaved, made to do larger works that mean more than their insignificant lives."

Brónmal shook his head. "There was no peace in the Reign, only suffering!"

"Lies! Only those who struggle suffer. Look at you. You march into this land under the whim of a foolish tyrant, and for what? To burn it? Why? Because they disagree? Because your people starve? There is plenty of land in Mednodorn. Only chains and whips can cure you of your madness and bloodlust. When you have only stones to move for the Breaker of Man, you will be simple, docile, like a domesticated animal."

"I will not be broken! I am no slave! You lie about peace!"

"You are a slave! If you do not listen, I will show you!"

Brónmal opened his eyes to visions of a past so forgotten that no culture of men remembered it. He saw Mednodorn before the Reign, before the unity of King Peregrine and the Mednohail Empire. Yet, something was different. This land looked like Western Mednodorn but nothing like he remembered.

Astrophel spoke. "Behold the time before the Reign, in western Mednodorn, known to you as Etutakur."

Brónmal's eyes widened. It was green, with rolling hills and beautiful forests, much like the rest of Mednodorn. The vision shifted. He saw villages, towns, and cities dwarfed by even the smallest city in modern Mednodorn. He saw men fight, all waving different banners and wearing different clothes.

"These are the men of the ancient times, the first men. They were all different. None spoke the same language or believed in the same god. They were damned to war until the end of time. Then came Arathmalok."

Brónmal saw clay men, thousands in unison, sweeping over the homes of the first men. They enslaved them, took them in chains, and forced them to build great, brutalistic monuments like the black church.

"The Breaker of Man, the Great Uniter of my time. He conquered the first men, from Etutakur to Heonar, to all the North, and the red desert of the Ahamari. There was no war between men in his time, only peace and order."

Brónmal saw men writing books, building monuments, forging new inventions, and performing magic. He saw progress. As the monuments grew, the cities inflated, and the land became gnarled and twisted by magic. He saw rivers floating in the air, rain falling upward, floating islands, and great plains of thistle-covered grass. The corruption of Etutakur growing like a cancer on the world.

"For six Aothills, Arathmalok lorded over the world. He gave us literacy, taught us architecture, showed us how to use new metals, and we learned magic that revolutionized our world. There was hope and promise. A bright future for all things."

"A future built by a false god! A tyrant!"

"Built by those who were fed, who were in peace! You do nothing but harm with freedom! Soon, you will see. All wars will end, all conflicts resolved, and all will wave the banner of the Great Uniter. I will personally have you tear down the idols of your false gods. It is too late for you to stop us. You are chained to your fate, destined to be broken. Now leave!"

Brónmal blinked, looking around in the black church. The soldiers that had followed him were dead, Astrophel and Lodhur gone. Men of clay tore themselves from the walls as he grabbed his sword and stood. They were stiff, moving machine-like as they approached with spears. They stomped over the corpses of his soldiers, surrounding him.

He swung into one. "Begone demons!"

The blade bounced off the hard body of the living statue. His hand rattled, Brónmal dropping the sword and clenching his hand. The statue swung, Brónmal ducking and grabbing a mace from a dead soldier. He smashed it through the head of a construct, turning to face a group of five. This battle was beyond him.

Brónmal swiped up the sacred sword of the Supreme General before he crashed through the church door and sprinted out into the mud. The constructs stormed after him. They were slower but unstoppable. Brónmal ran into the thicket, bursting through branches and jumping over the roots. The constructs followed, their heavy masses easily crushing through anything that blocked them.

More came out of the swamp. They rose from the ground, emerged from the waters, and tore themselves out of vine cocoons. Monstrous, they were ancient, so old that they seemed to have grown into their environment. Brónmal ducked as one came from behind a tree and swung at him. He smashed his mace through it. Its head shattered, the construct falling to the ground, dead.

Brónmal shouted. "Begone, servants of Dubilfen!"

More came. Brónmal kept sprinting, tearing off his helmet to see better. Was there anywhere to go? No matter where he turned or ran, the constructs kept following. He needed the army.

Brónmal screamed. "Hacarad! Men of the Three!"

Like a storm of bees, Mednohail soldiers rushed out of the fog ahead. "Charge! Protect the Supreme General!"

Dozens of clay constructs crashed into the Mednohail. The constructs were formidable. Blades and spears rang and glanced off them, doing nothing to their hard bodies. Soldiers with maces ran forward. Like enraged ants, they overwhelmed and smashed each construct into pieces.

Hacarad ran up to Brónmal. "Lord! Are you okay?"

Brónmal groaned. "I was a fool! We have a new enemy, and I just gave them the key to victory."

The soldiers cried. "More are coming from the fog!"

Brónmal groaned. "We need to flee this cursed place! Retreat! Hacarad, where is the road?"

Hacarad waved. "This way, Lord!"

Hacarad led them back onto the road. Relieved to have found the path, Brónmal led the army away from the black church and the constructs. Some stayed behind. They kept the living statues at bay, allowing the army to move forward through the swamp.

Brónmal glanced back. "Where is the end of this cursed road!"

Hacarad pointed ahead. "We passed the mountains some time ago. We should be getting to the end."

Brónmal moved faster, the army speeding up after him. More constructs came, meeting the pair and the escort. Brónmal raised his mace. "Swords are useless! Do not damage your weapons on these demons!"

One construct thrust a spear at him. Brónmal moved aside, grabbing it and ramming the mace into the devilish clay. He swung into another, ducking another blow and finishing a third. Soldiers with maces joined him, overwhelming the constructs and smashing them like vases.

Ahead, Brónmal caught a glimpse of light. "Move forward toward the light!"

Like a formidable tide, Brónmal and the soldiers with maces spear-headed their escape. Slowly, the swamp began to open up. Light got through the canopy, trees parted, and a great green plain could be seen ahead. It was morning, the light of the sun guiding their escape.

Like a flood, the army poured from the thick swamp onto the open plain. Brónmal waved. "Get into formation! Protect our men and keep the constructs at bay."

The army kept flooding out, a wall of soldiers holding the constructs at bay until everyone escaped. They retreated backward into the plain. Some of the constructs followed, quickly dispatched by thousands of men. No more came, the swamp calming as the Mednohail menace was driven out.

Brónmal, gasping and sweaty, fell to his knees. He drew his sword, held it before him, and stared. His ancestors' weapon, the Supreme General's divine blade, had failed him. He looked the blade over, his gaze crossing over a chip that had come off. It had been damaged.

Head bowing, he sheathed the sword. He would not use it, not anymore. It was far too sacred to be further destroyed. Brónmal needed to protect it, even in its failure. He closed his eyes.

"Three, thank you for saving me, for bringing my faithful men to my side in my time of need," Brónmal prayed.

While he prayed, the sound of armored boots approached him. Brónmal looked up, his eyes meeting Hacarad's.

Hacarad stared down at Brónmal. "What happened?"

25

The Recruiter

Brónmal and Hacarad strolled by the creek side. Coming into their mid-teens, it was soon time for them to become men. They had grown strong. Good harvests in the last few years had given them the bread, meat, and beer needed to create a soldier's body. Not all things changed with time. Brónmal had bruises and scars. As he grew more muscular, his father became harsher in his training, anticipating the day Brónmal would go to the great fortress of Baradun. Every faithful soldier of Mednodorn was made there, and soon, the pair would join the legions.

Hacarad looked at Brónmal's bruised face. "You okay?"

Brónmal shook his head. "I am fine."

Hacarad frowned. "Training was hard?"

Brónmal sighed. "Trained with a staff to learn how to use spears."

Hacarad shook his head. "Did... You learn anything new?"

"Some stuff. It's really just sharpening my skills. I look forward to going to Baradun."

Hacarad smiled. "Think we will get sent back here after training?"

Brónmal nodded. "Yeah. My dad got sent back home after the war."

Hacarad grabbed a stick and threw it into the river, scaring off some fish. The pair chuckled before Hacarad spoke. "Do you think we will ever fight the Heokolons again?"

Brónmal hummed. "I hope so. Those heathens cannot live with a victory over us. We are righteous. The Three are with us."

Hacarad smiled. "Can you imagine? Us at the castle of their Emperor, sharing a drink while their city burns?"

"Does such glory await us? It did not await Father," Brónmal thought. Despite his doubts, he pictured them sitting at the center of a city. Mugs in hand, they watched as soldiers burned the city and slaughtered its people. A glorious vision. He nodded. "I am not sure that they have castles."

Hacarad shrugged. "We have no idea. They never got past the mountains."

"Oh, can you imagine? Being the first Mednohail to truly march into Heonar? To conquer for the Three?"

"To make the Godspeaker and the Highlord proud."

"To make my father proud."

"I think you should do it for yourself. Your father's failures will be your victories."

"How could I ever walk without his shame?" Brónmal thought. He groaned and rubbed his face. "He says I will be nothing more than a foot soldier."

Hacarad scoffed. "I am the peasant boy here. I will be the foot soldier. Maybe you will be a commander, maybe even a province General one day."

"I hope we stay side by side the whole time. Who could stop a duo like us?"

"Nobody! Not even my angry grandma."

Brónmal snorted. "Your grandma gets displeased when I try to steal her pastries before she bakes them."

"You are so gross! How could you like dough?"

"It's good!"

Hacarad gagged. "Just shut up."

The pair crossed the river and went to Angmere. Home. Brónmal had found peace in this forest. Here, he hid away from his father, which granted the place a sense of freedom and holiness to him. This is where he was normal. For years, the pair had played here secretly, each coming up with clever ways to avoid their families and meet.

Hacarad pointed toward his distant home. "I heard the recruiter is coming today."

"Are they picking up new soldiers today?"

"Low Summer is coming, so they must be."

"Does that mean your older brother is going?"

Hacarad frowned. "I think so."

"You must feel honored. I do not have any siblings to pray for and none to pray for me."

Hacarad stuttered. "I-I am."

"You sound worried?"

"No! I just want him to be safe. I pray to the Three that he will, but I do not think I have to worry. He will go with his friends."

"Two years away for us, can you believe it?"

Hacarad shook his head. "I remember meeting you on the river's side here."

"I remember meeting your family. Do they still believe I am another peasant?"

Hacarad snorted. "Always."

Brónmal smirked. "A little mud in my face and some roughed-up hair works wonders."

"Speaking of which, let us give you your makeup to see if the recruiter has gone. Lose the shoes!"

Brónmal removed his shoes while Hacarad rubbed his dirty hands through Brónmal's hair and smudged his face with dirt. Removing his fancy clothes, Brónmal left himself in an oversized, raggedy shirt and shorts. The look of a peasant boy. His callused feet were like shoes. Following Hacarad, he stomped and ran over the terrain, not bothered by rocks or splinters.

The village of Angmere came into view.

Like many villages, Angmere was part of a vast collection of settlements. The villagers toiled daily, producing crops and children for the Empire. This was their lives, simple and faithful. They believed that, as long as they worked hard, everything would turn out right and that the Empire and the Three would protect them.

They were fragments of the Mednohail system. Hamlets and small settlements paid tribute to Angmere and its elders. Angmere paid tax to a local town named Aosgildath, whose mayor paid taxes to the city of Raothal and its king. Since Raothal was the province capital, all cities in the province and their kings paid their levies to it. Like all province capitals, Raothal paid tribute to Ardmunhaich and its Highlord, supplying wealth for the Empire.

The other village children greeted the pair as they entered. "Brónmal! Hacarad!"

They greeted each other. The peasant kids, like Brónmal and Hacarad, were dirty and ill-clothed. None of them even had shoes.

One of the peasant girls pointed to a road going east. "I heard the recruiter is coming today."

A boy spoke. "I thought that was tomorrow?"

Hacarad shook his head. "No, stupid! Today. Today marks the last week of High Spring!"

Brónmal shushed them. "There he is!"

Over the distant tree-flanked hills came a group of men: the recruiter and his recruits. The recruiter was dressed in noble clothing. He wore bright colors with golden buttons and fine craftsmanship in every weave and stitch. Behind him were recruits, each sixteen years old. They were primarily peasants, dressed in simple clothes with simple boots, still waiting to be handed their first spear.

Unlike the peasant boys, the recruiter had styled hair and a pointed beard. His face was clean, and his teeth decayed from sugary foods. The recruits had unkempt hair and the beginning of facial hair.

The village stirred. People ran and gathered in the village square. Brónmal and Hacarad followed the other children to watch. They were silent. Brónmal stood behind Hacarad, hidden out of view.

The recruiter waved upon entering the square. "Three bless, folk of Angmere!"

The village responded. "Three bless!"

In front of everyone was a line of eight boys, each sixteen. Among them was Hacarad's brother. Part of a small Mednohail family, he was one of six siblings. His parents stood behind with all the other parents, proudly gazing at the recruiter when he rode past.

The man had a sharp eye. He examined them from head to toe, looking for signs of stunted growth. He was picky. Bowed legs, weak backs, and lacking confidence could disqualify a possible recruit. Passion is what the recruiter looked for. He pointed. "You, you, you..."

He skipped two boys only, picking Hacarad's brother, among others. The recruiter looked at the two he did not select. "There is no shame in not being picked. You have next year to be chosen, which is your final year. Mednodorn still needs farmers, but if you want to be picked, I want you two to be stronger and to have a look of fire in your eyes. Be with your families now and cherish them."

The recruiter then rode to the children.

"*Three, hide me,*" Brónmal thought as he ducked backward, trying to avoid the recruiter's gaze.

The man gestured at them. "Look at these proud and strong children!"

The man pointed. "I am proud to see the next generation is even stronger and better than mine. Girls with faith and discipline, boys with strength and zeal! Sons and daughters of the Empire, are you proud to be one of the Mednohail?"

The children shouted. "Yes, Lord!"

The recruiter pointed. Brónmal's heart stopped when the man spoke. "You there, hidden among the others, why do you cower?"

Brónmal stuttered. "I–I..."

"Silence! Come forth."

Brónmal reluctantly walked forward and stood in front of the others. The recruiter squinted. "Raise your head, stand proud."

Instinctively, Brónmal assumed the disciplined stance of a soldier, back straight and head up. The recruiter smiled and looked him over. "You are a strong one. Bruises and scars like that of a fighter. You already have muscles like a man, and your eyes scream with spirit."

The recruiter got off his Auhmog. Brónmal's heart pumped as the man tapped his shoulder and chuckled. "Your father, whoever he is, would be proud. What is your name, boy?"

"Patrudir!"

The recruiter repeated his name. "Patrudir! A good name, a noble name."

The man kneeled and whispered. "I know who you are, Brónmal. You will be better than your father, boy. I know who you are, but I will say nothing. Do us all proud. Be what he failed to be."

Brónmal nodded. "Yes, Lord!"

The recruiter chuckled and stood. "You will be a soldier."

26

The Plains Beyond

Men sat in the fields. Exhausted, muddy, and sweaty, they drank and cleaned themselves off. Wagons were parked everywhere. The Auhmogs were released to graze as the army recovered from the swamp. Many of the men looked dull, as if tired and disheartened. By this time, fields were ripe and being harvested back in Mednodorn. The holiday of the Second Harvest left the men crushed and yearning for home. Brónmal walked among them, barking life into his tired men.

He pointed to the soldiers. "Set up camp! Get everyone rations. Tend to the wounded! I want patrols around camp and scouts sent to the East to see what's ahead! Rebuild the War Carriages!"

Hacarad spoke up. "What happened?"

Brónmal snapped. "Silence! You will come with me."

Hacarad nodded. Brónmal waved for him to follow, staring down at the other soldiers. "Get to it! Move with haste!"

The army fell into organized chaos while the men set up tents, started fires, made food, and carried out Brónmal's command. Orders and shouts filled the air. Brónmal walked away from the camp, Hacarad on his tail. "Lord, why do you keep your thoughts hidden from us?"

"Quiet. Wait until we are out of earshot."

Hacarad narrowed his eyes. Brónmal marched over two hills, leaving the camp behind as they crossed the Heokolon plain. It seemed like home. The

185

plain was grassy with a dream-like green. Though the land was smooth, flowers and rocks popped up amongst the twisting hills. It would all burn well.

Upon a hill stood a lone boulder. Brónmal approached and leaned against it. "We were fools, Hacarad."

"Fools?"

Brónmal nodded. "This war is a fool's errand, and we are the fools leading it. There is nothing here for us but death. We are doomed to do this."

Hacarad scoffed. "What do you mean, Lord? This is our rightful destiny. We are marching toward victory. We have broken the Heokolon armies."

"It is not! The weavings of destiny have been shown to me. The old chief, the witch, even in the black church."

"I lost you in the fog. I blinked, and the very mist itself stole you. What happened? What did you see?"

Brónmal's gaze grew blank. He looked off into nothing as memories of the cursed, black structure filled his mind. He spoke quietly as if his words would offend the wind. "A building of black with architecture colder than stone. It drained the spirit out of me when I set eyes on it. Within? Horror. One of the soldiers was a traitor, a servant of this unknown enemy the Empire has forgotten. And his master? An aberration, a man with skin like clay that fell apart. And within? Ash. He withered constantly, yet reformed as if he could not fall apart."

Hacarad narrowed his eyes. "I have never seen such a creature, not within the borders of Mednodorn or beyond."

"It had power, so much power. Black magic that made me a puppet to it. They completed that strange book the witch mentioned, the Skinbook."

"What does that mean, Brónmal?"

"This enemy we soon face may have already won. They seek to summon in some form of ancient evil."

"And what of the invasion? You say that it is folly?"

"The Heokolons knew we were coming. Do you not see? The first battle was a test we passed. They simply let us through after."

"Did they pull back to their capital, then?"

"I do not know. All I know is that even if it is folly, we must complete this invasion."

"Why?"

"It is worse if we do not. Every battle we win now is necessary."

"Necessary? We are burning men for nothing. We must return to the Empire to defend it."

Brónmal waved. "You fool! We must finish this. First, we deal this blow to the Heokolons and then go home."

Hacarad sighed. "Brónmal, are you sure? Were you told we must do this, or do you want to do this?"

Brónmal shook his head. "We must do this. If we come back against the wishes of the Godspeaker and Highlord, we will be executed for Esadif. Or worse, we will be branded and cast down with the heretics. We must make our fathers proud, then go home and fight for Mednodorn."

Hacarad frowned. "You are right. How did our people lead us into such things?"

Brónmal whispered. "We let men speak for gods."

Hacarad stared. "Even the wisest would not utter those words."

Brónmal furrowed his brow. "And I have spoken them."

Hacarad shook his head. "I listen and speak nothing. What else did you learn?"

"This Skinbook, the traitor, had a page for it. Dubilfen's wickedness, it must be. They said it will bring in the Second Reign."

"The Second Reign?"

Brónmal stared into the distant plain with horror. "The creature, Astrophel he was named, showed me visions of the first Reign."

"What did you see?"

Brónmal felt hollow, as if his will had been drained again as memories returned. He spoke softly: "The first men, before the Reign and King Peregrine, before the wall, when the cursed Western lands were green like the hills of home. They fought—centuries of fighting. Then came the Breaker of Man and the clay men. They broke the first men and built a black empire on the backs of slaves."

"Brónmal?"

"Horror. Horror untold in times of old. The demons of the past are awakening, Hacarad, and I fear they have already won."

"Nonsense! We are Mednohail. We rule this world. These forgotten demons, servants of a forgotten empire, can do nothing. Who else can stand against the Nine Armies, the endless legions of Mednodorn?"

Brónmal lowered his head. "I pray you are right, Hacarad."

A rumble echoed over the land. Brónmal looked upward at a wall of dark clouds rolling in from the South. A storm was coming. Hacarad looked up. "Wonderful, exactly what we need."

"May this pass. Fast," Brónmal muttered.

A man on an Auhmog rode from the camp toward them. "Supreme General!"

Brónmal waited for the man to ride up to them before he spoke. "What is it?"

"The Heokolons sent a messenger to us! He brought a box with the head of one of our scouts. They wish to meet us on the battlefield to the East. They said they will meet us if we do not meet them."

Brónmal clenched his jaw. "Has anyone else returned? What is there to the East?"

"Only one other has returned. He speaks of a village to the East. A mass of Heokolons waits there."

"Have the men ready in a few hours. I want them to be rested yet prepared to march at a moment's notice."

"Yes, Supreme General!"

"Away with you."

The man rode away. Hacarad looked at Brónmal. "It seems the Heokolons wish to test us again?"

"A village with an army? They will be nothing."

"The audacity to send us back a head. They are taunting us."

"Do not worry, Hacarad. I do not stand for such things. I will burn their homes, raze the foundations, and leave not a person living to tell the tale."

"I stand with you, Lord, but what about the men?"

Brónmal squinted. "What about them?"

"We have not stopped marching for two days. We had to fight our way out of the swamp. They are tired, Lord. Are you not? You are not well. I can see it."

Hacarad's words brought Brónmal's attention to his body. Fixating on his hands, he felt them pulse with pain. He had simply ignored his suffering. With his body achy and heavy eyes, it felt as if his head was wrapped with an iron band that squeezed. His tongue was dry, sticking to the roof of his mouth. Grime and sweat caked his body. Armor-heavy, he felt like he carried a pile of rocks on his body rather than the fine Mednohail steel that protected him. Exhausted, the lessons of his father shone through. He ignored weakness.

He scoffed and spoke. "I am well enough to fight. I can sleep when I am dead. The Heokolons force our wrath. We have routed them before; we can do it again."

Hacarad stared back at the army. "Perhaps it is wise to meet them. This plain offers us no advantage, especially being back against that wretched swamp."

Brónmal nodded. "We will crush them. The men are strong, Hacarad; we can do this."

Hacarad raised a hand. "As I said, I will stand by you, Lord."

Brónmal took his hand with a clap, nodding. "And I will stand by you, brother. Three shield us."

27

The Rape of Alterger

Brónmal and Hacarad rode forward to the sign by the road. With a rope, Brónmal led Azra to the sign and pointed. "Read this."

Azra looked the sign over and read. "Alterger, Supreme General."

Brónmal looked up from the sign. Beyond them was a large village that dominated the center of the plains. Distant mountains surrounded the plain, with three openings between the peaks. The swamp was to the west, and in the east were two spots where the mountains dipped.

The village was built in the typical Heokolon style, square homes with sloped roofs that curled into protrusions at their corners. Some were built like trapezoids, starting wide at their foundations and slightly narrowing toward their roofs. In the center was a larger rectangular building with a pyramid-shaped roof. The same Heokolon corner protrusion was seen at the edges of its base at all four edges.

Unlike the homes in the Khagoreti mountains, the village houses were not built from red stone and clay. Instead, they were yellow and white. Brónmal had noticed that the stones in the plains were usually whiter in color, telling a shift in the landscape. They were far from home.

"*What a gift to burn for the Three,*" Brónmal thought and glanced back. Behind the pair were the legions. They were called to fight again after only a few hours of rest. Among them were War Carriages. Though exhausted, the insatiable soldiers were eager to loot, pillage, and burn again. Brónmal

190

spoke. "Azra, what sort of village is this?"

"A farming village. This one is big, so it likely supplies the local city."

"Then it's worth burning."

Azra lowered her head. Tears formed and rolled down her cheeks, knowing she could do nothing to stop the coming onslaught. Brónmal gestured to Hacarad. "I see only a few soldiers."

Hacarad hummed. "And yet they sent us one of our scouts without a head. Perhaps they are fools. Or they wish to die."

Brónmal tilted his head. "No matter. It should only take so long to defeat them. Tell the men to take what they please and kill everyone. We do not need more slaves. Keep an eye out as well. I do not suspect this to be as easy as it looks."

"Very well, Lord."

Hacarad rode off to convey Brónmal's command. Meanwhile, the eight Generals approached Brónmal and waited behind him. Cosalmir of Beinthal spoke first. "Supreme General, is this stop worth our time?"

Brónmal nodded. "The slave says it's a farming center. We burn it, we weaken the Empire. Our men need some fun after marching through that wretched swamp."

Palagrad of Faothal spoke. "Supreme General, you should take a sailor's wisdom. Only a confident predator lures with something that brings courage in the prey."

Maomarad of Peresthal tilted his head. "This is no different from the Stygian Men. There's only a few hundred, I can see from here. They seem more savage than they are, but they are nothing compared to our iron tide."

Brónmal glanced back at them. "Why do my Generals worry about such a small place? The Heokolons have dared us to attack, and we will crush them for their arrogance. We will drink on Heokolon ruins tonight."

The Generals looked at each other and then cheered. "For Mednodorn!'

Brónmal gazed forward. "Ready your men. I want this village burned. I want nothing left."

The Generals together saluted. "Yes, Supreme General!"

"*Is that a sense of trust I find in my Generals? Is this what you once had, father?*

Trust? I will not fail that trust like you. I deliver these Heokolons as a sacrifice to the Three," Brónmal thought.

Thunder rolled in. Overhead, the clouds twisted and churned, releasing their black bowels upon the earth. Rain. It started slowly, ramping up with the wind. This would be a muddy, wet battle. The army came into formation behind him, rows of shields and spears forming a blockade. The War Carriages were in front. Men with Snakebows filled them, occasionally peeking out at the distant village. Hundreds of thousands to destroy hundreds.

Brónmal rode past the front line of his army. The men stared at him, waiting for his command. They were hungry, ready to draw blood. Impatiently, they squeezed their weapons and fidgeted. The Generals rode up to Brónmal. Hacarad joined and spoke. "The men are ready for your command, Lord."

"I want nothing left."

Hacarad nodded. "The men know."

Brónmal rode to the center of the army and drew his mace. "Men of Mednodorn! Do you hunger for battle?"

The men cheered. Brónmal shouted. "Do you hunger for blood? For glory?"

The army cheered once again before Brónmal continued. "Bleed the enemy for the Three! Feed the earth with their blood, give their spirits as sacrifice, blacken the air with ash! Carry out your divine destiny! March forward!"

He led the army forward slowly. While they marched, he shouted. "What do we say to the East?"

The army shouted. "Death to Easterlings!"

"Louder!"

"Death to Easterlings!"

"Louder!"

"Death to Easterlings!"

"Loud enough!"

The army increased its pace. The War Carriages sped up, creaking as they went over rocks and through the mud. Thunder echoed across the land as the rain grew more intense. As the village came into view, Brónmal could see the formation of a few hundred Heokolons outside. Archers stood on the roofs of buildings. Between the formations were wooden spikes, forming bottlenecks that would choke the Mednohail legions. Men screamed. The Heokolons were prepared. Soldiers stumbled on holes and fell into pit traps.

Then, the storm grumbled. Frogs rained down on the plain.

Brónmal looked up, shielding his face from a falling frog. "It's raining frogs!"

Hacarad looked up. "Frog rain?"

"*Dubilfen has cursed us,*" Brónmal thought.

Frogs covered the ground while the storm belched hundreds more onto the armies. Men tripped and fell in holes while falling amphibians knocked out a few soldiers and injured others. The legions stomped over the creatures. Their marching broke the soil, mixing the ground into slick mud.

Brónmal shouted. "No matter! Charge!"

The army crashed forward like an unstoppable tidal wave. The War Carriages led. Heokolon archers pelted them. Each side exchanged arrows and bolts while the magical machines took down archer after archer. Then, the armies collided. Blood sprayed as men screamed, spears piercing one another. Heokolon glass swords clashed with Mednohail axe and mace, shield walls pressing against each other as the two sides tried to plow through one another.

In the fray, frogs hailed down, amphibian and human blood soaking the ground into a muddy, bloody quagmire. For every Heokolon killed, two to three Mednohail paid with their lives. It did not matter. The Mednohail, endless as they were, surrounded the entire village within minutes. Uprooting the spikes, they flooded into the village. The Heokolons retreated between alleys, keeping up their shield walls while they retreated.

Brónmal shouted. "Burn them!"

Men with Flamebows pushed through the horde of soldiers, spraying down the Heokolons with fire. Others burned the houses. The village went up in flames. Not a civilian in sight. They had evacuated, leaving only their defenders behind.

Frenzied from fighting, the Mednohail began to chop down and crush the houses. They smashed walls, tore off doors, and hacked down pillars. Homes collapsed. Fire devoured the rubble, cooking the corpses of frogs, Heokolons, and Mednohail. The Heokolons did not surrender.

Brónmal rode into the town while it collapsed, the Mednohail covering it like termites. Among the alleys and small crevices were the Heokolons, fighting to the death to defend the place. They feared nothing. One by one, dozens of arrows, spears, and maces took them down.

"*I want nothing left—nothing of the Easterling legacy, no reminder of my father's failure, the mistakes of the past,*" Brónmal thought.

The defenders lasted only a short time against the attackers. Brónmal rode around the town, shouting to his men. "Burn it all! Leave nothing!"

Hacarad laughed. "Look at them go!"

Soldiers ran out of homes with whatever valuables they could grab. Those left destroyed the structures, crushing whatever they could until the flames devoured the buildings. In the center of the village sat the building with the pyramid roof. Brónmal rode toward it, watching it as men ran out of the building away from a pile of oil barrels.

A soldier shouted, "Clear the building! Clear the way! Flamebows, light the barrels!'

A pair of men carrying a Flamebow and a fuel tank spewed a cascade of fire at the building. Within, the pile of barrels lit aflame. All the soldiers stumbled back as the fire burst into an explosion, collapsing the structure. Brónmal shielded his face. A wave of dust and debris exploded outward. The crumbling building echoed as stone and wood fell, leaving a vast smoldering pile behind.

Brónmal lowered his shield. "Well done! Burn the rubble! Destroy everything you can!"

A soldier nodded. "Yes, Supreme General! You heard him! Destroy it all!"

Brónmal led his escort and Generals out of the village, riding to a small hill beyond it. A massive pillar of smoke rose from the village. One by one, the houses fell until the Mednohail flattened the entire settlement. It was precisely what Brónmal wished for. Nothing left.

Fire would eat the rest away. The rubble would smolder for hours, leaving nothing but a dent in the ground. Embers and smoke filled the air, frogs crawling everywhere while the rain pounded.

Hacarad smiled. "The work of good Mednohail never ceases to amaze me."

Brónmal chuckled. "This place was called Alterger. Now, it will be forgotten with nothing left."

Hacarad tilted his head. "I think I have already forgotten all about this place."

Brónmal grinned. "Perhaps we should do the same to their capital?"

Hacarad took off his helmet and scratched his chin. "Maybe? What is better, to erase their first city or rename it to something, Mednohail?"

Brónmal chuckled. "Perhaps I should ask the slave? We must erase their identities to help them convert, same with the Throfi."

Hacarad shrugged. "We were fools with the Throfi. The Heokolons deserve nothing less but total brutality in their conversion."

Brónmal hummed. "Perhaps. It is up to the Godspeaker to decide."

Hacarad narrowed his eyes. "Yes, that is true."

Brónmal squinted into the distance. "Do you see that?"

Hacarad urged his Auhmog forward and gazed, mouth agape. "Heokolons!"

Two armies of Heokolons approached from the East. One came from the northern dip in the mountains, another from the South—tens of thousands. They merged, chanting in their strange language.

Brónmal gasped. "Gather the Nine Armies! Battle approaches!"

Hacarad rode off. "Yes, Lord!"

"*Three protect us*," Brónmal thought as the enemy approached. The village was no gift to the Mednohail to burn for fun. It was a lure. With glass glaives and swords, the Heokolons waved the banner of the East without fear.

The Heokolon vengeance had come.

28

The Heokolon Vengeance

"Get into formation!" Brónmal shouted. "Get into formation!"
Thousands of soldiers moved into formation while the Heokolons marched upon them. Each side let loose volleys of arrows into the sky. With the rain of frogs, a grim shadow of death covered the army while arrows hailed down from above. Brónmal pointed. "War Carriages! Move forward! I want men supporting them! Move!"

The War Carriages went forward, Snakebows firing off bolts while soldiers with shields and spears marched after them in formation. Commands and shouting filled the air. The formations moved forward until, just slightly beyond the burned village, the two armies met with weapons of steel and glass.

Brónmal pointed to his escort and Hacarad. "To me!"

The group charged into the fray. The escort closed around Brónmal, shields up and swords weaving through the Heokolon foot soldiers. Arrows hailed down from above. Occasionally, a frog fell from the sky and hit them. Brónmal groaned as his armor absorbed frogs and arrows. He felt arrows ricochet off him, though some penetrated the plate suit and stuck. Caught by the chainmail and padding beneath, he felt their tips press on his skin. The cat-sized frogs were worse. Flying down like rocks, they hit him and rattled his suit. He shrugged off the hits, moving forward with his mace.

Brónmal's vision narrowed. There was nothing around him beyond the unlucky Heokolons that became trapped between him and his escort. He smashed through them. The mace did short work. Heokolon plate cracked under his wrath as he crushed bones and skulls. He ruthlessly beat down each victim, screaming and shouting with every strike.

The opposing armies pushed back and forth. Disciplined and trained far longer than any Mednohail, the Heokolon formations stood firm. The Mednohail fell apart. They fell back on their numbers, using their bodies to overwhelm shields and spears. Many climbed over the Heokolon shield walls, sacrificing their lives to disrupt the formations. This was their glory. Coughing up blood, organs cut out; they died swinging between the Heokolons.

The frog rain let up, and fewer and fewer frogs hit the soldiers. Like plows, the War Carriages pushed through the ranks of Heokolons, bolts firing out everywhere. Some grew too brave. Those that went too far lost the formations of men behind them. Heokolons climbed into the vulnerable War Carriages, slaughtering those inside.

Brónmal shouted. "Push forward! Protect the War Carriages!"

His shouts were not heard. The chaos grew as Flamebows entered the fray. The Heokolons shrieked in horror as fire bathed them. A Heokolon ran past Brónmal, flames eating him alive while he tore off his armor. Brónmal stared, numb to the horror.

Exhaustion slowly sucked the fight out of Brónmal. There were no tactics in the battle, no strategy. It was a meat grinder. The Heokolons had come upon them so fast that they barely had time to get into formation. Heat built up in his armor, sweat-soaked him, and his muscles burned. Brónmal shouted. "To me!"

The escort grew tight around him. Brónmal shouted again. "Hacarad!"

Hacarad approached, blood splattered across his plate armor. "Lord!"

"Where are the Generals?" Brónmal panted. The commanders? We need to envelop their army!"

Hacarad shook his head. "I do not know, Lord! We are pressing forward but losing hundreds for every step!"

Brónmal pointed. "I want the men to protect the Flamebows and War

Carriages! We march forward!"

"Yes, Lord!"

Hacarad ran off and shouted commands. Brónmal huffed and raised his mace, shouting to the men. "Men of Mednodorn! Fear no evil, fear no death, cut them down! Your bodies and spirits belong to Daonrex!"

Those who heard him cheered. "For Mednodorn!"

Brónmal cried out. "What do we think of the Easterlings?"

Some of those who heard shouted. "Death to Easterlings!"

"Louder!"

More joined in. "Death to Easterlings!"

"Louder!"

"Death to Easterlings!"

Soon, the entire army chanted, spears and maces heaving forward. Mednodorn's enraged spirit spurred men through glass and spear. They did not fear pain or death. They fought through their wounds, perishing only after being impaled and cut to pieces.

Brónmal looked up, his eyes drifting to a man in golden armor. He squinted. It was Temkemeletl. The man sat on his beast from afar, overlooking the battle. He seemed sour. His jaw clenched, his eyes narrowed. He was unhappy.

"*Your life is mine,*" Brónmal thought and pointed. "The head of the snake presents itself! Show the Heokolon scum the righteous justice they deserve! Push forward!"

As the frog rain stopped, the chants grew louder. "Death to Easterlings!"

With every chant, the Mednohail pushed forward like an ocean wave. Like a dam, the Heokolon formations cracked. Mednohail pushed between them, fires devouring Heokolon shields and armor while bolts came from everywhere. Thousands of Mednohail lay dead, blood and mud mixing. Yet, the legions kept pushing forward, stepping on the corpses of their comrades as they felled the Heokolons.

Brónmal pointed to the Heokolon General. "Push toward him!"

The escort veered, spears and shields going through the Heokolon line while hundreds of foot soldiers aided them. There was no Mednohail more crazed than those who fought beside Brónmal, each doing everything they could to kill. Fanatical rage made them go berserk. Bodies cut open; they fought until the blood drained from their brains or until they were cut down.

They pushed closer and closer, almost getting through to the archers. Brónmal stared up and made eye contact with Temkemeletl. The pair locked onto each other. Brónmal tore off his helmet. He was dirty, sweaty, and bloody, madness bleeding from his eyes. He stuck out his tongue, laughing like a madman. "I am coming for you!"

Temkemeletl recoiled before he pointed and shouted. Brónmal ducked as arrows flew toward them. A few of the escorts fell. As if a second wind came, Brónmal put on his helmet and charged straight into the fray. Hacarad cried out behind him. "After him! Lay down your lives for your Supreme General!'

Brónmal crushed the skull of one Heokolon and broke the leg of another in a frenzy. Looking up, soldiers surrounded him. Together, they pushed like a spear toward the Heokolon General. The fighting paused for a moment as a horn sounded. It was deep, echoing across the great plain. Brónmal stared at Temkemeletl as he lowered a horn from his mouth. He nodded to Brónmal before he rode away, his army following.

The Heokolons retreated, their army routing, while a few stayed behind to keep the Mednohail at bay. The Mednohail had won. They pushed forward, cornering those that stayed and chasing after those that ran.

The fighting stopped. Brónmal stared as the Heokolons retreated. They had survived, but at what cost?

29

You'll be a Soldier

Brónmal sat on the log and poked into the water with a stick. He felt hollow. His old life was ending. The age of sixteen held salvation. No more brutal training, beatings, trying to escape the estate, nothing. He would soon have a purpose, and his life as a soldier would offer greater freedom.

"*Can this day move any slower?*" Brónmal thought. He felt butterflies in his stomach and bounced his knee incessantly. The minutes crawled past. His escape was mere hours away.

Hacarad skipped rocks on the river while Brónmal sat. "I am so excited."

Brónmal glanced up. "Are you nervous at all?"

Hacarad flexed his arms. "Nervous? Absolutely not. The Three have blessed us to allow us to get so far. Just like my brothers, I will be a proud servant of the Empire! Why? Are you nervous?"

Brónmal shook his head. "I am not. I feel weird, like a free sensation I do not know what to do with."

Hacarad tilted his head. "Free?"

Brónmal nodded. "Free from my father, free from this life. I can move forward and do what I was meant to do. I can be better than him. I just want to leave here as soon as I can. I want to go to Baradun."

Hacarad smiled. "I am glad you get to move on from him. We get to go together too, like brothers."

"Like brothers. I cannot believe we met here by chance six years ago."

"I cannot believe a noble wanted to be friends with a peasant like me."

Brónmal snorted. "Oh, the amount of trouble. Remember stealing Old Fraimada's pies every time she left them to cool?"

Hacarad chuckled. "Remember the time we got caught?"

Brónmal nodded. "She chased us so far into the woods with her broom."

"At least she did not catch us. What if we did that one last time before we left?"

Brónmal shook his head. "She would know, she would know. It would be funny, though. What would she do while we are in Baradun? When we are soldiers? Is that not strange? We are going to be soldiers."

"I cannot believe it either. At least we will not seem like fools there with your training and what you taught me."

"So many months of fighting with sticks here. It is odd to think that was so long ago."

Hacarad sighed. "Felt like yesterday. I am glad you taught me how to fight. Might make the year in Baradun easier."

"There is nothing easy about Baradun. One year outside in all eight seasons, training every day while it rains, snows, or the sun boils us in our armor."

Hacarad scoffed. "Mother did not raise a weakling."

Brónmal chuckled. "I know she did not. She raised a stubborn idiot."

Hacarad shrugged. "If you are gonna be an idiot, you gotta be tough."

Brónmal sighed and rubbed the bridge of his nose. "That's for sure. Remember when you thought you could get rid of a headache by hitting it out of your head?"

"Hey, we don-"

"And so, you hit your head on a tree and knocked yourself out?"

"We do not talk about that!"

Brónmal laughed. "You did it!"

"How do you get rid of your headaches?"

"I do not. I just deal with them."

"Sounds like you are the idiot for not trying."

"Who's the one that ended up with a bruise the size of a boulder on his head?"

"The one with a brain."

Brónmal paused. "Right... You think it's getting time?"

"Time to go home before the recruiter comes?"

"Yeah. Go say bye to your family. I will meet you in the village."

"Alright, come here, noble."

Brónmal chuckled. "Stupid peasant."

The two hugged. They squeezed for a moment, then let each other go and went on their way. Hacarad ran back to Angmere while Brónmal ran back to the estate. His heart fluttered. The surrounding forest, the beams of sunlight piercing the canopy, the birds and the animals, none of it felt real. It was as if he was dreaming.

"My prayers have borne fruit," he thought. His destiny was at hand. His glorious service to Mednodorn, the Three, the Godspeaker, and the people were just within his grasp. If he so pleased, he would never have to see his father again.

The walls of the estate came into view. Taking the same way as always, he leaped inside the small compound and walked to the front. His father's voice echoed as soon as he passed the front of the house. "Where have you been, boy?"

Brónmal flinched. "The forest, Lord."

Remtaich, dressed in a fancy set of clothes, approached. They were red, a color many of the first war veterans wore on important occasions. He had a tunic parted in the middle by his hips into two tails with a golden, puffy belt around his lower waist. The tunic, made from a fabric harvested in Arn'eketh, had been made by Ahamari slaves. He wore no jewelry yet had black leather boots lined with silver. Wealth to stomp the peasantry. He stared hard at Brónmal. "You are more disciplined than that. Go get ready for the recruiter. I will not have my son stink of the forest. Go!"

* * *

Brónmal walked the halls of his childhood home. Every inch held a memory of pain. Visions of his mother haunted him. His father had beaten or yelled at him in every part of the home, making it a living hell. How could Brónmal think of anything else? There were glimpses of positive memories, yet none included his father. The place was a cage of nightmares, a prison for his whole life.

"*Can I do better than you, father?*" he thought. Could he do what his father raised him to do? Could he be better? Brónmal shook his head. Of course, he could. Remtaich was a failure and lived a life of shame. Many praised him, but some were present for his failure and the failure of others on the plains of Heonar. One day, Brónmal knew he would get further.

The slaves dressed Brónmal in blue clothes. Unlike his father, he wore a simple blue shirt and a vest embroidered with yellow fabric. The shirt ended in a split skirt that stopped by his knees, hanging over a white pair of pants that went into black boots. His hair was done, his body was cleaned, and a fresh smell followed him. He would undoubtedly stand out from the peasantry. Still, Baradun made all equal, even nobles and peasants. Slowly, he left the home and went to Remtaich.

An Auhmog waited for Brónmal. He hopped onto it, his father glaring before he rode. "I pray we are not late because of your little shenanigans."

"*Soon, I will hear no more from you,*" Brónmal thought and remained silent. They rode out of the estate and onto the path to Angmere. Such a familiar path. They had taken it many times. Once, there was a time when the road made his stomach turn. He feared being tied to his father in public. Now, he was relieved. It was the last ride he would ever have to take with his father.

They came to the village faster than Brónmal expected. It was surreal. The town already stirred as families presented their sons in a line in the village square. People chattered and spoke, waiting for the recruiter. When the pair rode into the square, the villagers bowed and cheered Remtaich's name.

Remtaich waved, then got off his Auhmog. Brónmal joined him, Remtaich leading him to the line of young boys. This year, the village had eight ready to go to Baradun, including Hacarad. Hacarad smiled at Brónmal, the pair nodding at each other as Brónmal joined the line.

While they waited, Remtaich stood behind Brónmal with the rest of the parents. Time slowed. The recruiter could not come soon enough. Brónmal's hands shook, his stomach dropped, and his palms became sweaty. Then he saw him. The recruiter rode over the same hill he did yearly, a trail of recruited sixteen-year-olds behind him.

The recruiter waved upon entering the square. "Three bless, folk of Angmere!"

The village responded. "Three bless!"

"May I be worthy. May the Three guide me, and may I honor them in humble service to the Empire," Brónmal prayed.

The recruiter wasted no time. He rode past the line of boys and examined each. This time, he said nothing while he passed each boy before riding to the center of the square. "I feel blessed this day by the Three to be in the presence of such a fine generation. No year has ever presented me with such strong young men. There is passion in all your eyes!"

The village cheered. The recruiter spoke again. "I have high hopes for you boys. Say goodbye to your families, then come with me."

Brónmal dropped his head back with relief, eyes closed and a smile crossing his face. His happiness filled his body, only to evaporate a moment later. Remtaich grabbed and pulled Brónmal away, though he was not rough this time. He took him away from the villagers and then spoke calmly. "We finally part, boy."

Brónmal said nothing. Remtaich let out a slow sigh and shook his head. "I am proud of you. I have worked hard to raise a faithful young man with courage and discipline. I am sorry I had to raise you like this. This world is hard, and it will break the weak. I want the best for you. I want you to succeed, go further than I did, and not bear my shame. I did what I did out of love."

Brónmal whispered. "You do not love me."

"What did you say?"

Brónmal stared, cold and unmoving. He had no words.

Remtaich's face wrinkled as he became red. He clenched his fists, only unballing them as the recruiter approached. "It is time to go, Brónmal."

Brónmal turned and walked away, joining Hacarad with the other boys. As he walked away, he heard the two men exchange words.

The recruiter spoke. "Is that regret, Remtaich?"

Remtaich spat. "I would watch your words."

"I do not fear a failure like you, Remtaich. You might have fooled these village folk into thinking you are a hero, but I know who you are. Your son will replace you. One day, his name will make yours forgotten."

"You–!"

"Save your words. I must be going. The better generation awaits."

30

The March to Nasalohotehr

The battle had been a disaster. The army had lost a fraction of its men to death and injury, leaving six hundred thousand left to fight. Worse still, High Autumn gradually ended, with Low and High Winter around the corner. Supplies and soldiers dwindling, the Mednohail felt dispirited. Brónmal's arrogance tormented him. He thought he could face the broken Heokolon armies on even ground. He gritted his teeth throughout the morning. Rage and shame mixed into a concoction in his head. The Heokolons did have fight left in them. And worse, a battle on even ground proved deadly. How, then, could they assault the central city of the Heokolon Empire?

Stubborn and zealous, they refused to go back. The army rested for two days before being rallied and packing the camp. The marching resumed. They would not turn around. Brónmal and many others refused to face the same shame as their forefathers. Death was better.

The Heokolon land shifted between swamps, plains, and slender peaks with rare plateaus among them. The army followed a stone path. The path twisted and turned, guiding them between great valleys as it followed the plains eastward into the heart of Heonar.

The first hints of Low Winter's approach had arrived. A steady, chill breeze danced along the hills and grass of the plains. The leaves of trees had begun to change, slightly yellowing and soon to die. Heonar was much different than Mednodorn. Brónmal recalled that the leaves would be in deep colors of red and purple by now back home. Clouds became more and more present, gray skies and rains awaiting them. When it rained, it was bitter, cold, and muddy.

Brónmal rode with a soured frown. The army followed. They left the plains behind and passed between mountains and through valleys. Hacarad rode up beside him. "Are you well, Lord?"

Brónmal shook his head. "No. I fear for us."

Hacarad tilted his head. "What do you mean?"

Brónmal glanced back at the army. "We have lost so many, and we will lose many more. How do we know we will live? The old chief in the Marcoili forest said that we would not conquer Heonar."

Hacarad scoffed. "We are Mednohail. Nothing can stop us as long as we are ready to lay down our lives for gods and country. Can the Heokolons say the same?"

Brónmal shrugged. "I do not think Heokolons fear death, either. I just feel shame. If we do not conquer Heonar, are we not better than our forefathers?"

Hacarad sighed. "Your father still gets to you. Remember how far west his defeat was? He did not even pass the Khagoreti Mountains. Our fathers failed to burn the plains and were pushed back over the river. They could not ever dream of marching so far into Heonar."

Brónmal nodded. "You are right. I still have victory over that old bastard, but I only wish I could bring the head of the Emperor back to truly show him."

Hacarad chuckled. "You can always hang over him that you became the General of Beinthal and the Supreme General of Mednodorn. He was only a commander."

Brónmal smiled. "You are right. At least I will always outrank him."

"Just remember, if you told him to fall on his sword, he would have to. Disobeying you is Esadif."

"Maybe I should go back and make him do that?"

"Let us finish the invasion first."

"You are right. Where is that slave? Azra? I wish to speak with her."

"I can fetch her."

"Do so."

Hacarad rode back into the line. Brónmal stared off into the nothingness, thoughts enveloping him as he waited. Was he a failure? His dreams of marching through the streets of Ardmunhaich with the head of the dead Heokolon Emperor seemed so distant. Dread filled him. What did the future hold? What burden would he carry if he lived?

A few minutes passed before the translator slave was dragged to Brónmal. Hacarad handed him a rope attached to a collar around her neck. Covered in rags, her hands were bound. Brónmal waved. "Thank you. March with the others. I wish to speak alone."

Hacarad nodded and joined the Generals. Brónmal looked down at Azra. "You have always been a strange one. How does a Heokolon know Medno-hail?"

The woman remained silent. Brónmal tugged on the rope. "Speak!"

She gasped, then spoke quietly. "My village used to trade with some of the villages across the river."

Brónmal narrowed his eyes. "That is forbidden."

"For Mednohail, yet some did it anyway. They favored what we could provide, and we favored what they could provide."

"Were you some merchant girl?"

She nodded. "My father was known throughout the western plains. I was to take his place."

Brónmal chuckled. "I am glad we burned your home, then. Seems I stopped a smuggling market."

She looked down, growing silent. Brónmal tugged again. "Do not be sad. I gave you a greater purpose, serving as a tool for the greatest empire in history."

"Why do you do this?"

Brónmal furrowed his brow. "Do what?"

"Why do you kill? Burn my home? So much destruction."

"We are leading Heonar into the light. First, we stamp out those who resist, then gently lead those who will listen into the embrace of the Three."

"You kill for your gods?"

"I kill for many things. It is our Daodamath, our divine destiny, to rule all over the world and shepherd all pagans and heathens into the one true belief."

"How do you know it's true?"

Brónmal stuttered. "B-Because it is. It is a pure belief, a holy belief, one with righteousness and grace."

"Because you were told?"

Brónmal harshly tugged the leash. "Silence! I will not be questioned in such a manner by a mongrel Heokolon."

She lowered her head again and did not speak. Brónmal continued riding, jaw clenched. "Bitch."

The land shifted from valleys between mountains into another great plain. In the center was a monolithic, lone mountain. At its roots sat a village, smaller than the village of Alterger. As they approached, they saw no one. Brónmal glanced back. "Hacarad!"

"Yes, Lord!"

"Send scouts to check out the village."

"Right away!"

Scouts went out from the army, heading toward the village. Within only half an hour, they returned. Nothing. No one remained. Brónmal gestured and marched forward with the army. There must be something left to take.

As they approached, the soldiers muttered in horror. The mountain itself had a stair wrapped around it. Along the stairs were thousands of rectangular holes carved into the mountain, each occupied by a corpse. Birds and bugs covered the mountain, picking at the bodies in the open holes.

Brónmal whispered. "What is this place?"

Azra looked up. "Vy'hoga, a death mountain. The village you see is a Vy'hogon, a death village that takes care of the mountain."

Brónmal looked down. "Death mountain?"

"It is part of Vy'hogul, the mountain burial. We Heokolons do not bury or burn our dead. Instead, we offer them back to the universe and the world. All the energy we take during our lives is returned in death, including our bodies."

Brónmal scowled. "How wretched. You leave your dead out to rot? To be fed on?"

"We live, and we take. We die, and we give back. Is feeding the world upon our passing and sustaining others wrong?"

"Savages."

"Savages? What do Mednohail do with their dead?"

"We mummify our dead in salt and put them in death altars in or outside our homes. We preserve the dead so they may stay with us longer, so we can remember them, grieve, and say goodbye. They also remind us of our mortality and our sins."

"Your dead remain? What do you do with the mummies?"

"Once another family member dies, the mummy is buried and replaced by the newly dead."

Azra's brow wrinkled. "Strange idea to keep the dead around with the family. They are gone. There is nothing else to do."

Brónmal glared. "They are family, even dead. Once they are buried, they pass onto the Three for judgment."

"You deny them an afterlife, then?"

"No, they simply remain with us until burial."

"I would rather me and my body pass on."

"That is where we differ, Heokolon."

The two grew silent. Brónmal watched from afar while the army went through the village and looted it. The men found some jewels and valuables. The town mostly held tools for dealing with the dead: things to clean, things to remove, and more. Soldiers avoided the mountain, disgusted and fearful of the idea of a pagan burial ground.

They did not even light fires. They took what they could and left, leaving the village alone. Eventually, the army marched once again. Brónmal waited while the army started marching. With hundreds of thousands, it took hours to pass through anywhere. His escort and Hacarad awaited as he stared upon the mountain.

Brónmal looked down. "Is this where all the dead in Heonar go?"

Azra shook her head. "No, there are dozens across the Empire. They are sacred sites, ancient and holy."

Brónmal tilted his head. "What makes them so special? How ancient are they?"

Azra narrowed her eyes as she gazed at the mountain. "Often, they are the places of ancient cities, places from ancient days before the Reign."

Brónmal looked up and across the plains surrounding the lonely Vy'hoga. He saw nothing but grass. "Where is the ancient city for this place then?"

"Long forgotten, devoured by the earth and time."

"For the best," he thought. It was better for these ancient relics to be gone, soon to be forgotten as the Mednohail tore apart Heokolon culture. It would be easier for them if they simply forsook their identity, something that the Throfi would learn, too. Who could resist the Mednohail's Daodamath? None.

"Why do you bring your dead to such a place? Why a mountain? Why would a city once be built around here?"

"The mountain rises toward heaven. It is a step into the universe, the stairway that carries the energy of our lives back to be recycled. The village is here to maintain the mountain and keep it clean for the dead. Do the Mednohail not have the same? Who takes care of the dead in the West?"

Brónmal squinted back at the army, staring at the wagons ridden by death priests who brought the dead home. He pointed. "They do."

Azra looked back. "Who are they?"

"They are the servants of the Three tasked with the mortal job of taking care of bodies. While the Three take care of the spirit, they take care of the remnants."

"What is their place of work?"

"Death churches. Often, cities will have a church with salt pools to mummify our dead. The death priests will live in these churches and ride across Mednodorn to collect the dead, usually after High Winter and High Summer."

Azra frowned. "They sound like sad places. Confined, like stone boxes, not free like the wind-swept Vy'hogar."

Brónmal shook his head. "There is no sadness in death, only in sin."

Azra looked at him. "How could you live lives consumed with such fear as sin? There is only good in accepting the universe and striving for order despite surrendering to chaos."

"Is it a life of fear, or is it a life of virtue? Virtue which you lack."

"And who are you to decide what is virtuous and what is not?"

"I am not the one who decides. It is up to the Three; their divine word is above all."

Azra lowered her head. "As you were told."

Brónmal narrowed his eyes. "Be silent. Your attitude will cost you your tongue if you speak more. Come, it is time we leave this cursed place."

He turned and rode out with the rest of the army, Azra following him along with the rest of the escort. They left the grave mountain, departing further into the unknown bowels of the East. Nasalohotehr awaited.

31

The Doorstep of Nasalohotehr

L ow Winter set in. The army marched forward, cold and hungry. The journey's end brought hardship, with most of their supplies diminished. Morale choked. Despite their fading spirits, they drew closer to their destination. The Mednohail swept through Heonar like a scythe. They pillaged villages, taking food, livestock, and slaves from every place they demolished. Conquest sustained them. Each village gave them the supplies needed to keep marching.

The Mednohail erased what they attacked. Villages with living, breathing histories were turned into piles of rubble. The cultures and families of these villages were annihilated. Nothing would stand in the way of the steel fist of the West. They were a scourge. Even after the disaster at Alterger, the army was so massive that they scarred the land with millions of footsteps. The ground was stepped into mud, leaving a scar of burned villages and torn-up land.

Brónmal sighed. "A winter in Heonar, how wretched."

Hacarad shrugged. "Is it any worse than a summer? We can always warm ourselves with Heokolon homes. Plenty of firewood."

Brónmal chuckled. "We cannot burn the whole country."

"Why not? There's plenty to burn."

"Well, I guess we could make space for Mednohail to replace them."

"Exactly."

Brónmal's gaze scoured the surrounding mountains. "We are going into more mountains."

Hacarad sighed. "Mountains this, mountains that. Reminds me of the North."

Brónmal chuckled. "You miss the Throfi?"

Hacarad shrugged. "Pagans are pagans. Weird lands are weird lands."

Brónmal tilted his head. "I just wonder where the pagans are hiding. Did we defeat the last army of the Heokolons? Or is there something worse waiting?"

Hacarad shook his head. "You will curse us with your words. I assume they have pulled back to defend their capital."

"I guess we would do the same."

"Absolutely. The safety of Ardmunhaich is above all other cities. We could never let the holy city of King Peregrine fall."

Brónmal nodded. "Azra told me that Nas... Nasalohotehr? Strange name."

"Right? I hate their language."

"As do I. As I was saying, she told me that the city was the city built by the first Heokolon emperor, Otev."

"How can a first emperor be so special?"

"Azra told me that Otev brought their god Vishil to the Heokolon people and united Heonar."

Hacarad scoffed. "And that is why their belief is false. We do not have stories of the Three being brought to us, but the Three making us."

Brónmal nodded. "Certainly, a demon of Dubilfen revealed itself to Otev and tricked him."

Hacarad shrugged. "How can we blame the ignorant? We will teach them."

"In time."

While the army marched, the two conversed. The land shifted. Ascending from a great plain into peaks, they entered another mountain range. These mountains grew dense, like the Khagoreti Mountains they had marched through so many months ago. The trees closed in. Even in Low Winter, with leaves changing and muggy, cold air, the mountains felt like a jungle. Fog settled on the mountain. It was difficult to see anything and impossible to hear for an ambush over the sounds of Heokolon birds.

Brónmal looked around, his spine tingling. "Wonderful..."

Hacarad glanced at Brónmal. "Think we should armor up?"

Brónmal shook his head. "Let us just get the escort to surround us."

He snapped and whistled. The escort—those who had survived—surrounded the pair. The jungle surrounding the road grew tighter and tighter until Brónmal glimpsed light. They rode forward.

The trees opened out into a gigantic basin within the mountains. Like a great fence, the mountain range wrapped around the basin. For at least a mile, there were plains filled with farmland, and beyond that were three grand peaks in the middle of the basin. The most prominent and central peak bore a city. The city of Nasalohotehr. It straddled the mountain, homes built on plateaus along it, while a great wall snaked like a skirt at the bottom of the city. A monumental stair ascended from the basin to the wall's gate. With Low Winter, the farmland had been harvested, leaving it barren. Thousands of homes were on the plain, yet no one occupied them.

Brónmal looked up at the city, mouth agape. "We made it."

Hacarad laughed. "By the Three! The heathen hive of Heonar itself!"

Brónmal drew his mace and pointed it forward, leading the army into the basin. As they marched, they formed formations. They became wider and wider until they spanned the width of the basin. Brónmal shouted. "What do we think of Easterlings?"

The army chanted. "Death to Easterlings!"

"Louder!"

"Death to Easterlings!"

The chant echoed off every mountain around the basin. The Mednohail announced their arrival proudly. Dust kicked up while they marched toward the city. They crossed the basin and stopped at the base of the grand stairs ascending into the city. Brónmal squinted up. Hundreds of archers manned the walls, the gates sealed.

Among the archers stood Temkemeletl. The Heokolon General glared down at Brónmal as if his stare would drive the Mednohail out of the Empire. Brónmal looked back and snapped. "Fetch the translator."

Within a few moments, Azra was dragged to Brónmal. He got off his

Auhmog and pulled her a few steps up the stairs, shoving her forward in front of him. "Translate loudly, slave."

Azra nodded. Brónmal spoke. "Cowardly Heokolons! Open your gates and face the might of Mednodorn! Your deaths will be swift and merciful!"

Azra translated, yet her words were met with no response. Brónmal looked up along the wall, then continued speaking. "Why do the mighty Heokolons cower behind their walls? You dare not face us on the battlefield, men to men!"

Brónmal watched Temkemeletl point down at the Mednohail. An arrow fell from the sky and landed before Brónmal. There would be no talk, no face-to-face battle. Brónmal spat on the ground and led Azra back to the army. Hacarad and the Generals approached.

Hacarad spoke. "What are you thinking, Lord?"

Brónmal glanced back. "Set up a siege camp. I want the city fully surrounded, no one in, no one out. I want scouts checking for any Heokolon armies or surprise attacks. We have them cornered. All we must do is wait and try to find a crack."

Hacarad nodded. "Yes, Lord."

Brónmal looked among his Generals. "We have come this far. I will not be defeated here at the throat of the Heokolon Empire. That city will burn."

The Generals raised their fists. "Praise Brónmal! Glory to Mednodorn!"

32

The Stranger

High Winter arrived. Day in and day out, the Mednohail held their siege. Now and then, they stormed the walls. They tried to climb in with ladders or break the gates, yet nothing worked. As the days rolled into weeks, snowstorms blanketed the land while it grew colder. The humid, wet air of Heonar created a raw cold. It pierced clothing and went into the bones. Thousands died of sickness, starvation, and frostbite. The Mednohail kept fires going all day, chopping the land barren and demolishing the farmhouses of the basin for fuel.

Another day, another battle. From the third peak outside the city, Brónmal watched from a plateau. They had set up the commander's tent to watch over the battle, and from there, they watched every plan and attempt to break into the city fail. Brónmal and his Generals had no idea how to besiege a city on a mountain.

Brónmal and Hacarad sat on chairs and watched while a formation of men with shields and ladders marched up the stairs. It was pointless. The Mednohail had nothing to break the gates in. The War Carriages could not go up the stairs, which left them with nothing but attempts to scale the walls. Brónmal squinted at the gates. They were gigantic and made of thick metal. Explosive barrels of oil did nothing.

Hacarad sighed. "Two months of this. Why do we even bother? Can we not starve them out?"

Brónmal shook his head. "We could, but it will take how long? If Ardmunhaich was besieged, it would take at least three years to starve us out. The Heokolons are not fools."

Hacarad leaned his head back. "We are the fools. We should have come prepared with something. Catapults!"

Brónmal shook his head. "The War Carriages were a hassle to carry through the mountains. Imagine catapults."

Hacarad groaned and stood. "I need beer."

"Bring me one."

Hacarad entered the commander's tent and emerged with a flask and two cups. He poured one for Brónmal and then for himself. "I wonder how many other Heokolon cities are like this?"

Brónmal shrugged. "If they are anything like us, most of them probably. Raothal took them everything."

"I wonder if we have truly defeated most of their army or if they have more."

Brónmal pointed. "By all the Three, I pray all that remains is within that city."

A voice shouted. "Supreme General!"

The pair turned to see a tired and sweaty soldier stumble toward them. "Supreme General!"

Brónmal stood. "What is it?"

"We have captured another Heokolon that can speak Mednohail!"

Brónmal recoiled. "What?"

"An old man! We found him walking toward the city from the North. He speaks Mednohail and said he wishes to speak with you!"

Hacarad and Brónmal exchanged looks before Brónmal nodded. "Bring him here."

The man ran away. Hacarad narrowed his eyes. "Another Heokolon like Azra? This far East? I doubt it. Could be a spy, a traitor, something."

Brónmal waved his hand. "I do not fear an assassin. Perhaps he will tell us something interesting."

"We will see."

They waited thirty minutes before two of Brónmal's escort brought the Heokolon to his feet. Their spears pointed at the man's neck, ready to pierce at any moment. Brónmal examined the Heokolon. He was like any Heokolon. His skin was pale greenish, his eyes golden, his teeth square, and his head hairless. He was old. His face had deep wrinkles, skin covered in spots, and decayed teeth.

Slowly, he bowed. "Three bless, Supreme General."

"*Another Easterling wretch,*" Brónmal thought. He leaned forward on his chair and stared at the man. "Who are you? What does a Heokolon that speaks my tongue want with me?"

"My name is Koakrysar, but you can call me Koa. I am looking to help the Mednohail."

Brónmal raised a brow. "Help us?"

"Yes. I would like to help you cut the head off the Emperor."

Hacarad snorted. "And how can an old man like you help us?"

While the trio spoke, Mednohail soldiers died to Heokolon arrows. The man feebly pointed at the city's gate. "By opening that."

Brónmal glanced back and then gestured to the two bodyguards. "Did you check him for weapons?"

The two men nodded. Brónmal waved, the pair lowering their spears. "Why do you want to help us, Koa?"

Koa hummed. "I have lived a very long life and no longer fear death or persecution. I fear dying, knowing I could have done more."

Brónmal scowled. "Be clear, Heokolon, or I will have you tossed off this cliff."

Koa raised his hands. "My apologies, blessed one. I do not agree with the current emperor. He is a tyrant who believes he can speak for Vishil, a man who believes he can speak for a god."

"*So even Heokolons can agree with me?*" Brónmal thought and narrowed his eyes. He, too, did not believe men could speak for gods. For the first time in his life, he held some semblance of respect for a Heokolon. "So, you wish for us to cut off his head? And then what? Replace him with a new emperor? We do not come to free Heonar from any sort of tyranny. We come to save it from its sin and its demonic god."

Koa shook his head. "I will not be around for those things. Perhaps my people will cast you out from our land. Perhaps you will conquer it and be new tyrants, but I hope the current emperor will be displaced. Men cannot speak for a god, and men cannot be gods. It is only right."

Brónmal squinted. "Very well. Get my Generals!"

* * *

General Baufrius of Eidthal scoffed. An older Northerner with the same reddish hue of brown hair as Cosalmir, he was the only General beyond Cosalmir and Trudamal that Brónmal respected. He was an amputee. Caught in a snowstorm years ago in the Northlands, he had survived the loss of a few fingers, his right foot, and some of his toes on his left foot. A metal boot replaced his right foot, a symbol of his fortitude. He pointed at Koa. "And how could we trust a Heokolon?"

General Cosalmir of Beinthal slammed the table in the center of the tent. "What choice do we have? We lose men daily, and we gain nothing for it!"

An argument broke out among the men, with some proposing to throw Koa from the cliff outside the tent and others advocating to trust him. Brónmal shouted in frustration. "I will have you all thrown from the cliff if you do not silence yourselves! I am tired of bickering! What is the worst that can happen? We die? The siege continues going nowhere?"

Hacarad nodded. "I do not fear the poisonous words of a Heokolon. If he turns out to be false, to be a trickster, I will be the first to cut off his head."

Half of the Generals cheered. Brónmal sighed. "Speak, Koa, tell us how you can help."

Koa stepped forward, two guards with spears ready to pierce him. He flinched, then spoke carefully. "I know the city better than most. Even Temkemeletl does not know of this ancient city's many secret passages and places. The mountain Nasalohotehr is built upon is Mount Tehkemoreti, one of the three sisters. Within it are many tunnels. Some are more secret than others."

Palagrad of Faothal growled, his sailor's patience thin from months on land. "Get on with it!"

Koa nodded. "There is one tunnel high up on the mountain's Eastern side. If we can open it, you can enter the city directly and open the gate from within."

Cangramal of Reinthal spoke, his history of attempts on his life shining through his words. "And how can we trust a strange tunnel not to be filled with Heokolon soldiers?"

Koa shrugged. "I cannot reassure you of that. I can only tell you that no soul in the city knows of the tunnel. Would you rather throw your bodies against the gate and hope it opens?"

Hacarad spoke. "If we must take a tunnel, I will take a tunnel."

Brónmal nodded. "It is better than nothing. You men will bring you and your escorts with me to this tunnel. Together, we will break into the city and open the gate. Cosalmir?"

Cosalmir nodded. "Yes, Supreme General?"

Brónmal pointed. "You will remain and lead the charge through the gates."

Cosalmir bowed. "It is an honor, Supreme General."

Koa raised a finger. "We cannot take too many through the tunnels, and the Heokolons cannot see us."

Brónmal tilted his head. "How many can be taken?"

Koa hummed. "Fifty men can be snuck past as long as their attention is focused on the gate."

Brónmal narrowed his eyes. "That can be done. Let it be known, Koa, if you deceive us, I will have Hacarad cut you to pieces."

Koa nodded. "Understood, Supreme General."

33

Mount Tehkemoreti

The night rolled in, and with it came winter's wrath. A cold, bitter wind blew through the Heokolon mountains, bringing snow down with it. Even in full armor, Brónmal shivered—just what his father had trained him for. The sounds of war echoed through the night as the Mednohail onslaught continued. Men fought and died at the gates of Nasalohotehr while the party of fifty snuck around the wall.

In the darkness, they were not seen. Brónmal, Hacarad, four of the Generals, and their escorts followed Koa as they ascended the steep mountain. Unlike many of the roads in Heonar, no one took care of this one. The path was ancient. The stones were overgrown with lichen and so worn that they blended in with the terrain. It inconsistently rose. Sometimes, there were flat stretches. Other times, the men crawled up steep inclines. With every step, the storm grew worse.

"*Three hide us from sight, and may we not be cast off this mountain,*" Brónmal prayed. Shivering, he spoke quietly. "How far is it, Koa?"

Koa glanced back. "We must climb high to where the birds rest. Do not worry. It will not take us long."

Brónmal sighed, cold, condensed air coming from his helmet. "I see. How do you know about this path?"

Koa replied. "I was a young boy when I discovered it. I lived on the farms below and loved to climb the mountain. We often dared each other to see who could climb the highest. One day, I found the path hidden among the rocks, amongst the birds. It was a wonderful place, secluded, untouched for hundreds of years. I did not even tell my friends about it."

Brónmal persisted. "Among the birds?"

Koa nodded. "The birds will nest high on the mountain to avoid other animals climbing up and eating their eggs."

"You mean the terrain is going to be steep and dangerous?"

"It will, but I know the safest way."

"We better get there in one piece."

"We will."

Brónmal lagged back slightly, Hacarad walking up beside him. "Do you trust this Heokolon, Brónmal?"

Brónmal shook his head. "I do not trust any Heokolon."

Hacarad looked down at the steep fall on their right. "I cannot see anything with this blizzard. This path is far too dangerous."

Brónmal stared forward. "Stay steady on your feet, and you will not fall."

Hacarad chuckled. "Imagine if I did. The great Hacarad, the companion of Brónmal, slips off a mountain."

Brónmal shook his head. "The great Hacarad better not. You are the only one I trust. The ones behind us are fools, and the one in front of us is a heathen."

Hacarad nodded. "Their usefulness wanes, but soon all will be over."

"I only pray the Heokolons break and surrender at the death of their emperor and the destruction of this wretched city."

Hacarad shrugged. "I am always willing to burn another city."

The party marched, climbed, and crawled up the mountain as it grew steeper and steeper. Eventually, the cliff they climbed grew smaller. The sheer drop drew nearer and nearer until they had to slide along the mountainside. Brónmal's heart pounded. Heights did not scare him, but he was not a fool. The path was slippery, the winds blew, and it felt like he could fall at any moment.

"*Save me from being cast off this wretched mountain, Daonrex,*" Brónmal thought.

Then, the path widened. The slippery rocks opened into a small plateau that barely fit all the men. They packed together, holding onto each other out of fear. Koa stood against the rock face. He trailed his hands along the wall, whispering as he scratched off lichen and dust.

Brónmal rested his hand on the hilt of his mace. "You said there was a path here hidden among the rocks?"

Koa glanced back. "Did I? Sorry, I meant a door. Stand back."

"*What treachery is this?*" Brónmal thought.

Koa opened his palms. Black energy flowed from his fingers. The energy seeped out like wisps of smoke. As more came, it condensed, soon growing into a thrashing pair of tendrils from each hand adorned with writhing branches. It convulsed and throbbed, penetrating the stone in front of him. Brónmal recoiled. This was not Anhanka's purple energy. The surrounding men muttered, scared and enraged by the sight of magic.

"Fos taotua," Koa whispered.

The wall shook. A circular slab rotated in the wall, lit with dark symbols and inscriptions. It turned, clicked as if unlocking, and fell backward into a dark tunnel with a loud thud. Koa gestured. "This way. Light some torches."

A few who carried torches, Hacarad among them, lit them and brought them into the tunnel. Brónmal led, following Koa with a hand rested on his mace. The tunnel was pitch black. The stone path within was composed of carved stone that seemed flawless. There was a strange musk in the tunnel. It was as if the air in here had been untouched for ages.

Brónmal glanced back while the men entered. The winds howled outside, the icy breeze following them into the mountain. Hacarad spoke. "What is this place?"

Koa shushed them. "These tunnels are ancient. They were constructed many Aothills ago and have not been opened for a long time. There are traps here, everywhere."

Brónmal narrowed his eyes. "How do you know that?"

Koa shook his head. "It is not important. Step with caution if you wish to live and burn the city."

"*You lie through your teeth, Heokolon. Dubilfen's embrace is all around you.*

224

I can see it," Brónmal thought. He looked back, the other men behind him exchanging glances with him. They were all nervous. The tunnel bent and curved, yet never forked or came to a crossroads. It was always straight. Despite this, now and then, they would walk into areas so large they could not see the walls anymore. Brónmal caught strange figures out of the corner of his eye, yet he never could look at one directly before it disappeared. Was this place cursed, like the path from the swamp months ago? His spine tingled, the same sense of dread he had at the black church returning to haunt him.

As they walked, Koa stopped at a strange statue of a handsome man wearing a crown. Brónmal had never seen such a finely detailed statue. It was as if a living man had been perfectly encased in stone. Unlike the rocks and walls of the cave, the figure was untouched by lichen, cracks, or any form of age. The crown was magnificent and pointed, with small details carved into it.

The man himself did not look like any Mednohail, Ahamari, Heokolon, or Throfi he had ever seen. He had sharp features, with prominent cheekbones and a pointed chin. Despite having eyes of stone, the statue had a confident, mesmerizing gaze. Brónmal felt like this statue could put him under a spell of domination. It was an evil so alluring that it did not even trigger Brónmal's faith. Instead, it triggered a deep dread, a sense that he would be powerless to the statue's will. Koa bowed deeply to the statue, then continued.

Brónmal spoke. "Who was that?"

Koa replied. "A very important man. It does not matter. Keep an eye out."

Brónmal recoiled. "An eye out? For what?"

Koa looked around. "Guardians."

The men behind Brónmal whispered. Brónmal furrowed his brow and spoke louder. "Be clear!"

Koa glanced back. "Quiet. We do not want to disturb this place."

A distant crack made them all stop. Koa sighed. "We may be too late."

Hacarad growled. "Too late for what?"

Koa turned. "They are coming."

Heavy footsteps echoed toward them from the darkness. Clay men appeared from the pitch black and attacked, wielding ancient spears, maces, and swords. Brónmal shouted. "Defend yourselves!"

The soldiers charged the clay men. Those with maces were the most effective, smashing through the heads and bodies of the monstrous guardians. Brónmal had faced these before. He drew his mace and crushed the guardians' limbs and bodies, avoiding spear and sword. Those among the soldiers who did not have maces helped the others by holding back the clay men or holding them down.

Throughout the fight, Koa stood undisturbed. More came, only to be crushed and defeated by the small army. Hacarad panted and looked around. "Is everyone fine?"

Domganmir of Gaothal shouted, wheezing from exhaustion. "What is this cursed place? Are you trying to kill us, Heokolon!"

Koa shook his head. "Nothing here can kill all of you. There should not be more."

Brónmal pointed. "Not a single one swung at you or even came for you. You are no Heokolon, are you?"

Koa chuckled and kept walking. "Come along. We approach the end of the tunnel."

Brónmal shouted. "You will not take one more step, or it will be your last!"

Koa sighed as he disappeared into the darkness. "You waste time, Brónmal! Come!"

The men followed, soon catching up again with Koa. Brónmal spoke again. "Who are you?"

Koa snorted. "I guess my disguise has fallen through? I am the last true emperor of Heonar."

Hacarad growled. "The Emperor! Take his head now."

Koa waved at him. "No, not the current fool who sits on my throne. The true last emperor. I was emperor nearly seven hundred years ago, a faithful servant of Arathmalok the Uniter during the Reign. I was the one who ruled this land for him, and it was a magnificent time for Heonar. There was plenty, there was progress, and great cities and monuments were erected. We had pride, but now we are condemned to be a lesser empire while an empire of slaves burns and pillages our land."

Brónmal growled. "We are not slaves!"

Koa scoffed. "You are, but you will be slaves to a better master soon."

Hacarad spoke. "You will not leave this tunnel alive."

Koa shook his head. "Words of ignorance."

Brónmal narrowed his eyes. "Why do you lead us through this tunnel? Do you take us to die?"

Koa shook his head once again. "No, at the end of this tunnel is the city. You will burn Nasalohotehr for me."

Hacarad spoke. "Why?"

"Because it will make retaking my homeland easier, especially without the false emperor on the throne. You get your victory. I get mine."

Brónmal ran forward. "You will not have your victory!"

Koa glanced back before he took off into the shadows with unnatural speed. Brónmal pointed and ran after him. "Slaughter the abomination!"

The small army charged through the tunnels, yet no matter how fast they ran, they did not see Koa again. They ran until a wall appeared before them, Brónmal skidding to a stop. "Halt!"

Everyone came to a stop at the end of the tunnel. Hacarad looked around, waving his torch. "Where is he?"

Brónmal groaned. "He's gone. Just like the demon in the swamp. This must be the door to the other side."

The stone wall had a circular door, just like the one at the tunnel's beginning. This time, the markings on it were visible. In the center was a round disc. Brónmal reached up to it and pressed it. It did not move inward but rotated. He turned it, rotating it many times before a click sounded, and the door began to fall.

Brónmal shouted. "Back in the tunnel!"

They all ran into the tunnel while the door fell with a loud thud. Light flooded in as the outside came into view. Brónmal turned, mouth agape. Beyond were buildings, walls, torches, and people.

The city of Nasalohotehr awaited.

34

The City of Nasalohotehr

Brónmal ran through the city with the small army. The city was built on plateaus, great squares dividing the city into levels. The Mednohail ran down the stairs, descending past ornate Heokolon buildings of fine stone with red roofs. No guards stood a chance. There would be no stopping them. Vicious, the Mednohail slaughtered the innocent and defenders alike, leaving a trail of blood. The wind bellowed as the clouds above let down flurries of snow. They continued until the city's lower part came into view.

Hacarad laughed. "We have won, Brónmal!"

Brónmal shouted. "Not yet, brother! To the gate!"

The men charged down the stairs and streets of the city and into the first square behind the gate. Temkemletl stood between the two towers guarding the entrance, shouting and pointing at the legions outside. He turned with widened eyes, screaming as Brónmal approached.

"*I have cornered you, fiend!*" Brónmal thought, pointing to his men. "Open the gate at all costs! Lay down your lives if you must!"

Archers turned to fire at them. Brónmal, brutal and savage, fought his way onto the wall. Hacarad followed. Together, they were unstoppable. Like the Heokolons, they, too, had years of training. The Heokolons approached with knives and glass swords as the Mednohail climbed onto the wall.

Hacarad shouted. "Together, brother!"

Brónmal responded. "Together!"

They smashed the archers to death, crushing their skulls and bones with ruthless strikes. With each man he killed, Brónmal grew more exhausted. He sweated in his armor, chest growing heavy as he exerted his wrath. He did not care. He would lay down his own life to open the gate. Pushing through exhaustion, Brónmal got to the first gate tower and fought his way inside. His escort and half of the men who went with him followed. They kept reinforcements at bay, keeping Brónmal safe while they searched the tower for a way to open the gates.

The Heokolons used mechanisms, chains, and heavy weights within the gate tower to open the gates. A pair of giant circular wheels with rods sticking out awaited the Mednohail. Another sat below while two more were in the other tower across the entrance.

Brónmal shouted. "The wheels! Turn them! Turn them!"

Some men, including Hacarad, joined in as they pushed. At first, they pushed the wrong way, meeting absolute stiffness.

Hacarad shouted. "The other way! Move it!"

They turned and pushed against the immense wheels. Each man pushed with all his might as others went down to the second knob and turned it. Across the gate at the other tower, the other half of the men turned their wheels.

A soldier outside the tower shouted. "The gates are opening! Keep pushing!"

A horn blasted in the distance. The knobs became still again as the gates opened. Mednohail flooded the city. The Heokolons had lost. There was no way out as thousands charged into the city, clashing with the defender. Brónmal walked out of the gate tower and watched while the insatiable, endless legion flooded the city.

"*I did it, mother. I won. I have found my glory,*" Brónmal thought.

Men with Flamebows burned houses. Mednohail soldiers tore apart Heokolon men, women, and children alike, killing anyone in their way. Brónmal and Hacarad looked at one another. Hacarad beat his chest plate. "We have won!"

Brónmal chuckled. "Let us go take our prize. The head of the Emperor awaits."

Together with the other Generals, they ran down from the walls. They joined a spear-headed assault straight to the palace at the top of Mount Tehkemoreti. Ash and snow mixed. Fires raged while they charged, the city falling as Mednohail filled it.

Fruitlessly, the Heokolons tried to get into formations, yet the Mednohail came from everywhere. Every street, alley, and corner were filled with wild, crazed Mednohail. They were so ferocious that they pushed their bodies through spears, glaives, and swords to cut down the Heokolons. Not a single formation kept them at bay while the horde surrounded and killed all resistance.

Brónmal shouted. "To the palace! To the palace! The Emperor's head is mine!"

Exhausted and sweating, Brónmal pushed forward up the steps and streets that curved around and hugged the mountain. Blood flowed down the streets, staining the newly fallen snow red. There would be no city left by noon.

Fighting each step of the way, the spearhead of the assault reached the palace. It was massive. Unlike anything in Heonar, the structure was grander than the castle at Ardmunhaich. Its many roofs were blue. It was more like a manor than a castle, with a tremendous pyramid-like roof with golden protrusions. Below it sat square layers, each corner occupied by a hexagonal tower with similar roofs. At the base of the building was a wall-like first level with a grand arch acting as the entrance to an inner, grand gate. The gate, made of a strange orange metal, was guarded by statues of beasts Brónmal had never seen before. At the base of the gate itself was a stone staircase. The structure was stunning. It would be a pleasure to destroy it.

The escort charged forward into Heokolons with golden armor - royal guards. There were dozens. They fought elegantly, moving like the wind to pierce and stab through cracks in the escort's plate armor. Still, they were outnumbered. Among the escorts were foot soldiers who threw down their lives just to get a stab at the royal guard.

The Mednohail burst through the formation and reached the palace steps.

There, in golden armor, stood Temkemeletl, flanked by two Heokolons in similar, ornate armor. All three wielded glass blades. They stared at the oncoming horde, fearless and unmoving in the face of certain death.

Brónmal shouted before the men charged. "Wait! I want him for myself!"

They stopped, allowing Brónmal to step forward and point at Temkemeletl. "Face me, coward! Far too long have you run from me! Prove yourself here and now!"

Temkemeletel looked between his two comrades and waved. The two stepped back, and the Heokolon General marched alone down the steps of the grand palace. In a small square, the two met—the duel of empires, the duel of leaders, the duel of two great warriors.

They circled. Brónmal raised his mace, Temkemeletl spun his glaive, neither attacking the other. The men watching grew silent. They swung, weapons clashing. The glaive was swifter and lighter than the mace. As the weapons collided, Temkemeletl grunted from the weight of the impact. Sparks fell.

Brónmal felt courage. They exchanged blow after blow. Temkemeletl moved swiftly and smoothly, while Brónmal struck with passion and vigor, relentlessly advancing. As he swung, Temkemeletl's foot kicked out his. Brónmal fell. The Heokolon brought down his blade. Brónmal rolled out of the way, the glass blade hitting the ground.

Temkemeletl advanced. Brónmal swung, mace flying through the man's defenses and denting the side of the Heokolon's breastplate. They grabbed one another, turning a few steps before Brónmal head-butted the General. They stepped back from one another, then clashed again.

Brónmal swung, Temkemeletl swung. In a blur, the Heokolon dodged the clumsy mace, his glaive's shaft striking Brónmal's helm. Brónmal spun, helmet torn off as he hit the ground. Enraged, he wildly kicked Temkemeletl back and stood.

Helmet off, Brónmal's exhausted face revealed itself. He panted heavily, yet he still had spirit. He spat and engaged again. The Heokolon dodged, yet his weapon could not entirely block the mace as Brónmal landed another dent on the man's arm.

Just as he felt confident that he was winning, the glaive came up. Brónmal cried out and stumbled back, blood pouring from a cut straight across his cheek. The world narrowed even more. "You wretched heathen!" Brónmal shouted.

He charged forward with reckless rage. He absorbed strike after strike, slamming his mace down until Temkemeletl raised his glaive to block. The mace smashed through it. A crack echoed as the mace slammed through the glaive's shaft and into the helmet of the Heokolon. A groan came as he fell.

Brónmal hopped on top of him and tore off his helmet. The two fumbled. The Temkemeletl reached up and tried to push Brónmal off, but Brónmal pushed his hands aside as he raised the mace.

A cry came from Temkemeletl. It was too late. With enraged shouts, Brónmal brought the mace down upon the man's skull. Again, and again, and again. A minute passed before the once-great General's head was nothing but a gory meat pile. Brónmal stood, blood covering his face and armor.

He raised his mace. "For the Three, for Mednodorn!"

The men cheered as they surged forward and clashed with the two twins. Meanwhile, Hacarad approached Brónmal. "Are you okay, brother?"

Brónmal blinked. "I-I am fine."

"Your face."

"It's nothing. My father did worse. Come, we have our prize to fetch."

The men fought the twin guardians while Brónmal, Hacarad, and others broke into the palace. Brónmal drew the jeweled sword of the Supreme General. He wanted to use the sacred blade. It was necessary, a divine weapon for a holy task of destiny. The inside of the palace was even more magnificent. Great pillars of white wrapped in crystal statues held up an even grander roof. They entered the throne room, beholding a huge throne carved from a strange purple crystal. Brónmal stumbled in, Hacarad beside him. Both stopped.

Brónmal looked around. "Where is he?"

More men entered the palace. Hacarad pointed to them and shouted. "Scour the palace! Find the Emperor. Keep him alive for Brónmal!"

"Yes, Lord!"

The pair joined the men as they checked every inch of the grand palace, coming upon more and more luxury and grandeur until they again met in the throne room. Hacarad walked up to Brónmal. "You find him?"

Brónmal shook his head. "No."

The pair stared at each other in disbelief. The Emperor was not here.

35

Looking Home

The sun rose. Nasalohotehr burned as the snowstorm subsided, smoke filling the sky. The Mednohail spared none. Dead Heokolons littered the streets. A river of blood flowed down the mountain, staining the snowy roads red. Soldiers ran everywhere, taking everything and destroying what they could not carry. They chopped down walls, burnt homes, and left nothing but foundations. Brónmal and Hacarad sat at the foot of the palace. A flask of Heokolon wine sat between them, freshly stolen from the Emperor's store.

Brónmal felt content for the first time in his life. He had truly bested his father. The glory of Heonar's conquest was his. His oath to his mother so many years ago had been fulfilled. He sat and smiled. Beaming with optimism, he did not care if the rest of Heonar did not bend to them even after the burning of the capital. He would gladly break them.

Brónmal sighed. "Is not it a sight?"

Hacarad poured Brónmal a cup of wine and nodded. "It is quite the sight. Our fathers would be proud."

Brónmal chuckled. "I would like to see Remtaich's face. His son made it to the capital of Heonar and burnt it to the ground."

"We are the better generation. Wine?"

"Sure."

The pair clinked the glasses together and sipped. "Blegh!"

They spit out the wine, gazed at each other in disgust, and threw the bottle down the stairs leading up to the palace. It shattered, wine flowing down the steps. Brónmal wiped off his tongue. "Wretched!"

Hacarad spat on the ground. "The Emperor drank that?"

Brónmal waved down to one of his escorts. "Fetch me something, Mednohail, and get yourself some!"

"Yes, Supreme General," The man shouted back.

The pair sat and waited. Hacarad glanced over at Brónmal. "How's the cut?"

Brónmal raised his hand to the cut. The physicians had done their best to close it with leather doused in sticky oil, taping it shut. The oil burned. He had begun to ignore it, yet the reminder returned the pain. "It hurts."

Hacarad chuckled. "You had us all scared. A duel against a Heokolon General? I would have stepped in if he had gotten anywhere near killing you."

Brónmal smiled. "I am glad to hear that. He scared me a little, but it was an honor to kill him. One less pagan."

The man returned with a bottle of Mednohail beer. Brónmal took it. "You are relieved. Go celebrate."

The man saluted. "Three bless, Supreme General!"

Brónmal poured Hacarad and himself a drink. The two clinked the glasses together and drank. Hacarad smiled. "Far better, far, far better."

Brónmal sighed in relief. "What do you think will happen now?"

Hacarad shrugged. "I am not sure. First, we must get the rest of the Empire to obey and then work on conversion. You and I must return to Ardmunhaich to announce our victory, then ask the Godspeaker what he wishes to do."

Dark thoughts of prophecy and destiny came to Brónmal's mind. They had only won one battle out of a great war. For a moment, his optimism dwindled. What of the Skinbook? What of the black church and the men of the West? The thoughts nagged.

Brónmal squinted. "The true enemy remains. Arathmalok. To think his servants were among our ranks."

Hacarad tilted his head. "To think one of his servants helped us take the city. Something is wrong with that, still."

Brónmal sighed. "We will find out soon enough. The war is not over for us."

Hacarad scoffed. "I do not want to think about that now. I wish to celebrate a successful invasion. What do you think we should rename this Nasalohotehr?"

Brónmal shrugged. "I am not sure."

"How about Brónthal?"

Brónmal chuckled. "Brón's city? Maybe something glorious, like Thuvinbrist?"

Hacarad narrowed his eyes. "Great conquest?"

Brónmal shrugged. "I am not a namer."

"Well, we must be as conquerors. It will be up to us to rename many of these places."

Brónmal nodded. "But we need something grand. This was the city built by the first emperor. How many Aothills ago? Before the Reign even."

"True. Can you believe it, though? It's been a long journey since that forest by Angmere."

"It has been many hard years getting here. We have been told of the first war and its failure all our lives, and here we are, drinking on the steps of the Emperor's palace."

Hacarad laughed. "Really showed everyone back home. All my family thought I would be a foot soldier, like my brothers."

Brónmal snorted. "I would not let that happen. A squire is not that bad."

Hacarad shrugged. "I did have to clean your shoes now and then."

"If you were better at it, I would not have the slaves do it."

"Excuse me! I clean shoes quite well."

"You are better at fighting, you stupid peasant."

Hacarad snickered. "Look at you, you pompous lord."

Brónmal pointed. "I will have you know I wash every day and lay in a bed of fine fabrics."

Hacarad rolled his eyes. "And your teeth rot from sugar, right?"

Brónmal tilted his head. "Duh. Nothing but pastries and cakes for me, like

Domganmir."

Hacarad sighed. "Pastries and cakes. I miss those. I look forward to retirement on a nice estate just like your father, with slaves to bring me nothing but food all day. I will be happy and fat by the time I die."

Brónmal nodded. "How about women?"

Hacarad shrugged. "I do not think about it too much. Maybe a nice wife, make her fat too."

Brónmal shook his head. "It just sounds like to me that you want to be lazy."

"Who does not? I have lived a peasant's and soldier's lives and would like to sit down."

Brónmal chuckled. "I do not blame you. I do not know where I want to retire. Perhaps I can get myself a castle. Maybe I should get a priest to write down our stories?"

Hacarad chuckled. "Write down our stories? Like a king?"

Brónmal nodded. "Exactly like a king! Brónmal the Conqueror and Hacarad the Great. Friends and brothers that destroyed the Heokolon Empire and brought its people to heel."

"That sounds wonderful. Another drink?"

"Absolutely."

They poured, clinked, and drank again. As Brónmal lowered his glass, he saw a sweaty Mednohail man run up the stairs. "What is this?"

Hacarad shrugged. "A messenger?"

The man ran up to them, exhausted. Sweat drenched his clothes, words falling out of him incoherently as he tried to speak. Brónmal stood and approached the man. "Calm yourself. Take a drink!"

Brónmal handed the man a drink. The man downed the drink ravenously and then spoke: "Supreme General, I bring news from the West."

Brónmal raised his brow. "Speak then!"

The man panted. "The Heokolons have crossed the Kabhain River! They are marching toward Ardmunhaich! The Throfi and the Ahamari are also invading from the North and South! The Godspeaker and Highlord call for the Nine Armies to return."

Brónmal stumbled back. It was as if he lost control of his legs. The world became blurry momentarily as he gasped and tried to maintain his balance. Hacarad stood. "The Heokolons went around us?"

The messenger nodded. It was all of Brónmal's nightmares come true. The Heokolons had simply marched around them. Brónmal stuttered. "G-get the men! Round up the army! We march back now!"

Hacarad nodded. "Yes, Lord!"

Brónmal sat down fully with widened eyes. His victory was flawed, taken just as predicted. The Mednohail were in peril, his homeland in danger. He had to return. Mednodorn teetered on the edge of destruction.

The sins of the past had grown too heavy, and the time for justice had come.

TO BE CONTINUED

Full Name Guide

People

- **Angamal** – "ANG-gah-mawl" – Raothal's Archbishop
- **Arathmalok** – "Ah-RATH-mah-lock" – Breaker of Man, The Uniter
- **Arderva** – "AR-der-va" – Brónmal's Mother
- **Astrophel** – "Ah-stroh-fel" – First of the Accursed, Servant of the Reign
- **Azratonoa** – "Az-ra-toe-NO-AH" – Easterling Slave
- **Baufrius** – "BOW-free-us" – General of Eidthal
- **Brónmal** – "BR-OOn-mawl" – Supreme General. Son of Remtaich, General
- **Bruidharir** – "BROO-ha-rear" – The Godspeaker
- **Cangramal** – "CANE-grah-mawl" – General of Reinthal
- **Clegdamar** – "KLEH-dah-mar" – Captain of the Kabhain Guard
- **Cosalmir** – "KOH-sal-meer" – General of Beinthal
- **Dachfranir** – "DACK-fraw-near" – Highlord of Mednodorn
- **Drakmanir** – "DRAK-mah-near" – General of Raothal
- **Domganmir** – "DOM-gan-meer" – General of Gaothal
- **Gu'hag** – "Goo-HAg" – Chieftain of the Mot'Algoniva from the Marcoili Forest
- **Hacarad** – "HACK-ah-rod" – Brónmal's Squire and friend
- **Koakrysar** – "Koa-kree-SAR" – Unknown Heokolon
- **Maomarad** – "MOW-mah-rod" – General of Peresthal
- **Ma'verd** – "Mah-VErd" – Marcoili Mot'Algoniva Hunter
- **Otevtecprov** – "Oh-tev-tech-PR-OH-V" – First Emperor of Heonar
- **Palagrad** – "PAL-ah-gr-ah-d" – General of Faothal

- **Remtaich** - "REM-tech" - Veteran of the First Heokolon War, Brónmal's father
- **Rosura** - "Rose-UR-ah" - The Old Witch, Servant of the Reign
- **Skalia** - "SKAW-lee-ah" - Mudtail Tradequeen
- **Tahitul** - "Taw-h-ih-TUHL" - Heokolon Translator
- **Talcemal** - "TAH-l-ke-mawl" - General of Munsthal
- **Temkemeletl** - "Tem-kem-eh-LET-EL" - General of the Heokolon Empire
- **Teohapnezal** - "Tee-oh-hap-NEZ-AL" - Emperor of Heonar
- **Trudumal** - "TRUE-doo-mawl" - Supreme General of Mednodorn
- **Wetemir** - "VEH-teh-meer" - King of Raothal

Places

- **Alterger** - "Ahl-teh-GER" - Unfortunate Heokolon Village
- **Baradun** - "BAR-ah-dune" - Mednohail War Citadel
- **Beinthal** - "BINE-tawl" - Northwestern Province of Mednodorn
- **Dronmar Towers** - "DR-OO-n-mar" - The Mednohail Towers on the Kabhain River
- **Eidthal** - "ED-tawl" - Northern Province of Mednodorn
- **Faothal** - "FOW-tawl" - Southeastern Province of Mednodorn
- **Gaothal** - "GOW-tawl" - Southern Province of Mednodorn
- **Hafornstalt** - "Hah-FORN-staw-lt" - Southern trade city on the edge of the Gisjaf Sea and Gribjdohen
- **Kabhain River** - "K-AH-b-hane" - River between Heonar and Mednodorn
- **Khagoreti Mountains** - "Ka-gor-REH-TEE" - Mountains between the Kabhain River and the rest of Heonar
- **Marcoili Forest** - "MAR-k-oil-ee" - Forest on the border between Ardmunhaich and Raothal
- **Munsthal** - "Moons-tawl" - Northeastern Province of Mednodorn
- **Nasalohotehr** - "Nah-sal-oh-HO-TER" - Capital of Heonar
- **Nehadrir** - "NEE-had-rear" - Priest in the Hafornstalt Temple

- **Raothal** - "ROW-tawl" - Eastern Province of Mednodorn
- **Reinthal** - "RINE-tawl" - Southwestern Province of Mednodorn
- **Peresthal** - "PEAR-es-tawl" - Western Province of Mednodorn
- **Tehkemoreti** - "Teh-kem-or-EH-TEE" - The mountain Nasalohotehr is built on

Lands

- **Arn'eketh** - "ARN-eh-KEth" - The Red Desert South of Mednodorn, home of the Ahamari
- **Darlamak** - "DAR-lah-MAH-k" - The White Desert South of Arn'eketh
- **Etutakur** - "EH-too-tah-ker" - The Cursed Land West of Mednodorn, home of the Stygian Men
- **Fjandgarth** - "F-YA-nd-gar-th" - Haundr's Spine, mountains West of the Gisjaf Sea, home to few Throfi
- **Gisjaf Sea** - "GI-S-yav" - Sea of Rot, the sea that separates Mednodorn and Gribjodhen
- **Gribjodhen** - "GR-IH-b-yod-hen" - Throfi-land, the Northlands, North of the Gisjaf Sea
- **Heonar** - "Hee-oh-NAR" - The Heokolon Empire, home of the Heokolons, East of Mednodorn
- **Maoran** - "M-OW-ran" - The Unknown Island
- **Mednodorn** - "MEHD-no-dorn" - Mednohail Empire, home of the Mednohail, Scourge of the Fourth Aothill, center of the known world
- **Mekden Sea** - "MEH-K-den" The Thorned Sea, the sea that separates Arn'eketh and Heonar, Faothal's Sea
- **Qiz'Abek** - "Kwiz-AH-bek" - The Unknown Wild, the land South of Etutakur and West of both Darlamak and Arn'eketh
- **Slesfarn** - "SL-ES-far-n" - The Frozen Sea, East of Gribjodhen and North of Heonar, home to few Throfi

Words

- **Ahamari** - "Ah-HA-mar-ee" - A person from Arn'eketh
- **Algoniva** - "Al-GO-NEE-va" - An umbrella term for a type of intelligent race that lives all across Adytum
- **Anhanka** - "Ann-hahn-KAH" - Heokolon Magic
- **Aogadraod** - "OW-gah-dr-ow-d" - The Sin of Magic in Tharifen
- **Aolfrao** - "OWL-frow" - The Sin of Deceit in Tharifen
- **Aothil** - "OW-till" - The Adytum version of a century which originates in the Reign, a length of 150 years
- **Apfaircada** - "AH-P-far-caw-dah" - Flagship of the Mednohail Fleet in the Gisjaf Sea
- **Aumog** - "AW-mawg" - Mednohail beast of burden
- **Bogarthdraod** - "BAW-gar-t-dr-ow-d" - An old form of Mednohail witchcraft
- **Cazatonia** - "Caz-ah-tone-EE-AH" - Heokolon concept of chaos, A Truth of Chekor
- **Ceborca** - "See-bore-KAH" - Heokolon concept. The Primal Forces of the Universe, A Truth of Chekor
- **Cetorvenna** - "Set-tor-VEN-AH" - Heokolon concept of perfection, a Truth of Chekor
- **Chekor** - "Che-CORE" - The central symbol and belief in Nepasni, a singular concept that combines six truths of reality
- **Crobestir** - "CROW-beh-stir" - Wild animals in Mednodorn usually hunted by the nobility
- **Cug Baolar** - "C-OO-g B-OW-lar" - The Sins in Tharifen
- **Daodamath** - "DOW-dah-math" - Divine Purpose, the Mednohail's religious drive to dominate the world and lead it under their faith
- **Eirsa** - "EAR-sah" - The Sin of Heresy, the worst sin in Tharifen
- **Esadif** - "EH-sah-dif" - The Sin of Disobedience in Tharifen
- **Gluvadraod** - "GL-OO-vah-dr-ow-d" - The "Sinless" Mednohail Magic by the Mednohail Church
- **Heokolon** - "Hee-oh-k-OH-LIN" - A person from Heonar, a person

from the Heokolon Empire

- **Mednohail** – "M-EH-D-no-hail" – A person from Mednodorn, a person from the Mednohail Empire
- **Mot'Algoniva** – "Mawt-al-go-nee-va" – Forest Algoniva, a specific type of Algoniva most prominent in Mednodorn
- **Sekur** – "Seh-ker" – The comet that burns through the sky every Aothill or every 150 years
- **Seletorvu** – "Cell-eh-tor-VOO" – Heokolon concept of connection between all things, a Truth of Chekor
- **Throfi** – "THR-AW-fee" – People of the north, a person from Gribjodhen, Fjandgarth, or Slesfarn
- **Zidra** – "Zee-dra" – Heokolon concept of life, a Truth of Chekor
- **Zidro** – "Zee-droh" – Heokolon concept of death, a Truth of Chekor

Religions

- **Adee'kuram** – "Ah-dEE-KUR-am" – Religion of the Ahamari
- **Elrivthin** – "EL-reev-thin" – Religion of the Throfi
- **Ma'eeg** – "Ma-EE-g" – Religion of the Mot'Algoniva
- **Nepasni** – "Nep-aws-NEE" – Religion of the Heokolons
- **Tharifen** – "TAR-ee-fen" – The Religion of the Mednohail
- **Gods**
- **Daonrex** – "DOWN-rex" – Supreme god in Tharifen, creator of man and patron of the nobility
- **Dubilfen** – "DO-bill-fen" – God of evil in Tharifen, patron of heretics, sinners, and criminals
- **Filahaich** – "FILL-ah-hike" – God of order and the world in Tharifen, patron of the peasant, commoner, and free folk
- **Vishilburkaili** – "Vih-shil-berk-AY-LEE" – Supreme god in Nepasni

Months

In calendar order, Mednohail pronunciation and translation

- **Laogorsh** - "L-OW-gor-sh" - Time of Free Rebirth
- **Trathuva** - "TR-AT-oo-va" - First Seed
- **Boheiruva** - "BOH-here-oo-va" - Second Seed
- **Aurhath** - "AR-hat" - First Harvest
- **Thorasora** - "TOR-ah-sor-ah" - Time of the Cruel Sun
- **Haichasora** - "HIKE-ah-sor-ah" - Time of the High Sun
- **Taorasora** - "T-OW-ah-sor-ah" - Time of the Merciful Sun
- **Trufuva** - "TR-OO-f-oo-va" - Third Seed
- **Coathfuva** - "KOO-ATH-f-oo-va" - Fourth Seed
- **Dornhath** - "DORN-hat" - Second Harvest
- **Uthbelk** - "OO-T-beh-lk" - Time of Dread Wait
- **Uthgelt** - "OO-T-g-eh-lt" - Time of Dread Arrival
- **Eurgbaslac** - "ERG-baw-slak" - Time of Early Death
- **Eurgbitmerk** - "ERG-beet-merk" - Time of Late Death
- **Markoram** - "MAR-oh-ram" - Time of Corpses
- **Beathiden** - "BEE-AT-ee-den" - Time of Mourning Rebirth

About the Author

TRANSLATING IMAGINATION INTO WORDS

E.T. Gunnarsson translates imagination into words. His debut book, Forgive Us, was awarded Best Sci-Fi at the 2021 San Francisco Book Festival and Best Post-Apocalyptic Book at the 2021 Fiction Awards.

Born and raised in the Rocky Mountains (9,000 feet altitude!), E.T. now lives in southern Sweden with his dwarfed Cane Corso and his lifelong interest in Norse myth and culture. A storyteller from an early age, Mr. Gunnarsson spent his formative years developing his writing skills on international role-play sites.

Outside of writing, E.T. is a well-versed individual. He trained with two different Olympic squads, is an expert in Norse mythology, an experimental cook, a woodcarver, an avid action role-play gamer, a Judo brown belt, and a Brazilian Jiu-Jitsu purple belt.

Finding E.T. on Facebook and Instagram is easy: search for his name. You can find his legendary interviews on YouTube and other websites. Or, visit etgunnarsson.com to reach his publisher.

You can connect with me on:

🌐 https://etgunnarsson.com

🐦 https://twitter.com/etgunnarsson

📘 https://www.facebook.com/etgunnarsson

🔗 https://www.instagram.com/etgunnarsson

🔗 https://www.youtube.com/@etgunnarsson

Subscribe to my newsletter:

✉ https://etgunnarsson.com/news

Also by E.T. Gunnarsson

Awards

Winner, Post-Apocalyptic – 2021 American Fiction Awards

Winner, Science Fiction – 2021 San Francisco Book Festival

Finalist, Science Fiction – 2021 Best Book Awards

Honorable Mention, Science Fiction – 2021 Hollywood Book Festival

Honorable Mention, Science Fiction – 2021 New York Book Festival

Runner Up, Science Fiction/Horror – 2022 New York Book Festival

Honorable Mention, Science Fiction – 2022 San Francisco Book Festival

Forgive Us

SILENT, EMPTY, AND CRUEL. THIS WAS THE NATURE OF THE WASTELAND.

Ignium was supposed to solve the world's energy crisis. Instead, it destroyed the planet. In the darkness of the 22nd century, survivors fight to endure what's left.

London, a wasteland veteran, struggles to keep his promise to protect his adopted daughter, Rose. After years of starvation, scavenging, and desperation, the two wanderers find a new hope: the growing nation of New Uruk. The city is an oasis of plenty and security, offering London a chance to fulfill his promise.

Little does he know that war is coming, seeking to end the sanctity they've long searched for.

Fans of *The Gunslinger* and *Mad Max* will love E.T. Gunnarsson's multi-award-winning book *Forgive Us*, a story of three men told in three interwoven timelines that readers call *"thrilling, brutal, awesome, and completely unique."*

Remember Us

"The Vessel? It must've been sent from God. It's the answer, the key to the peace I seek. Something to save or damn us."
– **The Father, leader of the Twilight Cult**

Remember Us is a thrilling journey through a post-apocalyptic world where every decision could lead to freedom or ruin, perfect for fans of *The Road* and *Station Eleven*.

Meet Simon, a former revolutionary from the space station *Arcadis*, now a reluctant Earthling in a world stitching itself back together with a blend of Wild West grit and forgotten technology. A haunting dream and a sky-shattering explosion propel him on a quest to uncover the fate of his old home, *Arcadis*, now a fallen star burning in the Earth's atmosphere.

Joined by Anna, a tough-as-nails wastelander and ex-soldier, Simon treks through a world where mysticism meets machinery. They race against the Twilight Cult and their enigmatic leader, The Father, who are convinced that the fallen meteorite is a divine vessel sent by God. The stakes are colossal as they journey through unforgiving landscapes and crumbling cities. Throughout it all, Simon finds himself navigating through a journey full of shamanistic visions and ancient monsters.

Abandon Us

How hard must a man fight when the apocalypse arrives?

Civil war ravages the country. The economy collapses. A plague spreads like fire, and pollution darkens the sky. This is the toxic world of Robert Ashton. A wasteland of broken dreams, death, tech, and mutants. But he is not alone.

Robert and his gay partner Zilv navigate life underground, where it is safer. Society has buckled, and working as a smuggler, Robert builds a criminal life to keep the two of them fed. But nothing lasts forever, and he is forced to return to the surface when the underground suffers a brutal military raid. What he discovers shocks a man who thinks he cannot be shocked anymore.

Robert emerges into the hellscape of the Third World War...

Printed in Great Britain
by Amazon

42902350R00148